P9-CFB-035

BAKING SPIRITS BRIGHT

Sarah Fox

BERKLEY PRIME CRIME
New York

BERKLEY PRIME CRIME
Published by Berkley
An imprint of Penguin Random House LLC
penguinrandomhouse.com

ISBN: 9780593546635

First Edition: October 2023

Printed in the United States of America
1 3 5 7 9 10 8 6 4 2

Book design by George Towne

For Jody Holford

Chapter One

THERE WAS NO PLACE MORE MAGICAL THAN LARCH Haven, Vermont, in wintertime. The canals that wound their way through the small town had frozen solid, providing a network of skating trails, and a thick layer of snow covered the cute cottages and the timber-frame buildings. With Christmas approaching, the postcard-perfect town had become even more magical, with twinkle lights strung along the main cobblestone walkways and all of the old-fashioned lampposts wrapped with red and white ribbons so they looked like peppermint sticks.

I loved my adorable stone cottage at all times of the year, but with snow on the roof, multicolored lights lining the windows, and a wreath on the front door, it looked like it belonged in the middle of a snow globe. Every time I arrived home to my cottage and my two cats, a warm glow lit up inside of me. I felt the same way whenever I entered my family's chocolate shop, True Confections. Moving back to my hometown in Vermont after living in Los Angeles for several years had definitely been a good decision.

"Ready?" my best friend Dizzy Bautista asked.

I finished tying up my skates. "Ready."

We left our snow boots in the shelter of my small boathouse and took our first strokes along the ice. The wind swirled around us, carrying the occasional snowflake with it and stinging my cheeks, but I didn't mind. We were on our way to get hot chocolate.

"There's something I want to show you," Dizzy said as we skated along the curving canal.

We glided beneath a stone bridge and then out into full daylight again.

Dizzy pulled a piece of paper from the pocket of her jacket. "A stack of these were dropped off at the library. I grabbed this one for you."

I accepted the slightly crumpled paper and unfolded it with my gloved hands. It was a black-and-white flyer.

While keeping one eye on the path ahead of us, I read the bold print at the top of the flyer. "'Third annual Baking Spirits Bright competition.'"

"Haven't you always wanted to take part?" Dizzy asked, almost brimming with excitement.

"Not exactly," I said. "I've never even heard of it before."

At this time last year I'd been in Florida, visiting my parents. For the two Christmases before that, I'd been in Los Angeles.

"Okay, but now that you have, you should definitely enter."

"I'm a chocolatier, not a baker," I reminded her.

After moving home, I'd trained as a chocolatier so I could work in my family's shop. Now I spent my days making bonbons, truffles, and chocolate versions of the gondolas that were always on the canals whenever the water wasn't frozen. Although I sometimes missed my first career as an actor, I loved working at True Confections.

"But you're a good baker too," Dizzy said. "And you

can showcase your chocolate skills during the competition."

"Okay, but this would be baking with an audience. Do you remember what happened in tenth grade cooking class?" I almost shuddered at the memory.

Dizzy and I had been partners for a project where we had to do a cooking demonstration for the class. Somehow, I'd managed to set the ends of my hair on fire. If not for Dizzy dousing me with a pot of water, I probably would have lost more than the three inches of hair that I'd had to have trimmed off.

"That was fifteen years ago," Dizzy pointed out.

"And I can still smell my hair burning like it was yesterday."

She rolled her eyes. "Becca, you've cooked and baked eleventy billion times since then without incident."

"But not with an audience."

Dizzy nudged my arm with her elbow. "You've acted on shows watched by millions of people."

"That's different. Give me a script and I'm fine."

"Then your recipes will be your script." Dizzy twirled on the ice. "You should enter. And you should make your candy cane bonbons. The judges will love them."

"I'll think about it," I promised.

We skated around a group of giggling and gossiping teenage girls. Then the way ahead of us was clear again.

"Well, while you think about it . . ." Dizzy tore off ahead of me. "Race you to the hot chocolate stand! Loser's buying!"

I stuffed the flyer into my pocket and chased after her.

GINGERBREAD AND CANDY CANES SMELLED LIKE Christmas, and that meant the kitchen at my family's chocolate shop did too. I had a batch of gingerbread baking in the oven, making my stomach grumble with anticipation, and I was in the midst of unwrapping a candy cane. Once I had it free of the plastic wrapper, I took an appreciative sniff of the peppermint candy before setting it aside. I loved working at True Confections all year round, but Christmas was my absolute favorite time to be in the shop and in the kitchen. Although this was my first Christmas as a professional chocolatier, I'd worked in the shop part-time while growing up and had often helped my grandmother in the kitchen. Now, the familiar holiday scents brought back fond memories of childhood Christmases, and there always seemed to be extra cheer and bustle these days as customers filled their shopping baskets with gifts for others and treats for themselves.

Adding to my buoyed spirits were the fluffy flakes of snow currently falling thickly from the sky. I didn't have a great view from the kitchen window, which looked out over the narrow alley behind the shop, but maybe that was for the best. If I could see the most beautiful parts of the town, I might not get much work done. Whenever I popped out to the front of the shop, I had a difficult time tearing my gaze away from the large window and the fairy tale–like scene beyond it.

For that very reason, I'd made sure to stay put in the kitchen for the past two hours. In that time, I'd made the dough for the gingerbread and had rolled it out and cut it into the shapes of gingerbread people and Christmas trees. I'd also made a batch of eggnog truffles, as well as several Santa Clauses and snowmen from both milk chocolate and dark chocolate. Now, while the gingerbread baked, I was busy making the ganache filling for my candy cane bonbons, the ones Dizzy wanted me to make for the Baking Spirits Bright competition.

I'd thought about the possibility of entering the competition several times since she'd suggested it the day before, but I still hadn't come to a decision. I enjoyed taking part in town events, but there were far better bakers in Larch Haven than me. Chocolates were my specialty. Everything else was an occasional hobby. Besides, the shop kept me busy, especially at this time of year.

I turned on one of the stove's gas burners and warmed up the cream in the top of a double boiler until it was just about to simmer. Then I removed it from the heat, dropped the candy cane into the pot, and left the cream to steep for several minutes. Once the cream was infused with the candy cane's flavor, I would heat it again before pouring it over a bowl full of chopped chocolate to make the ganache.

The oven timer dinged, so I grabbed a pot holder and removed the trays of gingerbread from the oven, quickly replacing them with two more trays of unbaked cookies. Once the gingerbread people had cooled completely, I would give them chocolate faces and buttons. For the Christmas trees, I would pipe on chocolate baubles and garlands. The gingerbread recipe was a family one, passed down from my great-grandmother, and the cookies were popular with the shop's customers as well as with my relatives.

I set the oven timer and checked on my steeping cream. It wasn't quite ready. I gave it a couple more minutes and tasted it again. The heavenly candy cane flavor was just right.

As I reheated the cream, my cousin Angela came into the kitchen. Our grandparents had started the family chocolate business decades ago, but they had finally retired—for the most part—and Angela had taken over the business side of things while I now filled the role of chocolatier.

"Becca, it smells amazing in here," Angie said as she eyed the baked gingerbread. "Let it be noted that I'm first in line for quality-control testing."

I grinned and turned off the heat under the cream. "You mean first in line after me."

"I guess that's fair, since you're the one who baked them." She held up a familiar-looking flyer. "And speaking of baking . . ."

"Dizzy told me about the competition." I poured the cream over the chopped chocolate and stirred. "Are you entering?"

"Me? No way. I can cook, but I don't bake much. There's no need when Lolly's always got something delicious to share. I was thinking *you* should enter," she said.

"That's what Dizzy said too, but the shop is crazy at this time of year. I don't think I'll have time for the competition." I gave the ganache a final stir and left it to cool and thicken.

"I bet Lolly would step in for you here for a couple of days. That's all you'd need, really."

She was probably right about that. Lolly—our grandmother—still enjoyed helping out at True Confections every now and then, even though she had plenty of other activities to keep her busy during her well-earned retirement. Still, I wasn't sure that I wanted to enter the competition. While I felt confident that I could wow the judges with my chocolates, I'd likely need more than that to do well overall.

"It's only two days?" I asked.

"Sounds like it. There's a preliminary round and then the top four move on to the finals. You have to make two items for the preliminary round. The finalists have to make a showpiece with several elements, but I'm sure it's nothing you can't handle."

I thought about it some more.

"It would be a great opportunity for True Confections," Angie pressed. "Especially since *Bake It Right* is covering the competition this year."

My eyes widened. "I didn't know about that."

Bake It Right was a popular New England magazine. Pretty much everyone had at least heard of it, and its social media posts always garnered plenty of attention and engagement.

Angie had a big smile on her face. "I heard that from

Jaspreet Joshi, one of the event's organizers. Isn't it amazing? It would be free advertising for True Confections. You don't even have to win to get in the magazine. They're going to profile all four of the finalists."

"Even making the finals could be a real challenge," I said, not quite ready to fully embrace the idea.

"Give yourself some credit. You're a good baker, an excellent chocolatier, and you've got great imagination and creativity."

I checked on the ganache. "Now you're buttering me up."

"Maybe, but it's all true. So, what do you say?"

I considered the idea for another moment. I enjoyed a challenge, and I always wanted to do what was best for True Confections, so maybe it wasn't a difficult decision after all.

"Where do I sign up?" I asked.

Chapter Two

AFTER I FINISHED WORK IN THE MIDDLE OF THE AFTER-
noon, I stopped by the town hall to enter my name in the
Baking Spirits Bright competition. Then I set off to meet
up with Dizzy at the local library, where she worked. Snow
still drifted down from the gray clouds overhead, but the
flakes had grown smaller and fell less thickly. The town's
employees had been out on their quads with snowplow at-
tachments, clearing the cobblestone walkways that lined
the canals.

Aside from golf carts and maintenance and emergency
vehicles, cars and trucks weren't allowed in the downtown
core of Larch Haven. When the canals weren't frozen, gondolas and whisper boats allowed for passage along the wa-
terways. Otherwise, people mostly got around on foot or
bicycle. That was one of the many things I loved about my
hometown. It was so peaceful, and the pace of life was so
much more relaxed than what I'd experienced while living
in Los Angeles.

When I reached the library's front steps, Dizzy was on

her way out the door, pulling a beanie down over her dark hair. She waved when she saw me, and hurried down the steps, tugging on a pair of gloves. We'd arranged to do some Christmas shopping together that afternoon, so we headed in the direction of Venice Avenue, where True Confections and many other shops were located.

"I'm so excited you're going to be in the competition!" Dizzy said after I told her about tossing my name in the hat. "You're going to do great!"

"I'm worried I might embarrass myself."

"You definitely won't do that. You're going to make the finals and get into that magazine."

I hoped she was right.

"What are you making for the first round of competition?" she asked.

"Candy cane bonbons, like you suggested, and mandelhörnchen."

"Oh, yum. Let me know if you need a taste tester while practicing."

I laughed. "I will."

We had almost made it to Venice Avenue when Dizzy drew to a stop outside Larch Haven's only art gallery.

"We should go in here," she said. "You need some artwork to put over your fireplace."

That was true. The cottage I'd purchased upon my return from Los Angeles was mostly furnished now, but some of the walls were still too bare for my liking.

"I'm supposed to be shopping for other people today," I reminded her.

"No reason why you can't do both."

I didn't resist when she tucked her arm through mine and tugged me toward the gallery.

A woman in a gray coat and gray hat stood outside the shop, facing the artwork displayed in the large front window. It wasn't until Dizzy and I reached the door that I got a look at the woman's face. She glared at the paintings in the window, as if they'd somehow insulted her. I might have thought she found the artwork distasteful if I didn't know that an expression of displeasure was typical for her.

"Hi, Irma," I said in greeting, and Dizzy added in a hello of her own.

Irma turned her glare on us. Even though she was shorter than me, she somehow managed to look down her nose at us as she strode off, never bothering to return our greetings.

"A bright ray of sunshine, as always," Dizzy said with a shake of her head.

"How can a woman who makes such delicious sweets and treats be so sour?" I asked as Dizzy opened the gallery door.

"I have no idea."

We stomped the snow off our boots and entered the gallery. Irma Jones owned the bakery situated a few doors down from True Confections. She always seemed to be in a bad mood, but I made a habit of letting her grumpiness roll right off my back. I did that now, forgetting about her almost as soon as Dizzy and I stepped inside the art gallery.

As the door drifted shut behind us, blocking the cold air, I tugged off my hat and did my best to pat down the staticky strands of my dark brown hair. There were two other customers in the gallery: a tall man in an expensive-looking, dark blue suit and wool coat; and a blonde woman who currently had her back to us.

In unspoken agreement, Dizzy and I turned to the left and focused our attention on the paintings and photographs displayed on the wall.

"Afternoon, ladies." The gallery's owner, Victor Barnabas, approached Dizzy and me. His thinning dark hair was slicked back and he wore a gray, three-piece suit and shiny black shoes. "Is there anything I can help you with?"

"We're just browsing at the moment, thanks," I said.

"Let me know if I can be of assistance."

He was about to leave us when Dizzy stepped closer to an autumn landscape practically bursting with fall colors.

"This is nice," she said.

Victor smiled. "You've got a good eye. Oil on canvas by Gregor Marriott."

"*The* Gregor Marriott?" I asked with surprise.

"The one and only," he confirmed.

Gregor Marriott was one of Vermont's most revered artists. He'd died a few decades ago, and I'd never seen one of his originals.

"I thought it was hard to find his work these days," Dizzy said as she continued to admire the painting. "Isn't most of his art owned by his descendants, private collectors, and museums?"

"That is the case," Victor confirmed. "But one such private collector passed away recently and his heirs want to sell off some of his collection."

I stepped closer to the card posted next to the painting so I could read the small print. My eyes widened when I saw the price of the landscape. It was definitely way out of my budget.

"I'm going to keep browsing," I said.

As I turned around, I noticed the man in the expensive suit watching us out of the corner of his eye. He quickly turned his attention to a photograph on the far wall when he realized I was looking his way.

The blonde woman I'd noticed upon first entering the gallery now stood at the sales counter. She glanced our way, catching Victor's eye, and I recognized her as a local. Her name was Paisley Hooper and she was in her mid-twenties, a few years younger than me, but that was pretty much all I knew about her. She had a small watercolor painting in hand, and Victor hurried over to help her with her purchase.

Dizzy and I moved along the wall, checking out all the paintings and photographs. I spotted several that I liked, but it wasn't until I'd almost made my way around the entire gallery when a piece of art tugged at my heart and took my breath away. The oil painting was a Larch Haven landscape, depicting one of the residential parts of the town in the springtime, with green grass growing along the canals and a gondola with a gondolier onboard making its way along the water. The trees bore bright green foliage and vivid flowers bloomed in well-tended gardens. But what really caught my eye was the fact that my very own cottage—known as Bluebell Cottage—was showcased in the painting.

"Oh my gosh!" Dizzy exclaimed when she reached my side. "It's like it was painted especially for you!"

"My heart skipped a beat when I saw it."

Reluctantly, I tore my gaze from the painting so I could look at the card with its details. I recognized the name of the local artist, Abigail Tierney. I'd admired her paintings in the past, but none had captured my heart quite like this one. I didn't want to check the price, because I was afraid I couldn't afford it, but I made myself look anyway. Unsurprisingly, the painting would cost me a good chunk of change, but it was far more affordable than the Gregor Marriott landscape across the gallery.

"You have to get it," Dizzy whispered.

I stared at the painting with longing. "It's more than I was planning to spend."

"But the price isn't outrageous."

"I think it's pretty fair, really," I agreed. "And I can afford it. It's just a matter of *should* I spend that much money?"

"For the absolute right piece of artwork? Yes."

I thought she had a point, but I wasn't good at making big purchases on a whim.

"I need to think about it."

"Don't wait too long," Dizzy advised. "You don't want anyone else to buy it."

An idea popped into my head and I looked around the gallery, spotting Victor behind the sales counter. Paisley had already gone on her way, leaving the man in the expensive suit and Dizzy and me as the only remaining customers. I approached Victor.

"Would it be possible to hold the Abigail Tierney landscape for me for twenty-four hours?" I asked. "I'm pretty sure I want to buy it, but I need a bit of time to think about it."

"I can hold it until tomorrow at noon," he offered.

That was about twenty hours, and close enough to what I'd asked for, so I agreed and thanked him.

I spent another minute or so gazing at the painting before Dizzy and I decided to leave and get on with our Christmas shopping. As we headed for the door, the well-dressed man pointed to the Gregor Marriott autumn landscape and said to Victor, "I'll take this one."

The man had good taste. Clearly, he also had plenty of money.

Chapter Three

THE DAY OF THE FIRST ROUND OF THE BAKING SPIRITS
Bright competition arrived with a clear sky and a cold, biting wind from the north. As much as I loved winter, I wasn't keen to leave my cottage, not once I saw the temperature on the weather app on my phone.

"I'm going to need extra cuddles to keep me warm," I told my two cats, Truffles and Binx.

Truffles, my gray tabby, sat at my feet in the kitchen and looked up at me with a meow, as if to say she was happy to oblige. I scooped her up into my arms as her brother, my green-eyed black cat, pounced on his catnip banana and somersaulted with the toy clutched in his two front paws. He then zoomed around the cottage. I laughed as Truffles purred against my chest. It took a couple of minutes, but I was finally able to lift Binx into my arms when he stopped for a breath. Only once I'd given him a hug was I ready to head out into the dark, cold morning.

Outside, the crescent moon glowed bright over the mountains and the biting wind wiped away the last vestiges of my sleepiness. Most of the shops and homes were still dark. The only light I could see on Venice Avenue—aside from that of the streetlamps—was a faint glow in the bakery. I was an early riser, but Irma was always earlier than me. She, like many bakers, probably started work in the middle of the night.

By the time I reached True Confections, my fingers and toes were almost numb. I quickly warmed up once inside and I spent the next couple of hours making chocolates to replenish the shop's supply. Lolly would come in later to relieve me, so I could take time away for the competition, but I wanted to get as much done as possible before then. Working also helped distract me and keep the worst of my nerves at bay.

After unmolding the last batch of chocolates I planned to make that morning—aside from the ones I'd make for the competition—I washed my hands, drawing in a deep, shaky breath as the warm water ran over my skin. Now that I'd stopped focusing on work, my nerves were taking over.

I heard footsteps out in the hall as I dried my hands. Seconds later, my friend Sawyer Maguire appeared in the kitchen doorway, wearing his police jacket over his uniform.

"Hey," he greeted. "I wanted to stop by to wish you luck. All set for the competition?"

"I think so?" I sounded as uncertain as I felt.

"You'll do great, Becca," Sawyer assured me.

"Thanks." I managed to smile. "I guess I should head on over to the town hall." That was the venue for the competition. Temporary baking stations had been set up in the hall's largest room, along with several rows of chairs for those who wanted to watch the competition unfold.

"What do you need to take with you?" Sawyer asked.

"Just what's in this box." I tapped the cardboard box sitting on the edge of the counter. We'd be provided with basic baking dishes and utensils at the competition, but I'd packed a few of my own favorite tools in the box along with my chocolate molds and all the ingredients I would need.

"Are you walking?"

"Yes." I was hoping the cold air and exercise would help settle my nerves.

I passed Sawyer and crossed the hall to the office, where I'd stashed my outerwear. He followed me and then leaned against the office doorframe. "I'll carry the box for you."

"You're on duty," I reminded him.

"I'm heading in that direction anyway."

"In that case, I won't say no to the help or the company."

I quickly stepped into my boots and pulled on my coat and hat. I stowed my shoes in a bag to take with me so I wouldn't have to wear my snow boots while baking. We crossed the hall and had just returned to the kitchen when my grandmother appeared in the doorway.

"Oh, good," she said when she saw me. "I was hoping I wasn't too late to wish you good luck."

I accepted a hug from her. "Thank you, Lolly. I hope I won't disappoint everyone."

Lolly patted my cheek. "That wouldn't even be possible."

I smiled at that, and then quickly brought her up to speed on what chocolates I'd made that morning and what still needed to be done. After that, she shooed me out of the kitchen, so Sawyer grabbed the box and we headed out the front door of the shop.

"Are you okay?" Sawyer asked after we'd walked along in silence for a couple of minutes.

"I'm nervous," I confessed. "Way more than I should be. I know it's not a huge deal if I don't make it into the finals, but I want to do well. If I let my nerves get the best of me, that might not happen."

"Maybe pretend you're playing the role of a baker in a movie," Sawyer suggested. "Would that help?"

I turned the idea over in my mind, remembering Dizzy's

tip about viewing my recipes as my scripts. "Actually, it might." The sharpest edge of my nervousness dulled and I smiled. "Thanks. That's a great idea."

My first career as an actor had given me plenty of experience with playing characters. I felt far more comfortable acting than baking in front of an audience, that was for sure. Sawyer's suggestion gave me a way to draw from that comfort.

When we reached the town hall, we stopped outside the front door. The first snowflakes of the day drifted lazily down around us.

"I wish I could stay to cheer you on," Sawyer said as he passed me the box.

"I appreciate you walking with me. And helping me with my anxiety."

Sawyer's radio squawked. He listened to whatever was coming through his earpiece for a second. "I need to get going," he said when he was done listening. "Text me to let me know how it goes?"

"I will," I promised.

After Sawyer left, I made my way into the town hall. I stopped inside the door, trying to do as Sawyer suggested and approach the competition like an acting role. When I felt like I had the right frame of mind, I moved toward the open door on the far side of the foyer.

I'd only made it two steps when the front door opened behind me, letting in a rush of icy air. I turned around to find Stephanie Kang entering the town hall, an overstuffed tote bag in each hand. Snowflakes dotted her long black hair and she wore a knee-length down coat.

She smiled brightly when she saw me. "Hey, Becca. You're in the competition too?"

"And hoping not to make a fool of myself." My nerves had made a sudden comeback. Stephanie owned a cake shop in Larch Haven and made the most divine cupcakes I'd ever tasted. I'd also caught a glimpse of Irma Jones through the open door to the next room. She might not win any personality contests, but as a professional baker, she'd be hard to beat. I was up against some stiff competition.

"That's not going to happen," Stephanie said, sounding certain. "You make the best chocolates I've ever tasted."

That brought a smile to my face. "Thank you. I can say the same about your cupcakes."

She beamed at the compliment, and her cheery disposition gave my spirits a boost. We entered the town hall's main room together, where approximately a dozen people had already gathered. Four baking stations stood at the far end of the room. Stephanie and I followed the aisle between the rows of folding chairs to reach a petite woman who stood by the baking stations with a clipboard in her hand. She had black hair in a thick braid that nearly reached down to her waist.

"You must both be competitors," she said when she saw Stephanie and me approaching. "I'm Jaspreet, one of the organizers. If you have any questions, you can bring them to me. But first, can I get your names, please?"

We provided her with the requested information and she ticked off our names on her list.

"We have sixteen people entered in the competition, so we'll have four rounds of four competitors," she explained. "Becca, you're in the first group, and Stephanie, you're in the second."

I'd already received that information by email the day before, and I was glad to be among the first up. Waiting until later in the day would have given me more time to stress about the caliber of my competition. Jaspreet directed me to one of the farthest baking stations and told me I could get myself organized. I was relieved to see that Irma wasn't getting ready to bake in the first round. Instead, she sat in the front row of chairs, arms crossed and eyes closed. I would have found it intimidating to have Stephanie or Irma in my group. Even though I was still technically competing against both women, I wouldn't be constantly comparing myself to them as I worked.

My relief was short-lived, however. Within minutes of my arrival, a dark-haired, blue-eyed man in his mid-twenties strode into the town hall, carrying a clear plastic tub with a black lid. He paused to talk to Jaspreet, who sent him to the baking station next to mine.

"Morning," I said with a smile as he set his tub on the counter.

He nodded in acknowledgment, his expression serious and intense.

I'm just playing the part of a baker, I told myself. *The part of a very competent, calm baker.*

The new arrival was Roman Kafka. He worked as a pastry chef at the Gondolier, one of Larch Haven's most popular restaurants, owned by my brother, Gareth, and his husband, Blake. I'd eaten several of Roman's desserts and knew he was highly skilled. I was starting to feel like I was in over my head, but after another minute of convincing myself that I *was* a competent baker, I got control of my nerves and began organizing my station.

Over the next five minutes, the remaining two bakers in my group arrived. One was a nervous-looking young woman who couldn't have been more than twenty years old. Her gray eyes darted left and right and she fidgeted almost constantly. Watching her made me feel nervous again, so I quickly shifted my focus elsewhere. The fourth member of our group was a gray-haired woman who looked to be in her seventies. I'd seen both women around town, but I didn't know either of them.

By the time I had my baking station all organized, about half of the seats in the audience had been filled. Three chairs had been set apart from all the rest, with a sign on each declaring that it was reserved for a judge. Jaspreet was in conversation with three people, who soon broke away from her and settled in the reserved chairs. One of the judges was Victor Barnabas, the owner of the art gallery where I'd bought my new painting. I'd decided to bite the bullet and had made the purchase the day after I'd first seen the painting. Now it hung over my fireplace.

The second judge, Natalia Mehta, was the head chef at the Larch Haven Hotel, and the third, Consuelo Diaz, owned a small café. I decided to ignore the three of them as best I could. I wanted to focus on baking rather than what the judges might be thinking at any given time.

As I waited for the competition to begin, my gaze traveled around the room and came to an abrupt halt on the well-dressed man I'd seen at the art gallery several days ago. Once again, he wore an expensive-looking suit. With his wool coat draped over his arm, he paused one step inside the main room before heading toward the rows of folding chairs.

At some point, Irma had stirred from her nap and left her chair. She intercepted the well-dressed man before he could sit down. I watched as she spoke quietly with him, a smug expression on her face. The man shook his head when she finished speaking and said something to her before calmly walking to the nearest vacant chair and sitting down.

Irma no longer appeared smug. She glared at the man's back before storming to the front row and dropping into the same seat as before. I didn't know how anyone could be in such a foul mood all of the time. I felt sorry for her. She obviously wasn't a happy woman. I doubted she'd think much of my pity, though.

I took in the sight of the rest of the small audience that had gathered in the room. Dizzy was at work, but she'd texted me earlier in the day, wishing me luck and telling me I was going to do a great job. A smile broke out across my face when I spotted my brother-in-law, Blake, seated in the back row. When I caught his eye, he grinned and gave me a thumbs-up. Having him there for moral support made me feel much calmer. Whatever the outcome, I was determined to have fun as I baked.

Jaspreet took the floor in front of the audience and gave a quick spiel about how the competition would work. Then she introduced me and my fellow bakers as well as the judges.

"Bakers, you will have ninety minutes to complete your bakes," she said. "Starting . . . now!"

Tuning out everything around me, I grabbed some ingredients and got to work.

Chapter Four

THE NEXT NINETY MINUTES PASSED QUICKLY. I HAD to switch back and forth between working on my mandelhörnchen and my chocolates, since both recipes required some waiting time at certain steps. The mandelhörnchen dough needed to chill, my chocolate needed time to set in the molds, and my candy cane ganache had to cool before I could pipe it into the chocolate shells. The day before, I'd typed up a list of what I needed to do and in what order. I told myself that as long as I followed my own instructions, I'd be fine.

The last of my nerves disappeared as my focus intensified. I worked quickly, knowing I wouldn't have any time to spare, but I'd made both items many times before and that gave me the confidence I needed to keep going. When Jaspreet announced that we had one minute remaining, I already had all of my chocolates out of the molds and displayed on a platter, along with most of the mandelhörnchen. As the audience counted down the final ten seconds, I dipped the last mandelhörnchen in chocolate and set it next to the others. I had just enough time remaining to wipe a smear of chocolate off the platter.

"Time's up!" Jaspreet called out.

Letting out a relieved breath, I stepped back and scrutinized my desserts. They looked good. Delicious, actually. I'd done my best and now my fate sat in the hands of the judges.

I waited with minimal nerves as the judges tasted all of the desserts. They kept their thoughts to themselves and their expressions didn't reveal much. Each judge had a clipboard, and they made notes as they tasted each item. When they'd finished, the four of us competitors loaded all of our dirty baking dishes onto rolling carts and a cleaning crew moved in to ready the stations for the next bakers. Once all four preliminary rounds were over, the baked goods and confections would be set out for the audience, volunteers, and competitors to feast on.

Roman and I wheeled our carts into the town hall's kitchen, followed by the two women from our group. I chatted quietly with the women as we sorted our own dishes from the ones provided by the competition. Volunteers got busy cleaning the provided dishes, but we were responsible for our own. Roman remained silent as he cleaned up and packed his belongings into his plastic tub.

When I had all of my items organized and back in my box, I carried it out of the kitchen's side door and down the hallway that led to the foyer, so I could enter the main room from behind the audience. Up ahead, Stephanie paced back and forth. I could almost feel the nervous energy radiating off of her.

"Hey, are you okay?" I set my box on the floor when I reached her.

Stephanie clutched my arm. "No! I'm really not!"

"What's wrong?" I asked with mild alarm.

"I can't bake in front of an audience!" she said, her voiced pitched higher than normal. "What was I thinking? This will be a disaster!"

Her lack of confidence took me by surprise. She always seemed so cheerful and composed.

I gently pried her hand off my arm, where I was sure she'd left marks beneath my sleeve. "What are you talking about? You bake every day. It's your career, and you're amazing at it."

"In the privacy of my own kitchen." She hooked a thumb over her shoulder, in the direction of the main room. "There are people in there, *watching*. And there are judges. *Judges!*"

"Stephanie," I said calmly, "I know it's a bit intimidating, but baking is baking. It doesn't matter if you have an audience or not. You still know exactly what to do."

I didn't bother to mention that I'd had the same fear before my preliminary round.

She drew in a deep breath and let it out slowly. I caught a glimpse of her usual, composed self behind the nerves.

"You're right. Thank you, Becca."

"You've got this, okay?"

She nodded, and stood taller. I grabbed my box and walked with her to the foyer. Irma came out of the main room and scowled at us.

"Can you believe who they've got judging this thing?" she said to Stephanie and me.

"What's wrong with the judges?" I asked.

"Victor Barnabas, that's what's wrong. What does he know about baking?"

"He's an artist," Stephanie said. "The desserts, especially in the final round, are going to be judged partly on presentation. That's probably why he's a judge."

"An artist?" Irma snorted. "I can think of better words to describe him."

With that remark, she stormed past us and down the hallway.

Stephanie and I shared a glance and an eye roll.

Halfway down the hall, two young blonde women emerged from the restroom seconds after Irma disappeared through the same door. Paisley, whom I'd last seen at the art gallery, hurried to keep pace with her taller companion, who had sleek, straight hair in contrast to Paisley's wayward curls.

The taller woman gave her hair a haughty toss over her shoulder as she breezed past us.

"Good luck in the competition, Amber," Stephanie said to her.

Amber paused long enough to smirk. "Thanks. But I won't need it." She resumed walking and added, just loud enough for us to hear, "But you sure will."

Paisley shot an apologetic look our way before scurrying after Amber.

"Wow," I said, staring after them. "She's not exactly Miss Congeniality."

"She never has been," Stephanie said with a sigh. "I'd better get back in there. Thanks for the pep talk, Becca."

I stayed put when I saw Blake heading my way. He stepped aside to make room for Stephanie as she passed, and then he joined me in the foyer. I set my box down again and he gave me a hug.

"You did great, Becca."

"Were you here to cheer for me or for your employee?" I asked, joking.

"I want Roman to make it to the finals. I want you to win the whole thing." He glanced over his shoulder, then lowered his voice and grinned. "But don't tell him I said that."

"Your secret's safe with me," I promised.

Blake had to get back to the restaurant, so he pulled on his jacket and left the town hall while I collected my box and found a seat in the back row of folding chairs. Stephanie stood at her baking station, checking everything she had set out on the counter. While there was a nervous energy to her movements, she seemed calmer than she had a few minutes earlier. Amber, who had been assigned the baking station next to Stephanie's, posed with one hand on her bright red mixer while Paisley snapped photos of her with a smartphone. Amber wore a navy dress with high-heeled boots and had silver hoops in her ears. Her makeup was flawless, and every blonde strand of hair was perfectly in place. After Paisley had taken several photographs, Amber tied her hair back into a ponytail. She produced a compact from her handbag and used the mirror to check her hair and makeup.

Soon, the next round got underway. It wasn't exactly riveting entertainment, although Jaspreet did occasionally speak over the whirring of mixers and food processors to tell the audience about the desserts each contestant was making. I knew I wouldn't be able to sit through all of the remaining rounds, but I wanted to stay for the current one.

Partway through the ninety minutes, somebody slipped into the chair next to me.

I smiled when I realized it was Dizzy. "I thought you were working," I whispered.

"I'm here for my lunch hour," she said in an equally quiet voice. "I wish I could have been here earlier to see you bake. How did it go?"

"I think it went well, but you didn't miss anything exciting."

Dizzy turned her attention to the bakers at the front of the room. "I didn't realize Stephanie Kang was competing. I hope she does well. But not as well as you, of course."

"She's going to be tough competition," I said, "but I really like her. If she wins, I won't be too disappointed."

Dizzy's eyes narrowed. "I sure hope Amber Dubois doesn't win. Her head is already too big."

"Who is she, anyway?" I asked, still whispering. "Her name rings a bell, but I don't think I've met her before."

"I'm pretty sure you'd remember if you had," Dizzy said. "She's a few years younger than us and she didn't move here until her teens. Now she's a food blogger and a self-proclaimed social media influencer."

Even though it was the middle of the competition, with time ticking away, Amber paused in her baking to pose again, this time holding up a mixing bowl to show its contents to the camera as Paisley snapped a photo.

"Is she a model or a baker?" I asked.

"Right?" Dizzy shook her head.

Two middle-aged women claimed seats in our row, so we fell quiet. I was glad to see that Stephanie appeared to be in the baking zone now. All traces of nervous energy had vanished and she worked calmly and steadily. Amber stopped to pose for photos a few more times, and I wondered if she cared about making it to the finals, or if she simply wanted photos of herself taking part in the competition and nothing more.

The large digital clock on display counted down the time. With two minutes left, the first crack appeared in Amber's composure. Photo ops apparently forgotten, she hurriedly piped decorations onto her cupcakes and quickly arranged them on the serving platter, setting the last cupcake in place as Jaspreet announced that the time was up.

Dizzy had to get back to work, so she headed out of the building while I left my box on my chair and worked my way toward the front of the room to see Stephanie.

"Your cupcakes look amazing," I told her. They certainly outshone Amber's cupcakes, which lacked the sophisticated finish of Stephanie's. "I bet they taste even better."

Stephanie's smile could have lit up the whole room. "Thank you! Once I got baking, I wasn't nervous at all. I probably will be again when the judges start tasting, though."

It was time for that to happen, so I retreated to the back of the room. After the judges had sampled everything, I decided not to stick around any longer. It would be at least another half hour before the next round got underway, and watching the judges taste the desserts had made my stomach rumble with jealousy.

With my box in my arms, I headed for the foyer, where

I nearly crashed into the well-dressed man I'd first seen at the art gallery.

"I'm so sorry!" I apologized, halting just in time to avoid a collision.

"My fault," he said, stepping aside to make room for me to pass him. "I was looking at my phone." He tucked the device into his pocket.

"I saw you at the art gallery earlier in the week. Are you new to town?" I asked.

"No, just visiting."

"I hope you're liking Larch Haven."

"It's hard not to," he said with a smile. "It's a very charming place."

Shifting my box into my left arm, I offered him my right hand. "I'm Becca Ransom. I hope you'll enjoy the rest of your stay."

He gave my hand a firm shake. "Daniel Hathaway. Good luck with the competition."

I thanked him and smiled before continuing on out of the town hall. I'd made it down only one of the front steps when Stephanie called my name. I turned around and found her standing in the open doorway.

She didn't have a coat on so I joined her in the foyer again so she wouldn't have to get blasted by the cold wind any longer.

"Everything okay?" I asked.

"Sure, but I saw you talking with that guy in the nice suit."

"Daniel Hathaway?"

"Is that his name? Rumor has it that he's the representative from *Bake It Right*."

"Really?"

He struck me more as a wealthy businessman rather than a writer or editor, but magazine employees likely didn't all fit into one mold.

"Actually, some people think he might be the owner of

the magazine," Stephanie said. "Did he mention anything to you about it?"

"No. We introduced ourselves and he said he's a visitor here in Larch Haven."

"Here on business?"

"He didn't say."

She shrugged. "Oh, well. I guess we'll find out soon enough if he's with the magazine. See you later."

She returned to the competition room and I set off into the cold again.

Her words stuck with me as I walked in the direction of True Confections. If Daniel Hathaway was with *Bake It Right*, did that have anything to do with Irma's conversation with him earlier? She'd started out looking smug, then ended up angry. Had she tried to curry favor with him, without success?

I decided it didn't matter.

The only thing I was concerned about right at that moment was finding myself some lunch.

Chapter Five

~~~~~~~~~~

I RETURNED TO THE TOWN HALL LATE IN THE AFTER-
noon to hear the results of the preliminary round of competition. By then Dizzy had finished work, so she met me
on the front steps and tucked her arm through mine as we
headed indoors.

"Are you nervous?" she asked.

"A little," I admitted. "But not as much as I was before
the competition started. I know I did my best. If I didn't
make it into the finals, that's okay."

She gave my arm a squeeze. "I bet you did make it."

All my fellow competitors had gathered at the site of the
competition again. Stephanie sat in the front row of chairs,
looking calm except for the fact that she kept tapping her
thumb against her leg. Amber and Paisley sat a few chairs
to the right of her, both focused on their phones. Roman
had claimed a seat two rows back, where he sat so still that
he could have passed as a statute. His sharp cheekbones
and angular nose only strengthened his resemblance to a
stone sculpture.

Dizzy and I slipped into chairs behind him, and Irma—frowning as always—plunked herself into a chair at the end of the front row. The other competitors, along with some friends and family members, also settled into chairs when Jaspreet stepped up to the front of the room.

"Thank you to everyone who entered this year's Baking Spirits Bright competition," Jaspreet said, addressing the audience. "I'm pleased to announce the four finalists who will advance to the next round of competition. Congratulations to Roman Kafka, Irma Jones, Stephanie Kang, and Rebecca Ransom."

I turned my wide eyes to Dizzy. "What?"

She let out a squeal and threw her arms around me, almost squeezing all the air out of my lungs.

Around us, people cheered and clapped.

"Way to go, Becca!" Dizzy said when she released me.

As my initial shock wore off, a smile spread across my face. "I can't believe I made it!"

Dizzy gave me another hug. "I can."

I faced the front of the room again in time to see Amber get up from her seat and toss her hair over her shoulder before stalking off, her nose in the air and her mouth screwed up like she'd bitten into a particularly sour lemon. Paisley hurried to catch up with her, and together they left the town hall without a backward glance.

When everyone had settled down, Jaspreet gave me and the three other finalists our instructions. The next and last round of competition would take place in two days. We would have five hours to create an edible outdoor scene. Each entry had to include at least three different types of baked elements.

Afterward, Dizzy and I picked up a pizza and took it to my cottage, where we had a brainstorming session while we ate. By the time Dizzy left to go home, I had a firm plan in place. I was going to create an edible version of a slice of Larch Haven in the summer. It would feature gingerbread shops and cottages, and chocolate gondolas on sugar-glass canals. The surrounding mountains and the island in the middle of Shadow Lake would be made of chocolate cake, decorated with Swiss meringue buttercream. I would mold green marzipan into trees, and brandy snaps would form the wooden boards for the town's main dock. It was an ambitious plan, but one that would look amazing if I could pull it off.

THE NEXT DAY, LOLLY HELPED OUT IN THE TRUE CONfections kitchen while I made patterns for my gingerbread elements and worked out the final details of my plan. I didn't have time to practice more than a few of the individual elements, so I simply had to hope that I'd be able to finish everything within the five-hour time limit.

That evening, the night before the competition, I picked up a golf cart from the rental agency at the edge of town and parked it behind True Confections. The finalists were allowed to take any dishes, tools, or ingredients over to the town hall that night so we would have less to worry about in the morning. Anything that required refrigeration, I would take over the next day, but I had plenty of supplies that could be transported early. I had far too much to carry on my own, so I figured loading up a golf cart would be the easiest way to go about it. Soon, I was trundling off along the cobblestones.

I parked behind the town hall and carried my first box of supplies in through the back door. As I stomped snow from my boots, angry voices caught my attention. I peeked around the corner and spotted Irma halfway down the hall, arguing with her adult daughter, Juniper, who was a few years older than me.

"Grandma left that jewelry to *me*." Juniper practically spat the words out, her face contorted with anger. "That means it's legally mine. You have no right to withhold it from me!"

"I'm not letting you get your grubby hands on something so precious," Irma said, her voice full of spite. "If my mother had any idea how lazy you would grow up to be, she never would have left you anything."

"I'm not lazy!" Juniper shot back as I ducked out of sight.

I decided to hang around by the back door until their fight was over. I had no desire to walk through the middle of their war of words and insults.

"You might not think that being an artist is a legitimate job, but it is," Juniper continued. "I work hard and I'm doing well. That's pretty incredible when you consider what a terrible role model I had growing up."

"You always were an ungrateful wretch!"

I heard the creak of a door opening and peeked around the corner again. Irma disappeared into the restroom.

"This isn't over!" Juniper screeched at the closing door. Then she spun around in my direction.

I quickly ducked out of sight and backed halfway out the door to pretend that I was just entering the building. Juniper stormed past me, not even sparing me a glance.

I hoped the cold air outside would cool her temper. She looked ready to explode.

With the coast now clear, I hurried along the hall, wanting to make it to my baking station without running into Irma. Feeling uneasy, I peeked into the main room before entering. The only person present was Eleanor Tiedemann. Eleanor worked at Irma's bakery as her assistant, and I pitied her for it. During some of my visits to the bakery, I'd witnessed Irma insult and belittle Eleanor. I wouldn't have been able to endure working for a boss like that, but somehow Eleanor put up with it. Maybe she needed the money too much to risk losing her job by standing up to Irma.

Eleanor was in her early fifties, and I thought she was a single mother, although I couldn't remember for sure. At the moment, she was rummaging through a brown handbag. As I walked into the room, she glanced up and froze,

wide-eyed, like a deer caught in headlights. She yanked her
hand out of the bag and took a quick step backward.

"Hello," I called out as I approached.

Eleanor offered me a shaky smile.

The guilt on her face set alarm bells ringing in my head.
I soon realized why. I recognized the handbag as belonging
to Irma.

When I glanced from the bag to Eleanor, she must have
realized that I'd made the connection.

"I was looking for a pen to borrow," she said so quickly
that I had trouble making out the words. "I'm sure I can
find one somewhere else."

She darted past me and speed-walked out of the room
like an Olympic champion.

Strange, I thought, but then I brushed off the incident.

Each baking station had a piece of paper taped to it with
a finalist's name written on it. I set my box on the station
I'd been assigned and then made another trip out to my golf
cart, thankfully without witnessing any further drama.

It was no secret around town that Irma and Juniper Jones
didn't get along, but I'd never witnessed one of their tiffs
before. I didn't know what had set the relationship on such a
bumpy track, but Irma wasn't an easy woman to be around.
Most likely she was even harder to live with. I didn't know
Juniper well enough to say whether she had inherited her
mother's personality or not, but she clearly wasn't above giving as good as she got while arguing with Irma.

Pushing thoughts of Irma and Juniper from my mind, I
surveyed my station and made sure I hadn't forgotten anything. I had my piping bags, my chocolate molds—including
my custom-made gondola molds—a chocolate chipper, an
offset spatula, my favorite rolling pin, and various other
items. Everything else I would either bring with me in the
morning or borrow from the provided supplies.

With my empty boxes stacked together, I headed out of
the room. My shoulders tensed when I passed Irma and

Roman in the foyer. They were in the midst of a quiet conversation, but they stopped talking as I passed by. I flashed them a smile, but didn't receive one in return. Irma looked annoyed and Roman had a stony expression on his face. I suppressed a shiver of unease when he briefly turned his cold, blue eyes from Irma to me.

Once past them, I picked up my pace, not slowing until I was out in the fresh, cold air. I stashed my boxes in the golf cart and zoomed away from the town hall. Only then did the tension in my shoulders dissipate.

I AWOKE THE NEXT MORNING WITH NERVOUS JITTERS in my stomach. At first, I didn't know the source of my anxiety. I blinked bleary eyes at my ceiling while Truffles pawed at my blankets and Binx walked up and down my legs. My sleepy mind became more fully awake and I finally remembered that it was the day of the finals of the Baking Spirits Bright competition.

Any remaining sleepiness vanished and I threw back my covers. I hurried through my morning routine—skipping my usual yoga-Pilates fusion workout—and rushed off to True Confections, where I packed up all my ingredients and quickly transported them to the town hall in my rented golf cart. Stephanie pulled a cart in next to mine. right after I parked behind the building.

I glanced up at the gray sky, hoping that any snow flurries would hold off until after I'd returned the golf cart to the rental agency. The canopy was up, but the sides were open, and I didn't want to have to shovel out the vehicle before I could drive it again.

"Morning!" I called to Stephanie as I grabbed my box of ingredients. "How are the nerves?"

"Not as bad as before," Stephanie said. "Somehow making it through the first round has put me more at ease."

"You're going to do great," I assured her.

"Thanks. I know you will too."

She grabbed a box from her golf cart, and we headed for the town hall's back door.

I spotted a smear of red on the snowbank next to the door. Blood. Maybe someone had suffered a nosebleed.

I hugged my box with one arm and opened the door, holding it for Stephanie before following her into the building. Another splotch of blood caught my attention inside the door. This time it was on the wall, level with my waist. Hopefully the nosebleed or whatever injury someone had sustained wasn't serious.

I pointed the blood out to Stephanie.

"Maybe we should check the washrooms to make sure no one needs help," I suggested.

Stephanie agreed, so we set down our supplies and she entered the women's washroom while I opened the door to the men's room.

I called out before entering, but got no response. When I ventured inside, I found the room empty.

"Nobody there," Stephanie reported as we returned to the hall.

"Same with the men's washroom," I said.

We picked up our supplies and carried on down the hallway.

Briefly, I wondered what kind of drama I'd have to dodge this morning on my way to my baking station, but I saw with relief that Stephanie and I were the only people in the hallway. I soon found out that was the case with the foyer as well. Maybe luck was with me and there wouldn't be any further drama aside from finding out the winner of the competition later in the day.

I entered the main room, with Stephanie on my heels. The overhead lights were on, but it looked as though Stephanie and I were the first to arrive, aside from whoever had unlocked the doors and turned on the lights. Maybe that same person was the source of the blood we'd seen.

Glancing down, I noticed a clump of snow on my boot. I backtracked to the foyer and stomped it off on the mat. Then I returned to the room, with Stephanie several strides ahead of me now. She'd been assigned the baking station behind mine, so she headed straight toward the back of the room. When she reached my station, she dropped her box to the floor and let out a scream.

I came to an abrupt halt, but then rushed forward as Stephanie burst into tears.

"Stephanie! What's wrong?" When I reached her side, my stomach roiled.

Irma lay on the floor in a pool of blood.

Chapter Six

STILL CLUTCHING MY BOX OF INGREDIENTS, I STARED
at Irma, even though I wanted to look away. She lay crumpled on her side, but I caught a glimpse of a nasty wound
on her throat. I swallowed hard and took two steps back. I
dropped my box on the baking station next to mine and
then tried to force my stomach to settle as I returned to
Stephanie's side. She now had her back to Irma, her hands
covering her face as she cried.

"Stephanie?" I took her arm, and gently pulled one hand
away from her face. "Call nine-one-one, okay?"

She nodded and dropped her other hand from her face.
Tear tracks meandered down her cheeks. With shaking
hands, she dug her cell phone from her purse.

I didn't bother trying to check for a pulse. The blood had
dried and Irma's skin was discolored. It was far too late to
help her.

Her handbag lay on the floor a few feet away from her
head, its contents strewn about.

She must have been murdered, I realized, with a fresh

wave of nausea. I didn't see how there could be any other explanation.

I backed up so quickly that I almost bumped into Stephanie. She was talking with the emergency operator, her voice shaky but clear. I took her arm and gently but quickly guided her away from Irma's body. My knees trembled beneath me. I was tempted to drop down into one of the folding chairs, but instead I quickened my pace, pulling Stephanie along with me as we passed the rows of chairs and left the room.

Stephanie lowered her phone from her ear. "Outside?"

I nodded and shoved open the front door.

Cold air hit me like a slap to the face. Even that wasn't enough to fully snap me out of my state of shock.

"Yes, I'm still here," Stephanie said into her phone. She glanced my way, her eyes wide and full of the same horror that I knew would be showing in mine.

It couldn't have been more than a minute before I heard sirens in the distance, quickly drawing closer. A police cruiser navigated its way along the wide cobblestone walkway and pulled up in front of the town hall.

I hoped Sawyer would be in the cruiser, but two other officers climbed out of the vehicle. Stephanie ended her call with the emergency operator while I told the officers where to find Irma. As soon as they disappeared inside, an ambulance came around a bend in the road and parked next to the police cruiser. A couple of pedestrians looked our way with curiosity as they walked slowly by, but otherwise the road was empty. That probably wouldn't last long. I didn't doubt that more curious onlookers would soon arrive on the scene.

One of the police officers came out of the building and separated me from Stephanie so we were standing on opposite sides of the steps. Then the officer spoke with the paramedics. Another police cruiser, this one with flashing lights but no siren, pulled up next to the ambulance.

A rush of relief left my legs trembling even more when I saw Sawyer climb out of the driver's side. I wanted to hurry over to him for a hug, but I held back. He was on duty, there to investigate and protect, not to comfort me.

His face was already serious, but it became even more so when he saw me. He altered his path to reach me and took hold of my shoulders. "Are you okay, Becca?" he asked, looking straight into my eyes.

"Yes. It's Irma. Stephanie and I found her."

"Stay here, all right?"

I nodded.

He held my gaze for another second before releasing me and jogging up the front steps after one of his colleagues.

Despite my winter outerwear, the cold soon seeped its way into my bones. Across the way from me, Stephanie shivered visibly. I had to move out of the way as one of the police officers ran crime-scene tape across the front of the building, blocking off the front steps. As I'd expected, the sirens and emergency vehicles had drawn people toward the scene. A small crowd was now gathering across the cobblestone walkway.

"What happened?" one man yelled.

Stephanie and I pretended not to hear him.

I wrapped my arms around myself, trying to stay warm, but it didn't do much good. My toes and fingers had started aching from the cold when a female officer came out of the building, ducking under the tape when she reached the bottom of the steps. The officer asked Stephanie and me to accompany her next door to the community center, where she then spoke to us separately.

She asked me to tell her, with as much detail as possible, about finding Irma's body. She also wanted to know about everything I'd seen and heard from the moment I'd arrived at the town hall. There wasn't all that much to tell, although I made sure to mention the smears of blood I'd seen in the hall and on the snowbank out back. Eventually, the officer told me I could go.

"Was Irma murdered?" I asked, even though I was sure I knew the answer.

The officer had been about to leave the room, but she paused and looked back. "The investigation has only just begun. I'm sure a statement will be provided to the local media later today or tomorrow."

With that, she crossed the hall to another of the community center's rooms to speak with Stephanie.

Outside, as I stood on the front steps, my attention immediately returned to the town hall next door. A couple of officers stood in front of the building talking, but I couldn't see Sawyer anywhere. When I realized that some of the onlookers had spotted me, I decided to make a hasty getaway. I didn't want to get pestered with questions about what I'd seen. Recounting the experience to the police officer had been bad enough.

I hurried away from the crowd, ducking around the nearest corner and crossing a bridge over the frozen canal. I could have headed home, but there was somewhere else I wanted to be. After taking another turn and following a curving cobblestone walkway, I arrived at my grandparents' cottage. The walkway had been shoveled, leaving a clear path to the front door as well as one to the back gate. I took the latter path, and made my way around the cottage.

When I knocked on the back door, Lolly opened it almost immediately.

"Rebecca," she said with surprise, glancing at the clock on the kitchen wall. "Shouldn't you be at the town hall? I was about to head for the shop."

I shut the door behind me, and as the warmth of the kitchen enveloped me, I couldn't hold back my tears any longer.

"Oh, sweetheart. What's wrong?" Lolly asked.

I collapsed into a chair and told her everything.

"You poor thing," Lolly said when I'd finished the grim story. She kissed the top of my head and then made me a cup of tea with plenty of sugar and a generous dollop of cream. "What a terrible thing to happen." She set the steaming mug in front of me. "And what a terrible thing for you to see. Do you really think Irma was murdered?"

"I'm pretty sure. Maybe there was some sort of freak accident, but I don't see how that could have happened. It's not like there was any dangerous machinery lying about."

Saying that out loud left me feeling certain that it was murder, even though I didn't want it to be.

Lolly kissed the top of my head again. "I'm so glad you're safe."

She made sure I finished my tea before I left. I considered going to True Confections and trying to lose myself in my work, but I let Lolly convince me to go home. A wave of weariness took me by surprise and I suddenly wanted nothing more than to curl up on my couch with Binx and Truffles.

I didn't want to walk past the town hall on my way home, so I took another route. I hadn't gone far when I spotted a police cruiser up ahead.

Apprehension slid cold fingers over my shoulders. Had there been another murder?

I picked up my pace and soon realized that the cruiser was parked outside of Irma's cottage. Not another murder, then. At least, probably not. The police were likely at Irma's cottage as part of their investigation into her death. I hoped that's all it was.

Keeping my head down and avoiding eye contact with anyone I passed, I hurried home to be with my cats. I spent the rest of the day on the couch, as planned, watching holiday movies and trying my very best to not think about what I'd seen at the town hall.

* * *

AFTER A RESTLESS NIGHT FILLED WITH UNSETTLING dreams and long spells of wakefulness, I made my way through the cold and dark morning to True Confections. Irma's bakery was completely dark, the usual glow of light from the back conspicuously absent. It was a stark reminder of what had happened to the baker the day before. Not that I needed a reminder. I could hardly think about anything else.

Once in the shop's kitchen, I took comfort in the familiar work of making chocolates. It was such a relief to be busy that I didn't pause for a break until nearly four hours had passed. After washing my hands and removing my apron, I cautiously peeked out into the shop area. Several customers browsed the shelves, but Angie and my aunt Kathleen were both working and had everything under control. I was glad of that. If I jumped in to help them out front, I'd run the risk of having to answer questions about Irma. No doubt most of the town knew by now that I'd been present for the grisly discovery.

I was about to retreat to the kitchen again when I spotted Eleanor Tiedemann approaching the sales counter. She set a box of chocolates down and started chatting with Angie.

"These are my son's favorites." She tapped the box at the top of her short stack. "But I had to get some of the candy cane truffles for myself, of course."

"You should never forget about treating yourself," Angie said as she scanned the boxes of chocolates. "Your son's in his senior year now, isn't he?"

Eleanor practically glowed with pride. "And heading off to college at the end of the summer."

Angie slipped the boxes into a bag. "I'm so sorry about what happened to Irma."

Eleanor's face fell. "Yes. It's a terrible business. I know

Irma wasn't the nicest person, but I still can't believe someone murdered her."

I tucked myself farther out of sight, listening in.

"So, it definitely was murder?" Angie asked.

"The police haven't said so yet, but I don't see what else
it could have been. Someone ransacked Irma's cottage
around the same time she was killed. That can't be a coin-
cidence."

I peeked around the doorframe in time to see Eleanor
shake her head.

"No," she said without a shred of doubt. "I'm absolutely
certain Irma was murdered."

Chapter Seven

I QUIETLY SLIPPED BACK DOWN THE HALL AND INTO the office across from the kitchen. Sinking into the chair behind the desk, I thought over what Eleanor had said. Someone had ransacked Irma's cottage. Did that mean the murderer killed her because they wanted something that was in Irma's possession?

A memory came rushing back to me.

I'd caught Eleanor rummaging around in Irma's handbag. She claimed she was searching for a pen, but I didn't really believe her at the time, and I still didn't. She'd appeared far too guilty for that to be the truth.

Had Irma later caught Eleanor going through her bag again? If that happened, maybe they got into a fight and Eleanor killed Irma. Then, not finding what she was looking for in Irma's bag, maybe Eleanor had gone to the cottage and torn it apart.

But what could Eleanor have wanted so badly?

I had no idea, but that didn't mean events hadn't unfolded as I'd just pictured them in my head.

I fought back a wave of queasiness. How coldhearted of Eleanor to kill a woman and then shop for chocolates the very next day.

I quickly reminded myself that I didn't know that Eleanor had killed Irma. It wasn't a good idea to jump to conclusions. After all, plenty of people had disliked the baker.

Not wanting to think about Irma's death any longer, I dug my phone out of my coat pocket. I hadn't checked it since I'd arrived at the shop early that morning. Now I saw that Sawyer had sent me a text message a few hours ago.

You doing okay? the message read.

Yes, thanks, I wrote back.

I didn't want to explain by text message that what I'd seen at the town hall still haunted me.

I received a message back almost right away.

I hate to ask this, but can you come by the police station today?

When? I wrote, even though I really wanted to ask why.

Any time.

A sense of trepidation crawled up the back of my neck. I didn't want to spend a chunk of the day wondering why he wanted me to visit the station, so I decided to get the visit over with.

I'll be there soon.

I sent the message and then got bundled up in my coat and boots.

I'D ALMOST REACHED THE POLICE STATION WHEN I spotted Stephanie and Juniper up ahead, walking in the same direction as me. I jogged to catch up to them.

"Juniper, I'm so sorry about your mom," I said as we stopped a stone's throw away from the police station.

She stared down at her boots. "Thanks."

She seemed subdued, but not distraught.

"Are you heading for the police station too?" I asked.

"We both got calls from Detective Ishimoto, asking us to stop by," Stephanie replied. "I guess the police have more questions for us." She cast a worried glance Juniper's way. "The detective talked to Juniper yesterday, but she wasn't feeling up to answering many questions."

Juniper tugged her hat down farther over her dull brown hair. "It's not like I can help the cops out much, anyway. It's no secret that my mom and I weren't close."

The three of us started walking toward the station again. When we reached the front steps of the brick building, I came to a stop. Eleanor was heading toward us along the canal.

"My condolences," she said to Juniper when she reached us.

Juniper mumbled her thanks, again staring at her boots.

"You've been called in to answer questions too?" I asked Eleanor.

"Standard procedure, I'm sure," she said. "Although, they might want our alibis."

"Alibis?" Juniper seemed startled by the word. "Yesterday the police wouldn't say for sure that my mom was murdered."

"Yes, well, perhaps you should prepare yourself for that possibility." Eleanor climbed the steps to the double doors of the police station, leaving us behind.

"Are you okay, Juniper?" I asked, concerned by the way the color had suddenly drained from her face.

She sucked in a sharp breath. "As okay as I can be."

"Do you have an alibi?" As soon as the words came out of my mouth, I wished I could take them back. That wasn't exactly a tactful question to ask in the circumstances.

Juniper's gray eyes widened.

"Of course she does," Stephanie said quickly before Juniper had a chance to say anything. "We were together at my place. Juniper came over in the early evening and then ended up crashing on my couch for the night. She didn't leave until I was ready to head for the town hall in the morning. Right, Juniper?"

Her eyes still wide and startled, Juniper opened her mouth and shut it again before finally speaking. "Right. We were together." Her words came out sounding stilted.

Stephanie tucked her arm through Juniper's and tugged her forward. "We'd better get this over with."

I stood at the bottom of the steps while the two of them disappeared inside the police station. As much as I liked Stephanie, I was certain that she and Juniper had just lied to me.

WHEN I ENTERED THE RECEPTION AREA OF THE PO-lice station, Eleanor, Stephanie, and Juniper were already gone from sight. I realized that I probably hadn't timed things well. If Detective Naomi Ishimoto wanted to talk to all of us in turn, I'd likely have to wait a while. I approached the front desk anyway. Maybe another police officer would ask me whatever questions needed asking and I could be on my way in short order.

The man behind the front desk told me to take a seat until an officer came to fetch me. I smiled when that officer turned out to be Sawyer.

"Hey, Becca," he said when he saw me. "Come on back."

I joined him by the door to the left of the reception area, and he rested a hand on my back as he guided me down the hallway and into a small interview room.

"You can wait in here for Detective Ishimoto." He pulled a chair out from beneath the small table for me.

I remained standing as disappointment pinged in my chest. "You can't ask me the questions?"

"Detective Ishimoto would like to be here."

Apprehension settled heavily in the pit of my stomach. That sounded serious. "It's a murder investigation, right?"

"Yes," Sawyer confirmed.

I sank down into the chair he'd pulled out. I really hadn't doubted that someone had murdered Irma, but hearing an official confirmation of that fact brought back what I'd seen at the town hall with far too much vivid detail.

Sawyer crouched down in front of me. "Hey. Are you really okay, Becca?"

I nodded and focused on him. That helped force the unwanted memories to recede. "I'm all right, but it was an awful thing to see." Even worse than the body I'd seen floating in the canal last summer. At least then there hadn't been much blood.

Sawyer touched my knee. "I wish you hadn't had to see it. It might be a good idea to talk to a counselor. I can put you in touch with someone."

I forced a small smile. "Thank you, but I'm all right."

Maybe it would have been good to take him up on his offer, but at the moment I really didn't want to have to talk about what I'd seen any more than absolutely necessary.

Sawyer held my gaze for a long moment, as if searching my eyes to see if I really was okay. Eventually, he nodded and stood up. "Can I get you something to drink while you wait?"

"No, thanks. I'm fine." What I really wanted was for him to wait with me, but I didn't ask for that. He no doubt had plenty of work to do that didn't involve keeping me company.

He rested a hand on my shoulder. "I'll check in with you in a bit, okay? Hopefully Detective Ishimoto won't be long."

I thanked him again, and he left the room, shutting the door behind him. I wriggled out of my coat and pulled off my hat and gloves, trying to get more comfortable.

For the next few minutes, I stared at the wall, fidgeted, and tried to think only happy thoughts. As time ticked by, I grew more restless, so I pulled out my phone. The organizers of the Baking Spirits Bright competition had sent out a text message to everyone involved in the event. The competition was postponed until further notice.

I wondered if they'd end up canceling altogether. I didn't know how long it would be until the town hall was no longer a crime scene. Even once the building was free to be used again, would any of us remaining competitors want to bake there again? I sure didn't. How could I bake cakes and make chocolates while standing in the exact place where Irma died? That wasn't something I even wanted to think about.

Thankfully, I had other text messages to distract me. Dizzy had stopped by True Confections a few minutes ago, only to find me gone. I quickly texted her back to let her know where I was and why. I'd spoken to her on the phone the night before and told her what had happened. Even so, I longed to see my best friend in person. We'd been friends since preschool, and Dizzy had helped me get through pretty much every difficult spell in my life so far.

I wouldn't get to see her for a while yet, though. She had the day off from work at the library, but she was about to drive to Burlington to pick up her parents from the airport. These days, they primarily lived in the Philippines, where they were from originally, but they usually visited Larch Haven for several weeks each year. This time they were staying until the middle of January.

Dizzy and I exchanged a few more text messages, agreeing to meet up in person later, and then I was left to wait without distraction again. I was about to find a game to play on my phone when the door finally opened. Detective Ishimoto entered the room, with Sawyer behind her. As he shut the door, I caught a glimpse of concern in his dark eyes. That set off a flare of worry in my chest. When Sawyer looked directly at me a moment later, however, I could tell that he was silently trying to reassure me.

Detective Ishimoto sat down across the table from me. She had a file folder, a notebook, a pen, and what looked like a clear plastic bag poking out from beneath the folder. She set everything on the tabletop. The detective's black hair was tied back in a twist, and she wore a gray suit with a blue blouse. Although she was probably a couple of inches shorter than my five feet, eight inches, she had a strong, authoritative presence that seemed to fill the room.

"Thank you for coming to the station today, Ms. Ransom," she said. "I just have a few questions for you."

"Okay." I glanced at Sawyer.

He stood next to the table with his back to the door. Again, I got the sense that he was trying to send me reassuring vibes.

I returned my attention to the detective. She opened her notebook and asked me a series of questions. Everything I told her I'd already told the other officer the day before, but I figured she was simply being thorough.

About a quarter of an hour later, I thought the conversation was winding down. Then the detective shifted the file folder off the plastic bag. It was an evidence bag, I realized. She pushed it toward the center of the table.

"Do you recognize this?" she asked.

My heart almost screeched to a stop before it lurched into a rapid dance. I wasn't sure if I was actually dizzy or if my thoughts were simply swirling so fast in my head that it felt that way. I wanted to look to Sawyer for reassurance, but I couldn't tear my gaze from the contents of the bag.

"Ms. Ransom?" Detective Ishimoto prodded when I didn't answer right away.

Black spots appeared in my peripheral vision and I reminded myself to breathe. I drew in a breath and then cleared my throat.

"Yes," I said, my voice sounding hoarse. "That's my chocolate chipper."

I'd recognized it right away. It had the letters *TC*—for True Confections—engraved on the wooden handle.

But now, what I really noticed was the dried blood on the tool's metal prongs.

Chapter Eight

"IS THAT THE MURDER WEAPON?" THIS TIME MY VOICE was hoarse *and* pitched higher than usual. I barely recognized it.

I wanted to look Sawyer's way, but I couldn't stop staring at the plastic-encased chocolate chipper.

"When did you last see it?" Detective Ishimoto asked, ignoring my question.

"Two days ago. I dropped off some of the things I was going to need for the competition, including the chocolate chipper. I left it on the counter at my baking station at the town hall."

The detective wrote something in her notebook. "What time of day was that?"

"Around six in the evening."

Finally, I managed to avert my gaze from the blood-coated prongs. Sawyer mostly had his professional mask in place. The only crack was in his eyes, which simmered with emotion.

Detective Ishimoto drew my attention back her way with her next question. "How well did you know Irma Jones?"

"Not well. I shop at her bakery and I saw her at the preliminary round of the competition, but that's about it."

"Did you ever have any problems with her?"

"No," I said. "I know other people did, though."

Detective Ishimoto asked me to explain, so I told her about the argument I'd overheard between Irma and Juniper. "Irma also wasn't very pleasant in general," I added. "I hate to say that after what happened to her, but she wasn't a happy woman."

Ishimoto asked for a timeline of my movements before wrapping up. "Thank you, Ms. Ransom. I appreciate you coming in today. Officer Maguire will see you out."

She gathered up her things and Sawyer opened the door for her. He shut it again once she was gone.

I turned so I was sitting sideways on my chair. "Sawyer . . ." I didn't know what else to say.

He grabbed another chair and pulled it close to mine before sitting down, facing me. "I'm sorry this is happening, Becca."

"The killer used my chocolate chipper to kill Irma." Even though Detective Ishimoto hadn't answered my question about the murder weapon, the blood on the prongs was answer enough. "If I hadn't left it there . . ."

"No." He leaned forward and took one of my hands, looking me right in the eyes. "Becca, it wasn't your fault. Not even a little bit."

"But if it hadn't been there . . ."

"Then the killer would have used something else. The only person who has any responsibility for this crime is the person who murdered Irma. Okay?"

I nodded, but my left knee started bouncing up and down, fueled by anxious energy. "Am I a suspect?" I was pretty sure I already knew the answer.

"Almost everyone is at this point," Sawyer said.

That didn't ease the sick feeling in my stomach, but then another thought perked me up and stopped my knee from bouncing. "Maybe I have an alibi. Do you know when she died, exactly?"

"Not yet. We'll know more once the postmortem is complete."

"When will that be?" I asked.

"Later today."

My knee started its jittery movements again. "I didn't kill her, Sawyer."

He rested his free hand on my bouncing knee, stilling the movement. "I know that, Becca."

I felt more grounded with him holding my hand and touching my knee. Some of the anxious energy drained out of me. "Okay, but Detective Ishimoto doesn't."

"She will."

He sounded so certain, and that eased more tension out of my shoulders.

"Thank you for being here," I said.

He gave my hand a squeeze before releasing it. "I wouldn't be anywhere else. Are you heading home or back to the shop?"

"The shop," I decided.

He stood up. "I'll walk with you."

I pulled on my coat as I got to my feet. "You must have other things to do."

"I'm heading out to talk to some of Irma's neighbors," he said. "A short detour won't hurt."

I mustered my first smile of the past hour. "Then I won't say no to your company."

As soon as we stepped outside, I wished I'd thought to grab a scarf before leaving True Confections. While I was in the police station, the wind had picked up, and it now swept around us, stinging my face and eyes, carrying snowflakes with it. As we descended the front steps of the station, the snow started coming down harder. I pulled my collar up as high as it would go and shoved my gloved hands into the pockets of my puffy, knee-length jacket.

"When are your parents getting into town?" Sawyer asked as we set off in the direction of Venice Avenue.

"They're flying in on the morning of the twenty-third and staying right through to the new year," I replied.

"You must be looking forward to seeing them."

"Definitely."

My parents had moved to Florida several years ago. My mom, a physician, had been offered a position at a Jacksonville hospital that she didn't want to turn down. So, she and my dad had packed up and moved south to the Sunshine State. Once there, my dad had quickly found a job as a hotel manager. As much as they enjoyed the Florida weather, I knew that my parents missed Larch Haven and would likely end up back here after they retired. For now, we made do with visiting one another a couple of times each year.

"How about your mom?" I asked. "Will she be coming to Larch Haven for Christmas?"

After Sawyer's dad passed away several years ago, his mom had shifted her home base from Vermont to Mexico, where she was born and raised. She did a lot of traveling the world these days, but she also spent long stretches of time in Mexico City, with her aging mother and aunts.

"Not this year," Sawyer replied. "But she's coming for a few days in the new year."

"That's good," I said. "I'd love to see her when she's here."

I stopped in my tracks and slapped a hand to my forehead.

"What's wrong?" Sawyer asked.

"I just remembered that I need to call the golf cart rental agency. I rented a cart to transport all my ingredients to the town hall, but it's still parked behind the building."

"You might be able to return it later today," Sawyer said. "I'll talk to Detective Ishimoto about it and let you know."

"Thank you." I resumed walking, and Sawyer kept pace

at my side. I still needed to call the rental agency, but I could do that once I was back at True Confections.

Thinking about the town hall drew my thoughts back to the subject of Irma's death. And the murder weapon. It took me a second to realize that I'd pressed one gloved hand to my throat, the spot where Irma had been attacked with my chocolate chipper.

"It wasn't your fault, Becca."

It was like Sawyer had read my mind.

I shoved my hand back in my pocket. "I know."

"Do you?"

I glanced his way and found him watching me closely.

"Yes," I said. "I'm starting to believe that now."

"Good, because it's the truth."

I managed a small smile. It faded as I remembered something else.

"I forgot about this once Detective Ishimoto showed me the chocolate chipper," I said, "but there's something you should probably know about Juniper and Stephanie."

I told him how I'd talked to both women outside the station, and how I was certain that Stephanie had made up an alibi for the two of them on the spot.

"Juniper seemed really surprised when Stephanie said they'd been together that night, but after that initial hesitation she quickly agreed with her. They're good friends, so . . ."

Sawyer finished the thought. "She might be willing to lie for Juniper."

I didn't like to think that was the case, but I couldn't help it. Stephanie and I weren't close, but we hovered somewhere between friends and acquaintances. Juniper, however, I didn't know very well at all, and she definitely didn't have a great relationship with her mother. Whether or not Juniper was the killer, Stephanie could get in a lot of trouble for lying for her. As much as I didn't want to be the one to get her into that trouble, I couldn't keep the information to myself.

"I'll have to see if they kept their stories straight when they talked to Detective Ishimoto," Sawyer said.

We turned onto Venice Avenue and my spirits couldn't help but brighten at the familiar sight of the colorful, timber-frame shops that lined the cobblestone walkway and faced the canal. Now topped with snow, the shops looked even more fairy tale–like than usual.

Sawyer drew to a stop at the corner. "I'll leave you here." He held my gaze. "But remember, Becca, nothing about this was your fault."

I nodded, not mentioning the fact that anxiety sat in my chest, worrying its way deeper inside of me. The crime wasn't my fault, but I had a cloud of suspicion hovering over my head, casting a dark shadow over me. Sure, Sawyer knew that I was innocent, but Detective Ishimoto didn't. In her view, there were probably three strikes against me: The murder weapon belonged to me, I was present when the body was found, and Irma was one of my Baking Spirits Bright competitors.

It would have been ridiculous and downright crazy for me to want to kill anyone to give myself a clearer path to winning the baking competition, but I knew that people had killed for less. Until I could prove to Detective Ishimoto that I had an alibi, I had no doubt that I'd remain on her suspect list. Even once the postmortem was complete and the police had a better idea of when Irma was killed, I might still be in trouble. If she was killed in the middle of the night, I didn't have an alibi. I was at home, alone, sleeping all night. Dizzy had dinner with me again, but nobody could vouch for me after 9:00 p.m.

My anxiety swirled around inside me, much like the snowflakes whirling about in the wind. Maybe there was something I could do to banish it. If I could prove my innocence, I'd feel much better.

Until I knew Irma's time of death, the best way I could think of to clear my name was to figure out the identity of the real killer. While I could come up with a few possible suspects—including my fellow competitors—the most suspicious person, in my mind, was Juniper.

As I stood there in the wind and snow, watching Sawyer walk off in the direction of Irma's cottage, I wondered if there was a way to find out if I was right about Stephanie and Juniper providing false alibis.

Chapter Nine

BY THE MIDDLE OF THE AFTERNOON, I HAD A PLAN. I also had several more batches of chocolates made, along with half a dozen new chocolate gondolas. Those would be filled with assorted bonbons before being packaged and placed on the store's shelves. Fortunately, I hadn't taken all of my custom-made gondola molds to the town hall for the competition. I didn't know when I'd get my belongings back, and the gondolas were always a popular product, so it was a good thing I still had a few on hand.

After cleaning up the kitchen, I once again got bundled up in my outerwear. Sawyer had texted me to let me know that I could pick up my rented golf cart from behind the town hall. I still couldn't go inside or retrieve my tools and ingredients, but at least I wouldn't have to keep paying for the rented golf cart I was no longer using.

My plan for the rest of the day started with returning the golf cart. Next up after that would be confirming—or poking holes in—Stephanie's and Juniper's alibis. With any luck, I'd have both those tasks crossed off my mental to-do list before darkness fell over the town. That didn't give me a lot of time, since some daylight had already faded, but I hoped to work quickly.

I passed through the shop on my way out and encountered a delay right away. As soon as I appeared, two customers immediately homed in on me. Internally, I groaned, but somehow I managed not to do so out loud.

Delphi Snodgrass had a multicolored, hand-knitted, and rather lumpy hat tugged down over her long, frizzy, gray hair. Her large glasses had fog on the lenses, which was slowly receding, suggesting that she'd only just arrived at the shop. Her best friend, Luella Plank, was at her side, as was often the case. Luella was a little shorter and rounder than Delphi, but they were two peas in a pod.

"Oh, Rebecca, we're so glad to see you're okay," Delphi said, grabbing my gloved hand and giving it a squeeze.

Luella's eyes gleamed in an unsettling way. "We heard about what happened. It must have been awful to see Irma's totally exsanguinated body."

"And you must have been terrified, what with the blood all over the room." Delphi patted my arm and looked at me with pity. "I suppose that explains why you didn't follow the bloody footprints."

Luella nodded. "It's a shame. If you *had* followed them, you might have caught the murderer making their escape and the case would be closed by now."

"Of course, nobody blames you, Rebecca," Delphi added, not sounding particularly sincere. "But the whole town would feel much safer if you'd had the presence of mind to follow the tracks."

"There were no bloody footprints," I said when I finally had a chance to get a word in, but the two women were no longer paying me any attention. They'd both turned toward a shelf of products, shaking their heads and whispering quietly to each other.

Angie hurried out from behind the sales counter and put

an arm around me. "Ignore them," she advised quietly in my ear. "You know what they're like."

Unfortunately, I did. Delphi and Luella were known around town as the Gossip Grannies. Their two favorite pastimes were gossiping and making up fantastical rumors, which they then spread around town with glee.

Angie gave me a squeeze. "Escape while you can," she whispered.

I took her advice, and practically barreled out the front door, causing the bell above it to jingle wildly. Even the biting wind was more welcome than facing the Gossip Grannies any longer.

After putting some distance between myself and Delphi and Luella, I brushed off my encounter with them. I walked at a brisk pace to the town hall, circling around to the back. Police tape remained across the back door, but there was nothing to stop me from accessing the golf cart. I noted that the one Stephanie had rented was already gone.

I did my best to sweep all the snow from the interior. Luckily, it was soft and fluffy snow and relatively easy to brush away. With that done, I climbed in and trundled off to the rental agency. I'd already explained the situation to the owner of the agency by phone, and he was kind enough to give me a discount when I paid my bill.

Then I set off on foot in the direction of Stephanie's cake shop. Most of the timber-frame shops in Larch Haven had living quarters above them on the upper two stories. I knew there were two apartments above Stephanie's shop, one above the other. She lived in the upper one, and a woman named Lois Marsh rented the other one. Lois was good friends with my grandmother, a fact I hoped would help me get the information I wanted.

Lois wasn't anything like the Gossip Grannies. She didn't make up ridiculous rumors and spread them around like they were the absolute truth. However, she did have a keen interest in everything going on around her, and she always seemed to know everybody's business, even more so than the average person in this town. On more than one occasion, I'd overheard her telling Lolly what various people in town were up to. She seemed to enjoy gossiping, but her variety tended to be true and not malicious in any way. If she, Delphi, and Luella were printed publications, Lois would have been a community newsletter while the Gossip Grannies would have been a tabloid.

As I passed by the front of Stephanie's cake shop, Love at First Bite, it took great self-restraint not to go inside. Stephanie made the most amazing cakes and cupcakes. My particular favorites were the chocolate hazelnut cake with gianduja Swiss meringue buttercream frosting and the chestnut cake, layered with chestnut puree and whipped cream and topped with glazed strawberries. Simply walking past the cakes on display in the front window was enough to make my mouth water.

I promised myself I could stop in at the shop after I'd spoken with Lois. That got me walking faster. I quickly reached the end of the line of shops and circled around to the narrow back alley with its rutted, unpaved tracks. A set of exterior stairs led up to the two balconies outside of the apartments above Love at First Bite. I climbed up to the first landing, holding tight to the metal railing so I wouldn't slip on any remnants of ice on the stairs. I could see a light on in the apartment, and that gave me hope that I'd find Lois at home.

Sure enough, when I knocked on the door, she answered within seconds.

"Becca, what a nice surprise." She stepped back and ushered me inside. "Come on in out of the cold."

"Thank you." I moved in far enough so she could shut the door behind me.

"Is everything all right with your grandmother?" Lois asked.

"Yes, everything's fine," I assured her. "I'm actually here in search of information."

I didn't think I imagined that Lois's blue eyes lit up at my last statement.

"Hopefully you've come to the right place. Come on in and get settled." She started toward the kitchen. "The kettle is about to boil. Would you like some tea?"

I accepted gladly, and removed my coat and boots. Then I joined her in her small kitchen, where she was pouring hot water from the kettle into a teapot decorated with a pattern of delicate pink roses.

We chatted about the weather while Lois set out the tea and a plate of homemade shortbread. Once settled at the table, she poured me a cup of the orange pekoe tea and I added some sugar and cream.

"I heard about how you were at the town hall when Irma was found," Lois said as she filled her own cup. "I'm sure that must have been difficult."

"It was," I said as I stirred my tea. "Irma's death is the reason I'm here."

"Are you involved in organizing a memorial?"

"No. I'm guessing her daughter will be the one to do that."

Lois raised one eyebrow briefly. "I wouldn't be too sure. Those two were like oil and water. It's a shame, but really not surprising, that they didn't get along. Imagine having Irma for a mother."

"That couldn't have been easy," I said, thinking that was probably a major understatement.

"I don't think I ever heard her say anything positive to Juniper." Lois shook her head sadly. "But if a memorial isn't what you're here about, what can I help you with?"

I took a sip of my tea, enjoying its warmth and sweetness. "I was talking to Juniper and Stephanie Kang earlier today."

A smile touched Lois's face. "Stephanie is such a nice young woman. She makes the most delicious cakes and cupcakes."

"She really does," I agreed, my mouth watering again.

I selected a piece of Lois's shortbread to tide me over until I could get myself a cupcake. I took a bite as I chose my next words.

"It was difficult seeing Irma that way. And I can't help but wonder who killed her. My first thought was that Juniper might have done it, but then I heard that she might have been at Stephanie's apartment when Irma was killed. Do you happen to know if that's true?"

Lois sipped her tea as she thought. "Let's see. That was two nights ago?" When I confirmed that with a nod, she continued, "As you know, anyone who takes the stairs up to Stephanie's place passes right by my kitchen window."

I glanced that way as she spoke. The window gave a clear view of the base of the stairs leading from the first landing up to Stephanie's door.

"I was doing some baking that evening," Lois said. "I made a few different things, including these shortbread cookies." She nodded at the plate in the middle of the table.

"They're delicious," I said before munching on the last morsel of the cookie I'd taken.

Lois smiled at the compliment. "Thank you, dear. Anyway, I did see Juniper arrive. Perhaps around five o'clock?" She thought for a second. "Yes, almost exactly. The five o'clock news had just come on the television." She angled her head toward the small flat-screen TV in the corner of the kitchen. "I like to have it on to keep me company while I'm baking. Either that or some music."

"So, it's true that she was at Stephanie's apartment," I said, mostly to myself.

"For a while, anyway."

I perked up at that. "Did you happen to see her leave?"

"I certainly did, as I was taking a batch of shortbread out of the oven. That must have been close to six."

I turned that information over in my mind. "Did you happen to see if she came back?"

"She didn't while I was here in the kitchen. It was shortly before eight o'clock when I finished cleaning up and moved into the living room to read."

"What about the next morning? Did you see Juniper leaving then?"

Lois shook her head. "Only Stephanie passed by the window while I was here eating breakfast. That was probably around six o'clock."

Stephanie had arrived at the town hall at around seven o'clock, at the same time as me. So, most likely, Lois had seen her on her way down to her shop to gather what she needed to take to the competition that morning. It was possible that Juniper had returned during the night and left very early, before Lois returned to her kitchen for breakfast, but that wasn't what Stephanie and Juniper claimed had happened. According to them, Juniper was at Stephanie's apartment all night, starting early in the evening.

So, as I'd suspected, they'd both lied.

Chapter Ten

I CONSIDERED CONFRONTING STEPHANIE ABOUT her lie right away. I'd made up my mind to do exactly that by the time I reached the front door of Love at First Bite, but I soon discovered that I had to scrap that plan. Stephanie's employee, Donna, was behind the counter, with no other staff in sight. When I asked if Stephanie was around, Donna told me she'd gone out and wouldn't be back that day.

Although I left the cake shop without any clues or helpful information, I didn't leave empty-handed. I couldn't make up my mind about what kind of cake I wanted, so I ended up buying four individual slices from four different cakes, as well as a whole chestnut cake.

While waiting for my purchases to get boxed up, I fired off a quick text message to Dizzy. She responded right away. She'd returned from Burlington, with her parents in tow, and told me that I was welcome to drop by.

With two bakery boxes stacked in my arms, I set off through the growing darkness to Dizzy's place. She lived in a cozy, two-bedroom apartment above the local bookstore,

Hooked on Books. The shop sat on a winding cobblestone road a short walk from Venice Avenue.

I admired my surroundings as I strolled along the canal. The strings of lights around the shop windows were lit up, as were the old-fashioned streetlamps with their ribbons and wreaths. The snow had let up, but the cold had only tightened its grip. My breath puffed out in little clouds as I walked, and I moved as quickly as I could without jostling the cakes, doing my best to keep warm.

I had almost reached Hooked on Books when I came to an abrupt stop. Up ahead, Eleanor Tiedemann stood on the cobblestones, talking to a guy in his late teens who had a snowboard propped up next to him. I figured he was probably Eleanor's son.

Eleanor said something to him, and he nodded. Then he grabbed his snowboard and set off in the direction of the parking lot at the edge of town. Most likely, he was heading up to Snowflake Canyon, the ski resort town a little farther up the mountain. I made a mental note to ask Dizzy if she wanted to go snowboarding with me sometime soon.

Eleanor disappeared into a yarn shop, and I got moving again. I wondered if Eleanor belonged on my suspect list. Irma certainly hadn't treated her well. I knew that from my regular visits to the bakery. Maybe all those years of insults and belittling had finally made Eleanor snap. Although that was a possibility, it didn't explain the ransacking of Irma's cottage. Then again, I did catch Eleanor searching through Irma's bag, and that same bag had been emptied at the crime scene. So maybe there was more to Eleanor's motive, or another motive altogether. What she might have been looking for, I didn't know, but I decided she did belong on my suspect list.

I hadn't told the police about seeing Eleanor searching Irma's bag. It hadn't even occurred to me to do so, but now I wondered if I'd accidentally omitted an important piece of information.

Setting my bakery boxes down on a bench outside the yarn shop, I tugged off my gloves and fished my phone out from my coat pocket. I typed out a text message to Sawyer, letting him know I needed to talk to him. He responded right away and we arranged to meet up that evening. The cold air nipped at my bare hands and did its best to cut through my down coat. I shivered and got my gloves back on as soon as possible. After wiggling my fingers in a vain attempt to warm them up, I gathered up my boxes and got on my way again.

As with Lois's place, a set of exterior stairs at the back of Hooked on Books led to Dizzy's apartment. While carefully balancing my boxes in my arms, I tugged off one glove so I could knock on the door. Dizzy opened it and made way for me to step inside as she called out, "Becca's here!"

"How was the drive?" I asked as Dizzy shut the door behind me.

"Not too bad. We made it back before dark, so that was good." She eyed the boxes in my arms. "Are those from Love at First Bite?"

"Yes, and the bottom box is for you and your parents." I shifted my grip to the top box as Dizzy slipped the other one out from underneath it.

"Thank you!" she said with excitement.

I set the other box on the small foyer table, just in time. Dizzy's mom appeared from down the hall and immediately pulled me into a hug.

"It's so good to see you, Rebecca!" Mrs. Bautista said, giving me a good squeeze.

"You too. How was your trip?"

"Long, but well worth it." She released me and stood back with a smile. She was a tiny woman—a couple of inches shorter than Dizzy's five feet, two inches—but she had a feisty and warm spirit that could radiate across a room of any size.

Dizzy's dad joined us in the foyer, and we went through another round of cheery greetings. Dizzy and her parents tried to get me to stay and share the chestnut cake with them, but I declined when I checked my phone and saw that I had a text message from Sawyer, saying he would stop by my cottage shortly.

"You must come over for dinner soon," Mrs. Bautista said as I gathered up my box of individual cake slices.

"That would be lovely," I said.

I waved to Mr. and Mrs. Bautista, and then stepped outside. Dizzy followed, tugging the door shut behind her.

"Did you see Amber's social media posts?" she asked. "She had a total hissy fit when she didn't make it into the finals of the baking competition. She even implied that the competition might be rigged."

"Seriously?" That struck me as ridiculous. "Talk about being a sore loser."

"She always has been." Dizzy wrapped her arms around herself. "Have you heard anything more about the murder?"

My stomach churned as I remembered my conversation with Detective Ishimoto. Maybe buying cake for myself was a mistake.

"Irma was killed with my chocolate chipper." I hated saying those words out loud.

Dizzy's eyes widened. "No! Becca, that's awful!"

"It just made the whole situation worse."

"I'm sorry, Becca. Are you okay?"

"I'm trying not to think about that aspect too much. But, yes, I'm okay."

Dizzy tucked her hands up inside her sleeves, shivering now.

"You'd better get inside before you freeze," I said. "Have fun catching up with your parents."

"Are you sure you won't stay?" she asked.

"I'm meeting up with Sawyer." I gave her a nudge with my arm. "Go on inside. Your lips are turning blue."

She slipped in through the door and then poked her head out again. "Call me if you need to talk more. No matter what the hour."

I gave her a grateful smile and counted myself lucky to have such a good friend.

MY CATS WELCOMED ME HOME BY WINDING AROUND my legs and meowing at me. As soon as I had my coat and boots off, I scooped them up, one at a time, for a good snuggle. Despite the cat cuddles, I couldn't shake the lingering chill in my bones, so I got a fire started in my wood-burning fireplace and put the kettle on. While I waited for the water to boil, I set out the individual cake slices on a large plate. Hopefully, if I provided Sawyer with cake, he'd be less likely to lecture me about staying out of the murder investigation. It probably wouldn't work, but it was worth a try.

I set the plate of cake slices on the kitchen table as a knock sounded on the front door. Truffles followed me down the hall to the foyer, but made no attempt to escape when I opened the door. She wasn't a fan of the cold weather and was spending most of her time indoors lately, rather than out in the catio Pops and I had built for her and Binx.

"Thanks for coming by," I said to Sawyer as he stepped inside.

He shrugged out of his jacket. He was off duty, wearing jeans and a gray Henley rather than his uniform. "I'm guessing the thing you want to talk about is the murder."

I took his jacket and hung it up in the foyer closet. "There's something I remembered this afternoon. Something I didn't think of telling Detective Ishimoto yesterday."

I led the way toward the back of the house. As soon as I set foot in the kitchen, I saw Binx up on the table, his green eyes fixed on the cake slices.

"No! Binx!" I lunged forward and swooped him off the table. "You're not supposed to be up there," I admonished.

"Can't say I blame him," Sawyer said, taking in the sight of the desserts.

With Binx in my arms, I carefully inspected each slice. All of the frosting appeared intact.

"Looks like I caught you just in time." I set Binx down on the floor.

"Better luck next time, buddy," Sawyer said to him.

Binx padded away and hopped up onto the couch.

I sent Sawyer a sidelong glance as he sat down at the kitchen table. "You wouldn't mind cat germs on your cake?"

"I've eaten worse."

"Ugh." I made a face. "Don't remind me. All these years later and I still can't believe you ate actual worms."

"One worm. One time. And I only did it to gross you out."

"Well, you succeeded," I said. "Twenty years later and I'm still grossed out."

"So, you don't want to eat any of that cake? Because I'll happily take all four slices off your hands." He tugged the plate across the table toward him.

"Nice try." I moved the plate back to the middle of the table. "Two of those are mine." I grabbed a small plate and fork for each of us. "However, you do get first pick."

"Does this mean I should be worried about what you're going to tell me?" he asked as he carefully maneuvered a slice of Black Forest cake to his plate.

"Of course not." I selected a slice of chestnut cake for myself and then told him about catching Eleanor searching through Irma's handbag at the town hall. "She claimed she was looking for a pen, but she had guilt written across her face. I'm pretty sure she was lying."

"Hmm," was all Sawyer said as he ate his cake.

"Don't you find that at least a little bit interesting?"

"Sure. I'm glad you remembered that. It might be nothing, but it might be something. I'll let Detective Ishimoto know."

I took a bite of the delicious chestnut cake, hoping the sweetness would help me withstand any disapproval that was about to come my way. "There's something else."

I told him about Lois seeing Juniper arrive at Stephanie's apartment the night of the murder, and leaving not long after.

"So, that's proof that they lied," I said to finish.

Sawyer set down his fork and sat back in his chair, his first slice of cake gone except for a couple of crumbs. He crossed his arms over his chest and regarded me silently with his dark eyes. I could tell a lecture was coming.

I pushed the remaining cake slices toward him. "Have another."

He raised an eyebrow. "Trying to distract me?"

"Is it working?" I asked, hopeful.

"No. But I will have another, thanks." He transferred a slice of chocolate mousse cake to his plate and then pointed his fork at me. "You know what I'm going to say."

"That I should mind my own beeswax?"

"That'll work." He sank his fork into the chocolate cake.

"But I came up with good information, right?" I snagged the last piece of cake—chocolate hazelnut—for myself.

He sighed and set down his fork without taking a bite. "That's not the point, Becca. Remember what happened the last time you got mixed up in a murder investigation?"

"All too clearly."

He met my gaze straight on. "I don't want anything like that happening to you again. Ever."

The intensity in his eyes sent a funny shiver through me. "Neither do I."

"Then don't do anything that will put a target on your back."

"I really don't think I have. Lois is the only person I talked to about Stephanie's and Juniper's supposed alibis, and Lois has no connection to the murder."

"So you assume."

"Seriously?" I said with disbelief. "Lois is one of Lolly's best friends. I've known her my entire life."

Sawyer took a bite of his cake, but then set down his fork again. "Okay, so Lois most likely had nothing to do with Irma's murder, but my point is that you can't know for certain who was or wasn't involved. If you ask questions of the wrong person, the next thing you know you could have the killer wanting to shut you up for good."

My shoulders sagged. "I know. You're right."

A hint of a grin tugged at one corner of Sawyer's mouth. "What was that?"

I glared at him. "Don't push it."

His half grin faded. "Seriously, Becks. I want you to stay safe."

"So do I. But I'm involved, whether we like it or not. Irma was killed with my chocolate chipper and I'm a suspect. At least, I think I still am. Do you know Irma's time of death now?"

"Not yet. There was a delay with the postmortem. It's been rescheduled for tomorrow morning." Sawyer picked up his fork and pointed it at me again. "And the chocolate chipper does not make solving the murder your responsibility."

"I know." But I didn't like having a cloud of suspicion hanging over me or anyone I knew. I kept that part to myself and ate a bite of chocolate hazelnut cake.

"You don't have a tree yet," Sawyer observed once he'd finished off his second slice.

"I need to do something about that."

"I haven't got mine yet either. If you want to go to the farm together, let me know. It'll be easy to get a couple of trees in the back of my truck."

My spirits rose. "That would be fun. Let's do that. Whenever you're free."

"Maybe at the end of the week. I'll text you when I know."

With that decided, Sawyer got to his feet. "Thanks for the cake, Becca."

"You can't stay longer?" I asked, standing up too.

"I wish I could, but I'm meeting up with a couple of buddies for some night snowboarding."

That reminded me that I'd forgotten to ask Dizzy about hitting the slopes soon.

"Do you want to come along?" he asked.

I eyed the crackling fire and my two cats snoozing on the couch. "Thanks, but I think I'll stay in tonight."

Sawyer's gaze landed on the Abigail Tierney painting above my fireplace. "That's new."

"I bought it a few days ago."

"It looks like it belongs there."

I smiled. "I think so too."

As I walked Sawyer to the door, my phone buzzed in my pocket. I took it out and checked my new email message as Sawyer pulled on his jacket.

"Hey," I said, my eyes still on my phone, "was Amber Dubois ever questioned in connection with Irma's murder?"

"Not that I'm aware of. Didn't she get cut from the competition in the first round?"

"She did," I confirmed. "But that could be the root of her motive for murder."

Sawyer zipped up his jacket. "Why do you say that?"

I handed him my phone, with the email still displayed on the screen. "Because the competition's back on, and Amber's got Irma's spot in the finals."

Chapter Eleven

I HAD MIXED FEELINGS ABOUT CONTINUING WITH THE Baking Spirits Bright competition. Sure, it was a great promotional opportunity for True Confections—as long as I participated in the finals, the shop would get mentioned in *Bake It Right*—but every time I thought of baking at my station again, the memory of Irma's dead body came rushing back to me. Even though the finals would now be held at Larch Haven's community center rather than the town hall, I didn't think I could erase that negative association.

Lolly told me that I could pull out of the competition if I wanted to, but I'd seen the disappointment in Angela's eyes when Lolly suggested that. My cousin and I both wanted True Confections mentioned in the magazine, and I figured I shouldn't let Irma's killer spoil that opportunity for us.

So, two days after receiving the email stating that the competition would move forward, I carried a box of ingredients over to the community center, with Angela and our teenage cousin, Milo, on either side of me, each with a box as well. With my relatives on hand to help out, I didn't bother with renting a golf cart this time. I was also making do without a chocolate chipper. Any chocolate I needed was already in small enough chunks to be chopped with a knife. I had no desire to get my old chocolate chipper back, and I wasn't in a rush to buy a new one either.

Nerves swirled around inside my stomach when we reached the community center, only partially triggered by the competition itself. I didn't know how badly the murder would affect me once I got to my baking station, but I hoped I'd be able to focus on the task at hand, rather than what had happened the last time.

Inside the building, we followed the signs on the wall that directed us down the hallway to the large room where the community center's cooking classes were held. The double doors to the room stood open, and several people had arrived before us. I spotted Jaspreet and Stephanie among those already present. When I got farther into the room, I also noticed Roman standing at one of the four baking stations, checking the cupboards, probably making sure he had everything he needed on hand.

"Rebecca, it's good to see you again," Jaspreet said. "Your baking station is at the back, next to Roman's."

I thanked her and continued in that direction. Angie and Milo followed, and we all plunked our boxes down on the counter.

So far so good. Irma's murder was a distinctly unpleasant memory, but it wasn't overwhelming me.

Angie gave me a hug. "You'll do great, Becca."

Milo offered me his fist to bump with my own. "Knock 'em dead." His eyes widened as soon as the words were out of his mouth. "Sorry."

"It's okay," I assured him.

He headed out of the community center, off to meet

some friends for a game of hockey on the frozen lake. Angie slipped out of her coat and set it across one of the chairs set out for the audience, claiming her spot.

I unpacked everything I'd brought for the competition and then stacked the empty boxes together. A couple of empty plastic bins already sat on the floor, along one wall of the room, so I set my boxes down beside them. I dropped my coat, gloves, and hat on top, and returned to my baking station, where I organized everything. Then there was nothing to do but wait for the competition to begin.

Angie was across the room, chatting with Stephanie, so I decided to join them. As I left my station, Amber Dubois arrived with Paisley on her heels. I'd checked Amber's social media posts the day before, out of curiosity. She'd shared the news that she was back in the competition, declaring that justice had been done. My idea of justice being done would have been seeing Irma's killer behind bars. Amber clearly had other ideas.

I'd also learned from Amber's posts that Paisley worked for her as her personal assistant. I didn't envy that position.

"Good morning," I said as I passed the two women.

Amber flipped her blonde hair over her shoulder and pointedly ignored me, while Paisley offered me a feeble smile. Fortunately for Amber, this wasn't a congeniality competition. She'd have no chance of winning one of those.

I stopped in my tracks when I heard Amber's shrill voice a moment later.

"Look at this!" she said loudly.

I turned around in time to see her thrust a piece of paper at Jaspreet.

"Someone wants me out of the competition!" Amber's voice grated against my eardrums. "I could end up dead like that other lady! How can I concentrate on baking when I don't even feel safe?" She planted her hands on her hips. "What are you going to do about this?"

Poor Jaspreet looked completely taken aback, but she

recovered quickly. After studying the piece of paper for a second, she spoke quietly to Amber, but not so quietly that I couldn't hear.

"I'll consult my colleagues."

"Your colleagues?" Amber echoed. "What about the police? This could be my life we're talking about!"

"I'll be right back." Jaspreet hurried off, the paper in hand.

When Paisley turned to follow Jaspreet's movement with her phone, I realized that she'd filmed the exchange. I was willing to bet that she'd done so at Amber's behest.

I decided to follow Jaspreet, and Roman apparently had the same idea. He strode past me, and I picked up my pace so I wouldn't get left behind.

Out in the hall, Jaspreet spoke quietly with a man with a gray-flecked, dark beard and a receding hairline. Both had serious expressions on their faces.

"What's going on?" Roman asked.

I added a question of my own. "Did Amber receive a death threat?"

"She received this note." Jaspreet handed it to Roman.

I moved closer to him so I could read it too.

"'Drop out of the competition or you'll be sorry,'" I read out loud.

The words were in a large computer font so that the short message took up most of the page.

A chilly sensation ran up the back of my neck.

"It's probably just a prank," Roman said with contempt, handing the note back to Jaspreet. "Can we get on with the competition?"

"In light of what happened to Irma, I think we should take the most cautious route," Jaspreet said. "I'm going to call the police and ask them what we should do."

"That's the right decision under the circumstances," her colleague agreed.

Jaspreet pulled out her phone, and Roman and I returned

to the competition room. Paisley passed us, going the opposite way. Curious glances came our way, but I didn't stop until I'd reached Angie in the second row of chairs. I dropped into the seat next to her and filled her in on what was happening. I noticed Amber across the room, talking with Ginny Ellis, a reporter for the local newspaper.

Angie noticed too. "Amber will milk this for all it's worth," she said. "In fact, it wouldn't surprise me if this was all a publicity stunt on her part."

"It wouldn't surprise me either." I watched as Amber posed by her baking station while Ginny snapped a quick photo of her.

Despite the scene she'd caused earlier, Amber didn't appear frightened or otherwise upset at the moment.

Maybe Angie was right and Amber had written the note herself. In these circumstances, though, Jaspreet had taken the right course of action. I wondered if the competition would be postponed again, or even canceled entirely.

Ginny moved off to the side of the room, typing notes on her phone. Amber took a seat at the end of the front row, and Paisley soon joined her there, whispering in her ear.

As time passed, more people arrived to watch the competition. The scheduled starting time came and went. There was already plenty of speculation getting passed around the room through hushed conversations, and the growing audience was becoming more and more restless.

Eventually, curiosity and impatience drove me out of my seat. "I'm going to see if I can find out what's going on," I said to Angie.

As soon as I stepped out into the hall, I spotted Jaspreet talking with Sawyer and one of his colleagues, Officer Ollie Nyberg. They wrapped up their conversation, and the three of them headed my way. Sawyer stopped next to me while Jaspreet and Officer Nyberg continued on into the room.

"Hey, what's going on?" I asked Sawyer. "Is the competition going ahead?"

"Probably," he said. "Nyberg and I did a circuit of the building to make sure nothing seemed out of place. Nyberg's going to have a word with Amber, and then a decision will be made."

"Do you think the threat is real?"

"I'm not sure, but we're treating it as real for the moment."

I followed him into the room, but then took a different path. I sat with Angie while Sawyer and Nyberg spoke with Amber, then Jaspreet again. After that, Jaspreet spoke with Amber.

Finally, Jaspreet addressed the room. "Thank you for your patience, and I apologize for the delay. The competition will begin in fifteen minutes."

Angie got up from her chair. "I'm going to call Lolly and let her know about the delay."

Lolly was holding down the fort at True Confections so Angie could watch the competition and take some photos to post on the shop's social media pages.

I'd grown tired of sitting and waiting, so I got up to work off some of my restless energy. Stephanie was across the room, chatting with Roman.

As much as I wanted to confront Stephanie about her lie, this wasn't the time or place. Even if I'd caught her alone before the competition, I wouldn't have brought it up. I didn't want to upset her right before we had to compete. I truly hoped that lying was the worst of Stephanie's misdeeds. I really couldn't picture her killing Irma—or anyone else—and I didn't think she had much of a motive. Winning the competition would be good for her shop, but I didn't think she'd resort to murder to better her chances at coming out on top.

I planned to join Stephanie and Roman, to chat about

anything other than Stephanie's lie, but I changed course before reaching them. A young man stood near the room's open doors, focused on his phone. He was the one I'd seen talking with Eleanor the day before.

"You're Eleanor Tiedemann's son, right?" I asked when I reached him.

He looked up from his phone. "Cameron, yeah." Recognition flashed in his eyes. "Hey, are you the chocolate lady who used to be on TV?"

"That's me. Rebecca Ransom."

"My girlfriend loves that show you were on. *Twilight* something? She's always watching the reruns."

"*Twilight Hills*," I said with a smile. "I'm glad she likes it." I quickly tried to steer the conversation in a new direction. "Is your mom going to watch the competition?"

He glanced around. "Yeah. She's here somewhere."

"How's she doing?" I asked. "Irma's death must have been hard on her. First the shock, and I'm guessing she's out of a job now."

A dark cloud crossed Cameron's face and a hint of anger underscored his next words. "I'm glad she's out from under that woman's thumb. My mom deserves better than to be treated like a servant. And, yeah, she's out of a job, but she's thinking of buying the bakery. You know, once the estate or whatever puts it up for sale."

Out of the corner of my eye, I saw Dizzy enter the room. She spotted me and waved. I waved back, and said to Cameron, "I hope that works out for her."

Then Dizzy was at my side, and we moved away from Cameron.

"I thought I was late," Dizzy said as Angie returned from making her phone call. "How come the baking hasn't started?"

I was about to respond when Amber bumped into me. Coffee from the cup in her hand sloshed over the front of my T-shirt. I gasped and pulled the fabric away from my skin. Luckily, the coffee was warm rather than hot, but the big, wet stain was still unpleasant.

"Oh, whoops. I'm so sorry," Amber said, not sounding sorry at all. "I didn't see you there."

Anger flashed in Dizzy's eyes. I put a hand on her arm before she could tear into Amber like I knew she wanted to.

"It's fine," I said through gritted teeth, knowing the supposed accident had been anything but. "I'll run to the washroom and get cleaned up."

"Better hurry." Amber smirked. "You wouldn't want to miss the competition."

With a swish of her glossy hair, she strutted over to her baking station.

Dizzy sent a death glare at Amber's back.

"She did that on purpose!" Angie said, indignant.

"I know." I looked down at my soppy, stained shirt. "I'd better try to clean this up."

Even as I said the words, I knew I wouldn't have much success.

"I'll come with you," Angie said. "There's nothing you can do for that shirt at the moment, but I'll give you my sweater to wear instead. It's light enough that you shouldn't get too hot while baking."

"Thanks, Ange," I said with gratitude and relief. "You're a lifesaver."

Out in the hall, we discovered that the women's restroom was currently closed for maintenance. We changed direction and headed up the stairs to the second floor, where I knew there was another washroom. I thought I heard someone coming up the stairs behind us, but I didn't bother glancing back.

In the restroom, Angie gave me her sweater in exchange for my stained shirt. "I'll go see if I can find a plastic bag for this," she said, bundling my T-shirt into a ball.

I thanked her again and she left as I adjusted my new attire and then tied my dark hair up in a ponytail. I'd dyed the ends purple in the summer, but the color had faded in recent weeks. It was probably time to get the ends trimmed off and maybe have the purple redone.

When I emerged from the restroom a few moments later, the second-floor hallway was deserted. A classroom door stood open to the right of the stairwell. A shadow moved inside the room, but I thought nothing of it.

I made a beeline for the stairs, not wanting to be late for the competition.

I'd only descended one step when a sudden shove from behind sent me flying out into space.

Chapter Twelve

I HIT THE STAIRS WITH A THUD AND TUMBLED THE REST of the way down to the landing. I lay there in a heap, aware of nothing other than the pain in my left wrist and several other parts of my body. Then I raised my head, and fear sent my heart pumping faster.

Someone had pushed me down the stairs.

I was alone now, but I thought I heard the sound of running footsteps on the second floor, retreating into the distance.

I wanted to scramble down the rest of the stairs, to find Sawyer, but my limbs wouldn't cooperate. The best I could do was to sit upright on the stairs rather than on the landing. I angled myself so I could see both up and down the stairwell. I didn't want to give my assailant another chance to creep up on me.

I tugged my phone from my pocket, relieved to find it hadn't been damaged. I was about to text Sawyer when Dizzy appeared at the bottom of the stairs. She stopped short when she saw me.

"Becca, what are you doing? If you don't hurry, they'll start without you." She realized then that something was wrong and she rushed up the steps toward me. "What happened? Are you okay? You don't look so good."

"Someone pushed me down the stairs."

Dizzy's jaw dropped. Then she snapped it shut and concern quickly replaced her shock. "Are you hurt?"

"Not badly. Just some bumps and bruises, I think." Even as I said that, I cradled my left wrist. It was protesting the most by far.

Dizzy was already heading back down the stairs. "I'll be back in five seconds."

I didn't want her to leave, but she was gone before I could ask her to stay or try to go with her.

Either she ran like lightning or Sawyer was close by, because she really did return within a matter of seconds, Sawyer half a step behind her.

I grabbed the railing with my right hand and pulled myself to my feet as Dizzy and Sawyer hurried up the stairs.

"Becca, are you okay?" Sawyer asked, taking me by the elbow as I made my way down to the first floor.

"My wrist is sore, but otherwise I'm just bruised."

"Maybe I should call you an ambulance." Sawyer reached for his radio.

I put my right hand to his arm to stop him. "Please don't. I'm fine." I wiggled the fingers on my left hand. "Nothing's broken and I want to compete."

"I think it would be best to call the whole thing off."

"That's not really necessary, is it?" Despite my earlier mixed feelings about continuing the competition, I now felt determined to bake my heart out. Quitting or canceling would mean my assailant had won.

"Someone tried to kill you, Becca," Dizzy said with a worried frown.

"I'm sure they weren't trying to kill me. They probably

just wanted to hurt me enough to stop me from baking." I looked to Sawyer. "Please don't call it off."

"I think your fellow competitors should have a say in what happens," he said. "If all four of you want to continue, I'll get another officer over here to help keep an eye on things."

"Thank you," I said, appreciating his willingness to compromise.

Sawyer walked us to the competition room and then jogged up to the second floor. I doubted that he expected to find the guilty party upstairs, still lurking around, but knowing that he was being thorough helped settle my worries. As much as I claimed that I was completely fine, the incident had shaken me up and my left wrist ached more than I wanted to admit. I had to be careful not to move it too much as I washed up at the sink at my baking station.

While I dried my hands with a towel, I looked around at my fellow competitors. Amber struck me as the most likely to have pushed me down the stairs. After all, she'd spilled coffee on me, and I didn't doubt that she'd done that on purpose. Maybe she decided to stoop even lower and use more force to put me off my game.

I stared hard at her for a long moment, but she didn't so much as glance my way. I turned my attention to the other finalists and sized them up too. Stephanie appeared nervous, but I hoped that was solely as a result of the competition and had nothing to do with causing my accident. Roman's face looked like it had been carved from stone, as it often did. Maybe he was the one who had pushed me down the stairs. He probably could have done so without changing his expression in the slightest.

After Sawyer returned from the second floor and sent a subtle shake of his head my way, he and Nyberg spoke to Stephanie, Roman, and Amber. Even after hearing what had happened to me, they all wanted to go ahead with the competition. I decided to push my suspicions to the side until I'd finished baking. Worrying and wondering wouldn't do me any good.

We all took up our spots at our stations and, finally, it was time to bake.

I checked the to-do list I'd made for myself. Instead of reading the first item and tackling it right away, I made the mistake of running my gaze down the entire list. There was so much to get done in the next few hours. Suddenly, I felt overwhelmed.

I looked out at the audience. Dizzy and Angie smiled and waved at me from their seats. I caught sight of Sawyer off to the side of the room and he gave me a subtle thumbs-up. Their support helped ground me, and the worst of my anxiety fizzled away. That allowed me to tune out everything around me and get to work.

The gingerbread and cakes needed my attention first. I wanted to get them baked as soon as possible so they had time to cool before I moved on to the construction and decoration phases. My aching wrist made it difficult to roll out my dough, but I tried not to let it slow me down too much.

While my cake and gingerbread baked, I got to work on tempering dark chocolate for the gondolas. While I planned to use only two gondolas, I made three in case one broke. For my other chocolate element, I painted cobblestone molds gray and filled them with tempered white chocolate. Once I had the chocolate out of the molds, I would place the rectangles together to create the cobblestone walkways along the canals.

As I worked, an unfamiliar, dark-haired man made a circuit of the baking stations, snapping photos with an expensive-looking camera. I glanced up when he snapped a photo of me.

"Sorry. Don't mind me," he said. "I'm Rodrigo Rivera

from *Bake It Right*. I'm taking a few photos of everyone as they work."

"Is Daniel Hathaway with the magazine too?" I asked as I scraped excess chocolate from the cobblestone molds.

"Never heard of him," Rodrigo replied. "I'm the sole representative here from the magazine."

It seemed the rumor about Daniel Hathaway was just that and nothing more. I glanced around the room and noted that he wasn't present. Most likely, he was simply a tourist and had already left town.

Refocusing on the task at hand, I got to work on my canals, made of blue sugar glass. By the time I finished that, my gingerbread and cake were cool enough for the construction phase.

I took a moment to step back and stretch out my neck and shoulders. I wished I'd taken something for the pain in my wrist before getting started, but now I didn't want to waste the time it would take to fetch an ibuprofen from my bag. Even though I truly believed I hadn't broken my wrist, it hadn't stopped aching and it had slowed me down, despite my best efforts to not let that happen. I reminded myself to simply do the best I could in the circumstances.

The judges had been wandering the room earlier, along with Rodrigo and his camera, but now they'd settled in their chairs in the front row, with cups of coffee in hand. I hoped they'd love my model of Larch Haven. I wanted to present them with the best edible display that I could, so I rolled my shoulders one last time and got back to work.

I cut, shaped, and stacked my cakes to form the mountains that would act as the backdrop for the rest of my scene. I planned to pipe green buttercream all over the mountains, but not until I'd put together my gingerbread shops and cottages. First, I tackled the line of shops along Venice Avenue, using caramel to hold the pieces together. Then I constructed four small cottages along the canals.

When Jaspreet announced that only ninety minutes remained, I had to fight off a wave of panic. I still had so much left to do. A quick glance at my competitors let me know that they all felt as panicked as I did. Somehow, that made me feel better.

I picked up my piping bag and got back to work, doing my best to ignore the nagging pain in my wrist. I used several different colors of icing to decorate the gingerbread shops so they would be easily recognizable as the ones on Venice Avenue, each of which was a different color. Then I piped some details on each of the cottages.

When I released my chocolates from their molds, I was relieved to find that all three gondolas had turned out well. I chose the best two and situated one out in the middle of the canal and another by the dock, made of brandy snaps. I'd hoped to make mini, multicolored meringues to fill the flower gardens around the cottages, but it looked like I'd have to scrap that idea. I wouldn't have enough time for that element. If I had a few minutes to spare, I could always pipe some buttercream flowers instead. It was more important for me to get my frosting on the cake mountains, so that's what I tackled next.

I still had a patch of bare cake when Jaspreet announced that we had one minute remaining. I piped as fast as I could and managed to cover the last bare spot as the competition drew to an end.

Dropping my piping bag on the counter, I stepped back and blew a wisp of hair out of my eyes. I was happy with what I'd created, but not ecstatic. I hadn't managed the flower gardens in any form and there was a small patch of sloppy piping on the back of one mountain where I'd rushed to finish up, but otherwise the elements I'd completed looked good.

Stephanie came over to my station and took in the sight of my edible Larch Haven. "That looks fantastic, Becca!"

"Thank you. I didn't quite finish, though."

"What a shame," a smug voice said.

I knew before turning around that it was Amber who'd spoken.

She smirked at me before flipping her ponytail over her shoulder and walking away. It wasn't hard for me to picture her giving me a shove down the stairs, but that didn't mean she'd done it.

"Ignore her," Stephanie advised.

I decided that was a good idea and focused on Stephanie's creation.

"Wow!" I moved closer for a better look. "Stephanie, this is incredible."

A hint of pink brightened her cheeks. "Thanks. I'm pretty happy with how it turned out."

"You should be," I said.

Stephanie had created an edible and adorable version of Whoville. There were gingerbread homes, bunches of colorful cake pops turned into whimsical trees, and a large evergreen in the middle, made from stacks of green macarons of decreasing sizes. Like me, Stephanie had made a mountain out of cake, but she'd decorated hers to look like a snowy one. Perched on the mountain, heading down toward the town, was a gingerbread sleigh complete with the Grinch and his dog, both made out of colored marzipan. All of Stephanie's piping was exquisite, and I knew everything would taste great too.

When I finally tore my gaze away from Stephanie's model, I checked out Roman's and Amber's. Roman had constructed an edible amusement park, while Amber had made an enchanted fairyland. Both of their creations looked good, but Roman's struck me as more sophisticated. Amber's model had cute cupcake toadstools, but some of her piping work was sloppy and the gingerbread tree house she'd constructed looked like it might fall apart at any moment.

Despite that, I had no idea who would win. Creativity

and presentation would count for part of the scores, but taste would also play a big role.

With the help of trolleys, volunteers carefully transported the models to a room across the hall, where Rodrigo would snap more photos for the magazine. Then the judges would move in to inspect everything before tasting all of the components. The judging would be done in private, so the rest of us waited in the room where the competition had taken place.

Dizzy had saved me the seat next to her, and I dropped down into it.

"You did amazing, Becca," she told me.

"We're so proud of you," Angie added. "And I managed to snap some great pictures for the shop's social media accounts."

I rested my sore wrist on my lap, happy despite the dull, aching pain. I might not have added every detail to my model that I'd wanted to, but I'd done enough to feel satisfied. Whatever happened now was out of my hands, and I was okay with that.

"There's something I need to tell you," Dizzy whispered.

"What is it?" I asked.

"Not here." She kept her voice so quiet that I could barely hear her. "I'll tell you later."

"You know I'm not good at being kept in suspense."

"Sorry. Too many ears around."

That only made me all the more curious. What could she want to tell me that she didn't want anyone else to hear?

I'd have to find out later, unfortunately.

"Did you hear about Amber's note?" I asked her.

"Angie filled me in." She lowered her voice again. "I bet Amber wrote it herself."

"It wouldn't surprise me," I said. "It also wouldn't surprise me if she was the one who pushed me down the stairs."

"Me either," Dizzy said. "Especially after the coffee incident."

As we waited for the judges to come to a decision, I watched Stephanie. She kept darting nervous glances at Officer Nyberg, who stood by the door. She drew in a deep breath and seemed to steel herself before quickly walking past him and out into the hall.

"I'll be right back," I said to Dizzy and Angie, before following Stephanie.

I made it into the hall in time to see her disappear into the women's restroom, which was no longer closed. I caught the door before it shut and slipped inside. Stephanie stood at the sink, washing a smear of what looked like buttercream frosting from her arm. We had all washed up at our stations earlier, but I wasn't surprised that she'd missed the spot. As soon as I saw myself in the mirror, I realized I had a smear of chocolate on my cheek and a bit of buttercream in a lock of hair that had escaped from my ponytail.

"Oh, hey, Becca," Stephanie said when I joined her by the sinks. "I'm so nervous that I couldn't sit still."

"Is it the competition making you nervous or the police presence?" I asked, watching her in the mirror as I dabbed at the chocolate on my face with a damp paper towel.

Her cheeks turned pink. "What? Why would the police make me nervous?"

"I thought maybe you were worried that they knew you lied for Juniper."

Stephanie stared at my reflection in the mirror, shocked. Then tears welled up, making her eyes shimmer.

"Oh no." The tears broke free and rolled down her cheeks. "I did lie, Becca. What am I going to do now?"

Chapter Thirteen

"DO THE POLICE KNOW?" STEPHANIE ASKED, TEARS still flowing.

"They at least suspect." I didn't know if they'd confirmed the information I'd passed on to Sawyer or not. If they hadn't, they probably would soon.

Stephanie covered her face with her hands. Her shoulders shook as she cried. "What am I going to do, Becca? Will I go to jail?"

I avoided her last question, voicing one of my own instead. "Did you kill Irma?"

Stephanie dropped her hands from her face. "No! Of course not!"

"But you thought Juniper needed an alibi?"

She wiped tears from her cheek. "She's one of my closest friends, and I wanted to help her. I knew she'd be a suspect because she didn't have a good relationship with Irma. I thought I could spare her the stress of police scrutiny, but I've probably made things worse."

"What's the truth?" I asked. "Where was Juniper that night?"

Although I knew she'd gone to Stephanie's apartment for a short while, I didn't want to let on that I'd questioned Lois.

Stephanie grabbed a paper towel and wet it with some cold water. "Juniper did come over to my place, but she only stayed an hour or so. She was upset about an argument she'd had with her mom."

"About jewelry?"

Stephanie paused with the paper towel pressed to her cheek. "How did you know that?"

"I overheard them arguing at the town hall."

She went back to dabbing away her tear tracks. "It was the jewelry, all right. The latest in a long line of things they argued about. Anyway, Juniper and I talked, had a glass of wine each, and then she left."

"Do you know where she went after that?"

"Home. That's what she told me when I asked her after we talked to the police yesterday." Stephanie crumpled up the paper towel and tossed it into the garbage bin. "Do you think I'll get arrested for obstructing justice or something?"

"I don't know, but I think you should tell the police what you just told me."

She looked about ready to cry again. "I don't want to get arrested. I couldn't survive jail time."

"It'll look far better if you come clean to the police rather than them confronting you with your lie."

Stephanie released a heavy sigh. "I know you're right, but Detective Ishimoto intimidates me. She's not mean or anything, but she makes me nervous."

"Same," I said.

Detective Ishimoto's authoritative presence was far larger than her physical stature.

"You could start by talking to Sawyer," I suggested.

"He can be intimidating too, when he gets that face."

I smiled, knowing exactly what she meant. "I call that his cop face. But he'll be as fair as he can be."

Stephanie regarded herself in the mirror. "I guess I could talk to him." A ghost of a smile showed on her face. "He's very good-looking."

I wasn't sure what to say to that, even though I agreed with her, so I put an arm around her and guided her to the door. "Let's go talk to him now and get it over with."

Although reluctant, Stephanie didn't resist. When we returned to the competition room, everyone was still waiting for the judges to finish deliberating, so I caught Sawyer's eye and waved to him to join Stephanie and me out in the hallway.

"Everything okay?" he asked with concern when he stepped out of the room. "How's your wrist, Becca?"

"It's okay," I said, even though it still ached. "Stephanie has something to tell you."

Stephanie managed not to cry this time as she repeated what she'd told me in the restroom. After she finished, Sawyer asked for precise times for when Juniper showed up and later left. Stephanie couldn't be exact, but she gave the best estimates she could. They lined up with what Lois had told me.

Sawyer jotted down a few quick words before tucking his notebook away. "I'd like you to come to the station and speak with Detective Ishimoto."

"Am I going to jail?" Stephanie asked, her apprehension obvious.

"You've never been in trouble with the law before," Sawyer said. "And it helps that you came clean. I can't make any promises, but I doubt Detective Ishimoto will want to arrest you."

A relieved breath whooshed out of Stephanie just as the judges emerged from their deliberation room.

"Is it okay if I wait until after the judges make their announcement?" she asked.

Sawyer nodded. "That'll be fine."

Stephanie followed the judges into the competition room.

"No signs of more trouble?" I asked Sawyer.

"Not even any littering." He frowned. "Nobody seems to know who might have been missing from the room when you were pushed down the stairs."

"I'm not surprised. Most people were busy chatting, not watching the room as a whole. My main suspects are Amber and Roman."

I told Sawyer how Amber had spilled her coffee on me shortly before I'd taken my tumble down the stairs.

"And Roman is pretty intense," I added. "He really wanted to win the top prize. Maybe he decided to up his chances by taking out one of us other finalists."

"I'll talk to the guy with the camera," Sawyer said, nodding at Rodrigo Rivera from *Bake It Right*. "He might have time-stamped photos that could help me figure out if any of the bakers were away from their stations while you were upstairs. Of course, the person who pushed you might never have been in the room," he added. "But I think that's less likely." His gaze traveled down to my wrist. "I still think you should go to the hospital."

I shook my head. "I'm fine. I'll take a couple of ibuprofen when I get home. That's all I need."

I moved past him into the room, hearing Jaspreet calling for everyone's attention. I slipped into my seat next to Dizzy as Jaspreet held up a small trophy for everyone to see.

"The winner of this year's Baking Spirits Bright competition is . . . Stephanie Kang!"

The crowd broke into cheers and applause. I joined in, happy for Stephanie and hoping I hadn't spoiled the joy of her win by upsetting her minutes before.

She looked stunned as she made her way up to Jaspreet,

and tears welled in her eyes, but when she accepted the trophy and people cheered again, a genuine smile brightened her face.

Several people rushed up to congratulate her. I got up from my seat and noticed Amber across the room, glowering at Stephanie and the people gathered around her. As I watched, Paisley put a hand on Amber's shoulder and spoke to her quietly, as if trying to calm or reassure her.

I dodged around a few people who were getting out of their seats and moved closer to the two blonde women.

"This is ridiculous," Amber groused, shrugging Paisley's hand off her shoulder. "The competition must have been fixed."

"We still got lots of great photos and videos for social media," Paisley said.

Amber made a noise of disgust and flounced out of the room, Paisley on her heels.

They passed by Roman on their way out. He stood by the wall, his arms crossed and his expression stony. I gathered from my few encounters with him that he wasn't much of one for smiling, but he appeared even more dour than usual. I could only assume that was because he hadn't won the competition.

Many of the spectators crossed the hall to the judging room, where they could get a closer look at the edible scenes before they were cut up and doled out for eating. Dizzy and Angela wanted to see all of the creations up close, so they joined the flow of people crossing the hall, and I followed. Before long, Jaspreet and her fellow organizers passed out samples of the cakes, cookies, and other desserts on paper plates.

Even though I hadn't won, several people came up to me and congratulated me on my model of Larch Haven. They loved how it looked and how it tasted. That left me feeling happy and satisfied, despite the fact that I hadn't won the top prize.

Eventually, the crowd thinned out and Angie and Dizzy helped me gather up the remains of my model and pack it into plastic containers. I sent some of the food home with Angela so she could share with her husband and two kids. The rest I decided to take home and share with friends and family over the next couple of days.

Dizzy, worried about my wrist, insisted on carrying most of what I was transporting home. I didn't see Sawyer again, and Stephanie had disappeared too, so I wondered if they'd gone together to the police station. I hoped Stephanie would be okay. I really didn't want her getting arrested for obstructing justice.

As for Juniper, I wondered what she would have to say when the police confronted her about her actual whereabouts around the time of her mother's murder. Maybe I could get that information from Stephanie later.

While we walked to my cottage, I filled Dizzy in on my conversation with Stephanie.

"It's good that she confessed to the police about her lie before they called her on it," Dizzy said. "Hopefully that will work in her favor."

"I've got my fingers crossed for her."

"We might have a new angle to look at." Dizzy glanced around to make sure no one was within earshot. "You know how Angie and I were sitting right behind the judges?" When I nodded, she continued, "I overheard them gossiping during the competition."

"Gossiping about the murder?" I guessed.

"Almost as fervently as the Gossip Grannies."

"I hope their theories weren't as wild."

"I don't think so," Dizzy said as we crossed a stone bridge. "I heard Consuelo say to Natalia that Irma might have been killed because of the information she wrote in her notebook."

"What notebook?"

"That's exactly what Victor asked," Dizzy said.

"And?" I prompted, eager to hear more.

"Natalia and Consuelo both seemed to know about this notebook. Apparently, Irma liked to keep notes about people here in town, especially when they did something she frowned upon."

"I'm guessing that was fairly often."

"Probably a safe bet," Dizzy agreed. "Anyway, Natalia said she'd never heard of anyone actually being blackmailed by Irma, and Consuelo hadn't either. It seems Irma simply liked intimidating people with the fact that she knew their secrets or whatever."

"But she *could* have blackmailed someone," I said, thinking out loud. "Or maybe the simple fact that she knew something was enough to set the killer off."

"Exactly what I was thinking."

"That theory would explain why Irma's handbag was emptied out and why her cottage was ransacked."

"Right?" Dizzy said. "I think Natalia and Consuelo are really onto something. Maybe they should join our sleuthing club."

"We have a club?"

"If we don't, we should."

I smiled. "Sawyer would love that."

Dizzy laughed. "We could make him an honorary member."

"Except I don't want us to be responsible for his blood pressure shooting sky high."

"We do drive him crazy sometimes." She seemed pleased by that fact.

I tried to rein in my smile, but failed, even as my thoughts returned to their previous path. "I wonder if the police know about Irma's notebook. I'm kind of surprised I've never heard about it before."

"I've heard it mentioned in the past, but not for a while," Dizzy said. "And I'd completely forgotten about it until today. But aside from going to the bakery on occasion, my path didn't really cross with Irma's."

"Same," I said. "And most of the time when I went into the bakery, I saw Eleanor rather than Irma."

Dizzy nodded. "Irma definitely wasn't a people person. She liked to stick to baking and let Eleanor handle the customers."

"Unless she was gathering juicy information, apparently."

"I wonder how she got her information," Dizzy mused. "By sneaking around? By eavesdropping?"

"I don't know." I turned my mind to another question. "Did Consuelo or Natalia happen to mention the name of anyone Irma had written about in her notebook?"

"I wish," Dizzy said with a shake of her head. "But maybe we can ask them more about it."

"Sawyer doesn't want me asking questions."

"He doesn't want you getting hurt again, and neither do I." Dizzy shifted the box in her arms. "Which is why we should do this together."

"Then you could end up with a target on your back too," I pointed out. "And I don't want that happening."

Dizzy looked at me like she was worried I was about to disappoint her. "You're not saying you want to stay out of this, are you?"

"Have you forgotten who you're talking to?" I asked.

"I was afraid you were trying to suppress your inner Miss Marple."

"I'm not sure that's even possible."

Dizzy grinned. "Glad to hear it."

"So, we should try to speak to Consuelo or Natalia."

"Let's start with Consuelo. I bet she hears a lot of gossip at her restaurant."

"Good call," I said. "I'd suggest a lunch date at her café, but we might not be able to talk to her privately there and we don't need all her customers getting wind of the fact that we're asking questions."

If I couldn't follow Sawyer's advice to stay out of the murder investigation, I could at least try to be careful when digging for clues.

"Consuelo is an avid reader," Dizzy said. "She comes into the library every week, sometimes twice. Next time I see her there, I'll let you know."

"So I can accost her in the mystery section?"

"Romance section," Dizzy corrected. "She's all about the romance."

Chapter Fourteen

~~~~~~~

DIZZY AND I SNACKED ON THE LEFTOVER CAKE, GIN-
gerbread, and chocolates I'd brought home from the competition while Binx and Truffles lounged on the couch with
us. When I got up to take the remains of our decidedly
unhealthy snack to the kitchen, Dizzy caught me cradling
my wrist against my stomach.

She jumped up from the couch. "Okay, that's it. We're
going to the hospital."

"We don't need to do that," I protested as I rinsed our
plates one-handed.

"It's swollen and bruised, Becca, and you're in pain.
Don't bother denying it."

She was right on all counts. Despite the ibuprofen I'd
taken as soon as I'd arrived home, my wrist still ached.

"I really don't think it's broken," I said in a last ditch effort to avoid a trip to the hospital. "Probably just sprained."

"Can we at least get that confirmed?" Dizzy requested.
"Otherwise, I'm going to worry."

"You're even worse than Sawyer," I said, smiling to soften my words.

She held up her phone and gave it a wiggle. "We may have been colluding."

"Texting about me behind my back?" I pretended to be miffed. "The betrayal!"

"If you think it's a betrayal now, you should see what Sawyer said about you."

My jaw dropped and I made a grab for her phone with my good hand. She darted out of my reach.

"Nope. Sorry," she said, not sounding the least bit apologetic. "Those texts are staying private until you go to the hospital and get checked out."

I planted my right hand on my hip. "That's playing dirty."

"Clearly, that's what it's going to take."

"Ugh. Fine," I said, relenting. "I'm not going to get any peace until you get your way, am I?"

Dizzy gave me a devious smile. "Nope."

I snapped the lid on the last of the plastic containers and shoved the remains of the cake into the fridge. Truffles traced figure eights around my ankles. I would have much preferred staying at home with my cats, but with Sawyer and Dizzy ganging up on me—in the sweetest of ways— there was no point in resisting any longer.

"Why don't we make the trip more fun by having dinner in Snowflake Canyon once you've been checked out?" Dizzy suggested.

The nearest hospital—where my mom had worked for many years—was in the ski resort town up the mountain.

"My parents are hanging out there this afternoon," she added. "I could text them and see if they'll meet us for dinner."

"Actually, that sounds great," I admitted, no longer dreading the trip quite so much. "How about we meet them at the Spaghetti House?"

"Yum. Good idea." Dizzy took hold of my right arm and steered me toward the front of the cottage. "Okay, let's go."

"You're not wasting any time," I said as she pushed me along the hall.

"No way am I giving you a chance to change your mind."

I rolled my eyes, but got bundled up in my winter gear.

The sun was sinking low in the sky as we walked to the parking lot near the highway, but plenty of people still skated on the canals and enjoyed hot chocolate from one of the outdoor vendors scattered around town. Maybe it was silly, but the postcard-perfect sight gave me a warm and fuzzy feeling. I really loved my hometown. Even though I missed my acting career at times, I knew I'd made the right decision by moving back to Larch Haven.

"My parents will meet us for dinner," Dizzy said as she checked her phone once we'd settled in her car. "I'm supposed to text them again when we're done at the hospital."

"How are they enjoying their visit so far?" I asked as Dizzy pulled out of the parking spot.

"I think they're having a good time."

I knew her well enough to know that she'd left something unsaid.

"But?" I prodded.

Dizzy bit down on her lip as she checked both ways before turning out onto the highway. "I think something's wrong."

"Wrong with your parents?" Apprehension tensed my shoulders. "What do you mean?"

"There's something they're not telling me. It's not like them to hold things back from me, so I can only assume that it's something bad. Like, maybe one of them is sick and they don't want me to worry. What if it's really bad, Becca?"

"Hold on," I said quickly, doing my best to sound calm and reasonable. "Let's not jump to any conclusions. Have you asked them outright what it is they're not telling you?"

"This morning, when I asked about their plans for the

day, they said they'd be Christmas shopping in Snowflake Canyon in the afternoon, but other than that they were pretty evasive. I asked if something was wrong, but they denied it. I'm not sure I believe them, though."

"Let's not assume the worst," I said. "Maybe we can get more out of them over dinner."

Although all the worry didn't disappear from her face, Dizzy smiled. "Thanks, Becca."

I desperately hoped that when we got the answers Dizzy needed, she'd have nothing more to worry about.

We pulled into the hospital's parking lot a few minutes later. I thought we might have to wait hours before getting seen by a doctor, but only one hour passed before my name got called. It took another ninety minutes for us to leave the emergency department, but I considered that a short visit, especially in the middle of ski season, when Snowflake Canyon was full of tourists, many of whom spent their days barreling down the slopes on skis, snowboards, or sleds. Best of all was the fact that I didn't have any broken bones. I'd sprained my wrist, as I'd suspected, but the doctor expected it to heal quickly, as long as I didn't aggravate the injury.

"So now I get to read Sawyer's texts," I said as soon as we stepped out of the hospital.

Dizzy handed me her phone. "Go ahead."

I accessed her text messages and brought up her conversation with Sawyer.

See if you can work your magic and get Becca to the hospital, Sawyer had written. I'm worried about her.

I'm worried too, Dizzy had written back. I'm on it. Please find who pushed her.

On it, Sawyer had texted in response, echoing Dizzy's words.

I handed the phone back. "He didn't say anything mean."

Dizzy tucked her phone into her coat pocket. "I never actually said that he did."

"You tricked me."

Dizzy didn't deny it.

"I could point out that you both overreacted." I held up my left wrist, which was now wrapped with an elastic bandage. "No broken bones."

"Think about it this way," Dizzy said, "you've given Sawyer and me peace of mind."

I couldn't really argue with that. "Thanks for looking out for me."

She smiled. "Always."

We climbed into Dizzy's car and I sent a quick text message to Sawyer, letting him know that my wrist wasn't broken, and thanking him for worrying about me.

"Hey, look." Dizzy slowed down as we drove along a road not far from the hospital. "There's my parents."

I looked in the direction she was pointing. Sure enough, her parents stood on the sidewalk in front of a row of town houses, illuminated by a nearby streetlamp.

Dizzy's forehead furrowed. "What are they doing here? They told me they'd be Christmas shopping."

We were in a residential neighborhood, not a single shop in sight.

"I'll see if I can find a spot to park." Dizzy drove past her parents, who didn't notice us, and found a free space by the curb farther along the street.

I opened the passenger door and climbed out onto the sidewalk.

"Too late," I said, looking back the way we'd come.

Dizzy's parents had already disappeared into their rental car.

I got back into the passenger seat, shut the door, and buckled up my seat belt again. Dizzy's parents drove past, not noticing us, despite the fact that we waved at them.

Dizzy grabbed her phone from the center console. "I'll let them know we're finished at the hospital."

After she'd sent the text, Dizzy pulled out onto the road.

Her parents' car was already out of sight. We'd almost reached the restaurant when Dizzy's phone chimed with an incoming text. I checked it at her request.

"Your mom says they're at the restaurant," I told her.

A couple of minutes later, we got there too.

Dizzy's parents had already secured a table for us, so we settled into the booth with them. After the waiter had taken our orders, Dizzy took a sip of ice water and addressed her parents.

"Becca and I saw you at those town houses over by the hospital. We waved, but you didn't notice."

"Oh?" Mrs. Bautista shared a brief glance with her husband. "That's too bad that we didn't see you."

"What were you doing over there?" Dizzy asked. "I thought you were shopping."

"We were, mostly," her dad replied.

"There aren't any shops over that way," Dizzy said, watching her parents closely.

Her mom busied herself with unwrapping her cutlery from her napkin. "We met up with . . . an old acquaintance and had a bit of a chat."

The waiter appeared then with the hot drinks we'd ordered. After the waiter left our table, Dizzy's parents firmly shifted the conversation in another direction, asking me about my family and True Confections. We went along with the shift, but not before Dizzy shot me a brief but pointed look.

After we finished dinner and parted ways with Dizzy's parents, we walked along the street toward Dizzy's car.

"I'm right, aren't I?" Dizzy asked as soon as we were alone.

"They definitely wanted to dodge the subject of what they were doing by the town houses," I said. "Maybe they're working on a Christmas surprise for you?"

Dizzy shook her head. "I don't think so. Becca, those town houses were within walking distance of the hospital."

I considered her words. "Your mom said they met with an old acquaintance. You think that was a lie and they actually went to the hospital?"

"I think she was dancing around the truth. Maybe they had an appointment with a doctor they know." Her eyes filled with tears. "What if it's really bad, Becca?"

"Hey." I squeezed her arm with my good hand. "We don't know if it's bad at all."

"Then why are they keeping secrets from me?"

My heart ached for Dizzy. I hated seeing her upset.

"I think you need to sit down with them and tell them straight up that you know they're keeping something from you and it's scaring you," I said. "Making wild guesses will only tear you apart."

Dizzy blinked away her tears and nodded. "You're right. I'll do that."

The worry didn't disappear from her eyes, but she seemed calmer.

"Let's focus on something else." She pointed at a poster hanging in a shop window. "Like Snowflake Canyon's annual snowmobile parade."

We stopped to read the poster, which gave the date and time of the event.

"I haven't seen the parade in years," I said.

"Want to go?" Dizzy asked.

"For sure."

We started walking again.

"And we should try the ice slide." Dizzy inclined her head toward the top of a snowy hill, which was visible over the line of shops across the street.

Every year, a winding slide was built into the hillside. It resembled a waterslide but one made out of snow and ice. For a small fee, people could ride down on carpet sleds. It was always a popular attraction, another one that I'd missed out on over the past few years.

"But not until your wrist is better," Dizzy added.

"I was also thinking we should go snowboarding."

"Again, when your wrist is better. You don't want to risk aggravating the injury."

"You're right. What a drag." I sighed. "But it could have been worse," I reminded myself out loud.

Dizzy hit the button on her key fob to unlock her car.

"We need to figure out who pushed you down the stairs," she said once we'd climbed into the vehicle.

I fastened my seat belt. "Sawyer's working on that, remember?"

She glanced my way before starting the engine and pulling out onto the road. "That's going to stop you?"

"No," I conceded, "but I thought it would be the responsible thing to bring that up."

"Okay, but now that we've got that out of the way . . ."

"I'm thinking we can use tactics that aren't available to Sawyer."

Dizzy smiled, a mischievous glint in her eyes. "I'm liking the sound of that."

"If Irma was killed because of her notebook and not because of the baking competition, then it would probably be safe to assume that Amber's threatening note and my tumble down the stairs aren't related to the murder."

"Then we need to figure out the motive for Irma's murder so we can know if that's the case," Dizzy said, picking up my line of thought. "How are we going to do that?"

"I don't know yet," I said. "But I bet we can figure it out."

Chapter Fifteen

~~~~~

DIZZY AND I DIDN'T HAVE ANY FLASHES OF INSIGHT
on our way back to Larch Haven, but I hadn't lost hope. I
knew we would come up with a sleuthing plan before long.

In the meantime, I needed to focus on the job that actually paid my bills—making chocolates. While fine snow
fell outside the next morning, dusting the cobblestones, I
got myself set up in the kitchen at True Confections and
soon had the tempering machine running. I needed to replenish our supply of holiday favorites, like candy cane
bonbons and eggnog truffles, as well as year-round flavors
like almond creams and peanut butter pretzel truffles.

By the time Angela arrived and opened the shop, I'd
already put in two hours of work and my wrist ached in
protest. I'd removed the elastic bandage to take a shower
before going to bed the night before and hadn't put it back
on. That might have been a mistake.

I'd brought the bandage with me to the shop, so I crossed
the hall to the office, where I'd left my coat. I dug the bandage out of my coat pocket and attempted to wrap it around

my left wrist. I was in the midst of doing a sloppy job of that when Sawyer appeared in the office doorway. He wore his uniform, and a few scattered snowflakes were melting on the shoulders of his jacket.

"Hey," I greeted. "What brings you by?" The smile that automatically appeared on my face upon his arrival faded away. "Do you have bad news?"

"I'd call it good news." He took off his police-issue beanie and dropped it on the edge of the desk before holding out his hand. "Let me do that."

I gave up on my pathetic attempt at wrapping my own wrist and allowed him to take over.

"I'm glad it isn't broken," he said as he gently but expertly bandaged my wrist.

My gaze traveled up Sawyer's face, past the stubble on his jaw, up to his dark brown eyes, and then to his almost-black hair, which was sticking out in different directions. When my gaze moved back down, he caught it with his own.

"Is that okay?" he asked.

It took a split second for me to realize what he was talking about. My wrist was now perfectly bandaged. "Yes, thanks."

I stood on tiptoe and used my good hand to tame his hair into a tousled but less wild style. It surprised me that he didn't swat my hand away.

"Winter hazard," he said with a wry grin. "I'll be putting the hat back on in a minute anyway."

I released his hair and rocked down off my tiptoes. Our gazes locked and my heart stumbled when I realized how close we were standing. I breathed in the mingled scent of his soap and the fresh, cold air that still clung to him. It was a heady combination.

Flustered, I took a quick step back and steadied myself.

"Did you have something to tell me?" I asked, glad but surprised that my voice sounded normal.

"Irma's time of death has been narrowed down. She was killed between seven and eight in the evening, before the building was locked up for the night. The janitor didn't go in that room because everything was supposed to be left as it was for the competition."

"So she was lying there all night." That thought made my heart heavy.

Sawyer nodded. "The good news is that she was killed while Dizzy was with you at your cottage."

"So I'm in the clear?"

"Another officer is confirming your alibi with Dizzy but, yes, it's safe to say you're off the suspect list."

"That's a relief. Thank you for letting me know."

Regret flickered across his face. "As for whoever pushed you down the stairs, we don't have much to go on. The guy from the magazine didn't take any photos during the relevant window of time."

"I don't suppose there are any security cameras inside the community center," I said.

"Not inside or outside."

No help there, then.

"I'm not in any danger now, though, am I?" I asked. "If everything that's happened recently was about the baking competition, then everyone should be safe now, right? After all, the competition is over."

"I'm not so sure that everything is connected."

My faint hope fizzled away. "Neither am I."

"That being said," Sawyer continued, "what happened to you probably was about the competition. But until we know that for sure, I want you to be careful. Try not to go out alone, especially after dark, and don't put yourself in any dangerous situations."

"Would I do such a thing?" I asked with mock innocence.

"Don't get me started." He pulled his hat back on his head. "I'd better get going."

"Come into the kitchen first," I said, leading the way across the hall.

"About our trip to the Christmas tree farm," Sawyer said as he followed me, "does the day after tomorrow work for you? In the afternoon?"

"Sounds perfect."

I selected a few of what I called misfits—chocolates that weren't perfect enough to sell for full price—and packed them into a small paper bag. I made sure to include some peanut butter pretzel truffles—Sawyer's favorite—and I also added a couple of holiday flavors.

"You shouldn't be giving me free chocolates every time I stop by," he said when I offered him the bag.

I pressed it into his hand. "Maybe it's my way of making sure you come back so I get to see you on a regular basis."

He captured my gaze with his. "You don't have to give me chocolate to make that happen."

My heart did a fluttering dance in my chest. It was getting in the habit of doing things like that when Sawyer was around, a phenomenon I didn't want to think too much about.

"I'll walk you out," I said, unable to look away from him until he finally blinked.

I led the way into the shop area, where Angela was ringing up a purchase for a young couple with Snowflake Canyon ski passes clipped to the zippers of their jackets. Three older local women had gathered on the other side of the shop, boxes of chocolates in hand while they chatted. I was about to ask if they needed any assistance, but then they noticed Sawyer and didn't give me a chance.

"Sawyer, have you caught the killer yet?" The question came from Mrs. Henzell, who was around my grandmother's age. Her husband often went bowling with Pops.

"The investigation is ongoing," Sawyer replied as he tucked the bag of chocolates into the pocket of his police jacket.

The bell above the door jingled as the young couple left the shop, and a blast of cold air swirled around us.

Ms. Fernstrom, a retired teacher, spoke up next. "I hope you're looking into Irma's daughter. Those two did *not* get along."

The third woman, Mrs. Lawrence, chimed in, "And I have it on good authority that Juniper is Irma's sole beneficiary."

Mrs. Henzell nodded. "I've heard the same. My niece Diana is dating one of the lawyers at the firm looking after Irma's estate. She dropped by to meet her young man for lunch and saw Juniper there. Diana struck up a conversation with her, and got the information right from the horse's mouth."

Sawyer was about to say something when Ms. Fernstrom cut him off.

"Quite surprising, don't you think?" she said. "Considering the bad blood between Juniper and her mother."

"But who else would Irma leave her estate to?" Mrs. Lawrence asked. "If not Juniper, then she'd have to leave it to charity. Irma wasn't the charitable sort."

"That's certainly true," Mrs. Henzell said, and Ms. Fernstrom nodded her agreement.

I wasn't sure if the women remembered that Sawyer and I were even present.

"I have to be on my way," Sawyer said.

Although he kept his expression neutral, I knew he was itching to get away from the women.

"Is this place gossip central?" he whispered to me as I walked with him to the door.

"Some days."

"Oh, Rebecca," Mrs. Lawrence called out from behind us.

I turned back, and Sawyer paused with his hand on the doorknob.

"I have something for you." Mrs. Lawrence rifled through

her handbag. "Now, where did I put that paper?" She produced a small square of white paper. "Ah, here it is." She pressed it into my uninjured hand.

I glanced down at the paper. It had a phone number and the name Brian written on it.

"Brian's my nephew," Mrs. Lawrence said. "He's a lawyer in Burlington."

"A lawyer?" I echoed, confused. "I have an alibi for Irma's murder, so I don't need a lawyer."

Mrs. Lawrence waved off that statement. "No one thought you killed Irma, dear. I'm giving you that because you and Brian would make a great match."

"Sorry?" I was too taken aback to say anything else.

I glanced at Sawyer. He'd taken his hand off the doorknob, no longer on his way out. His neutral expression had changed to one of simmering irritation.

Mrs. Lawrence patted my arm. "I know you went through a terrible heartbreak in the summer with all that Hollywood drama, but it's time to move on."

"She doesn't need a matchmaker," Sawyer said, his irritation obvious in his voice.

Mrs. Lawrence gave him a stern look. "There's no shame in getting a helping hand. You could use one yourself. I know a nice young woman—"

"I've got somewhere to be," Sawyer said, cutting her off. "Ladies," he added as an afterthought, nodding at Mrs. Lawrence and her companions. Then he disappeared out the door as if carried by a swift gust of wind.

Mrs. Lawrence didn't seem perturbed by his abrupt departure. She tapped the paper in my hand. "You won't be sorry if you call him."

She and her friends carried their boxes of chocolates over to the counter, where Angela waited to help them. I hurried past them into the office, where I dropped the piece of paper into the recycling bin. I didn't dare go back out front until I heard the bell over the front door jingle again.

I peeked into the shop area in time to see the three women leaving.

Before the door latched, Rodrigo Rivera from *Bake It Right* entered the shop. I came out of hiding to greet him. He had a fancy camera around his neck and had arrived to take photos and get information for the magazine article about Baking Spirits Bright. He snapped a few pictures and then asked me questions about the shop, my life, and the competition.

When he left, Angie did a happy dance. "I'm so excited that you and the shop are going to be in the magazine!"

I was about to voice my own excitement when Paisley came into the store.

Angela immediately calmed herself and called out a greeting. Paisley smiled before starting to browse.

I surveyed the shelves and made a mental note of which products needed restocking. Then I dashed into the back and returned with several chocolate gondolas filled with bonbons, as well as chocolate snowmen and several gingerbread cookies. As I arranged the items on the shelves, Paisley approached the display case and requested a box of a dozen assorted chocolates. She pointed out what she wanted, and Angela boxed them up for her.

"I saw you at the Baking Spirits Bright competition," Angie said as she secured a lid on the box. "You're friends with Amber Dubois, right?"

"Best friends," Paisley said with a smile. She glanced my way and her smile faded. "The judges got it wrong. Amber should have won the competition. She's so talented."

"Stephanie is too," I spoke up.

Paisley looked my way again, just long enough for me to catch her rolling her eyes.

A group of four tourists entered the store then, and I greeted them with a smile. Gallery owner and Baking Spirits Bright judge Victor Barnabas arrived on their heels, and the door had barely latched when it opened again. Amber stepped inside, annoyance on her face.

"Are you done yet, Paisley?" she asked with obvious impatience.

Paisley finished paying for her chocolates and gathered up her True Confections bag. "Sorry, Amber. We can go now."

Amber turned for the door and caught sight of Victor. As she left the shop, she sent a vicious glare his way.

If looks could kill, I thought.

Cold air swooped into the store as Amber and Paisley left, but I wasn't sure that was the sole cause of the shiver that scurried up my spine.

Chapter Sixteen

THE NEXT MORNING I COULDN'T RESIST GETTING OUT on the frozen canals. As soon as it was light out, the snowy landscape called to me through my cottage's windows. With more snow in the forecast, I wanted to get out and skate while the canals were clear. I'd arranged to meet Dizzy at Gathering Grounds, a local coffee shop, before she started work at the library, so I tucked my boots under my arm as I set off on my skates.

The icy wind that had swept through town for the past few days hadn't yet let up and I was the only person brave enough—or crazy enough—to be out skating this early. Despite the cold, I relished having the winter wonderland to myself. I couldn't believe how lucky I was. How many people could skate around their town? I'd always loved Larch Haven, but since moving back from California, I appreciated it even more.

When I reached the main dock, I sat down and traded my skates for my boots. I tied the laces of my skates together to make them easier to carry, and then I set off on foot to the coffee shop. The wind cut through my layers of clothes, setting off shivers, but that made the warmth of the coffee shop even more inviting.

Dizzy had already claimed a table for us when I arrived, so I dropped my skates off with her before joining the short line at the counter. Once I had an eggnog steamer in hand, I settled into a chair across from Dizzy and shrugged out of my coat.

"Suspect at twelve o'clock," Dizzy whispered. "My twelve o'clock, that is."

I glanced behind me to see Juniper Jones entering the coffee shop. She stopped on the mat inside the door and tugged off her gloves.

As she passed our table on her way to the counter, I spoke up.

"Hey, Juniper."

She stopped walking and looked our way. "Hi," she returned without a smile.

"I'm sorry about your mother," Dizzy said.

A series of emotions flickered across Juniper's face, each one appearing and disappearing so quickly that they were hard to identify. I thought I saw annoyance and fear in the mix, but I couldn't be sure.

"Thanks," she said, her voice flat.

She was about to continue on past us, so I quickly spoke again.

"I hope the police haven't given you too much of a hard time."

Her eyebrows drew together. "Why would they?"

"I heard Stephanie lied for you," I said. "About your alibi. I know she did it to protect you, but I guess it might have landed you in hot water. Unless, of course, you have a real alibi?"

Juniper frowned. "People in this town gossip too much."

"Where did you go after you left Stephanie's place that night?" Dizzy asked. "Did anyone see you?"

Juniper raised her chin and looked down her nose at us. "I don't see how that's any of your business."

With that, she turned on her heel and approached the counter, keeping her back to us.

Dizzy raised her eyebrows. "Touchy subject."

"Understandably so," I said. "But if she had a real alibi, wouldn't she want everyone to know that?"

"You'd think so. I mean, who wants the whole town suspecting you of murder?"

"I wonder what she said to the police when they confronted her about Stephanie's lie," I said before taking a drink of my eggnog steamer.

Dizzy produced her phone. "I'm going to ask Sawyer."

"I'm sure he won't tell you."

"I'm sure you're right," she said with a grin, "but I'm going to ask anyway."

I enjoyed my steamer while she typed her message. She set her phone on the table when she was done, and it chimed less than a minute later.

"Sawyer?" I guessed. "What does he have to say?"

"'You deal with librarian stuff and I'll deal with police stuff,'" she read. "That's a precise quote."

"No surprise there."

Dizzy gave me a conspiratorial smile before taking a drink of her peppermint latte. "I bet our librarian and chocolatier selves can solve the murder before the police do."

"I don't know," I said, feeling dejected. "There's not a lot to go on."

"But you still want to figure it out, right? Even though you're not a suspect anymore?"

I'd shared that bit of good news with her by text the day before.

"I do," I admitted. "I hate that my chocolate chipper was used as the weapon."

"Not your fault."

"Maybe not. But even if the weapon hadn't belonged to

me, I wouldn't be able to stop thinking about the murder and who the killer might be."

"That's because we're mystery lovers. And we want to feel safe in our own town."

She was right on both counts.

I took another sip of my steamer and watched Juniper. As soon as she had her take-out cup in hand, she rushed out of the coffee shop, giving our table a wide berth.

"Hey," Dizzy said, directing my attention back her way. "The Christmas craft fair at the community center starts tomorrow. Want to go?"

"Sure, but can we go the day after tomorrow? Sawyer and I are going to the Christmas tree farm tomorrow afternoon. Do you want to come with us?"

"My parents and I are going later today. And sure, I'm fine with the day after tomorrow for the craft fair."

We chatted about how much Christmas shopping we'd done and how much we had left to do, until a conversation at the table behind Dizzy caught our attention.

"Juniper certainly doesn't seem cut up about her mother's death."

I realized it was Ms. Fernstrom speaking. She wasn't with the same ladies who'd visited True Confections with her the day before. Instead, she shared a table with none other than the Gossip Grannies, Delphi Snodgrass and Luella Plank.

"She's probably relieved to be free of her." Luella leaned forward eagerly. "Do you think Juniper will take over Irma's business?"

"I don't think Juniper knows the first thing about baking," Ms. Fernstrom said before taking a sip of coffee.

"Not *that* business," Luella said. "The other one."

Dizzy and I exchanged intrigued glances as we quietly listened in.

Ms. Fernstrom asked the question I knew both Dizzy and I wanted the answer to. "What other business?"

"She was washing money for the mob," Luella replied with authority.

Dizzy let out a giggle and slapped a hand over her mouth to stop it. I had to bite down on my lip to keep from laughing.

Ms. Fernstrom's eyes widened. "Really? Is that why she was killed? Was it a mob hit?"

Delphi shook her head, annoyance pinching her narrow features. "No, no. It's the cupcake girl who's working for the mob."

"Stephanie?" Dizzy mouthed at me.

I shrugged my shoulders. I didn't know who else they could be referring to, but I highly doubted that Stephanie—or Irma, for that matter—had any ties to the mob.

Did we even have a mob in Vermont?

"Irma was killed because of that infernal notebook of hers," Delphi continued.

"Maybe Irma made notes about the cupcake girl's ties to the mob," Luella said in a hushed voice.

Dizzy was struggling harder than ever to contain her giggles. "Are you done?" she managed to ask me as her shoulders shook.

I tossed back the last of my eggnog steamer and jumped up, remembering at the last second to grab my skates. We practically raced out the door, bursting out laughing as soon as it shut behind us.

"*Washing* money for the mob?" Dizzy said once we finally got our giggles under control. "Those ladies are too much."

"I don't think Irma would launder money for anyone except herself," I said. "And Stephanie working for the mob?" I shook my head. "I don't know how the Gossip Grannies even come up with this stuff."

"Hopefully they won't spread that story about Stephanie any further," Dizzy said, sobering. "Some people in this town are crazy enough to believe it."

I knew that was the truth. After I broke up with my boy-friend in the summer, the Gossip Grannies had made up their own, far wilder version of the incident and several of their faithful followers had taken it as the gospel truth.

Dizzy had to get to work, so she set off in the direction of the library while I returned to the main dock. As I tied up my skates, I decided to pay my brother a visit at his restaurant. Even though the Gondolier wasn't open at this hour, I figured there was a good chance I'd find Gareth there. I skated northward, heading for Giethoorn Avenue, which faced Venice Avenue across the network of canals.

When I reached Giethoorn Avenue, I changed back to my boots and approached the handsome timber-frame building that housed the Gondolier. At this time of year, the patio was closed, but during the warmer months diners could sit outside, with a view of both the canal and Shadow Lake.

Now, with Christmas approaching, big red bows adorned the wrought iron railing surrounding the patio and white lights outlined the front windows. I was willing to bet those touches were courtesy of my brother-in-law, Blake. Gareth, a chef by trade, focused mostly on the food side of the res-taurant, while Blake looked after the other aspects of the business.

The front door was locked when I tried it, but I could see a light on inside, so I tapped on the glass. A shadow shifted back near the bar, and then Blake appeared. When he rec-ognized me, he picked up his pace and unlocked the door.

"How are you doing, Becca?" he asked as he let me in-side. "I hear you fell down some stairs at the community center."

"I had some help with the falling."

"Are you saying someone pushed you?" The question came from my brother, who emerged from the back hall-way. "Who?"

He sounded a bit like a growly bear. If I didn't know him

like I did, I might have found him intimidating in this mood. He, like Blake, stood well over six feet tall. They both worked out regularly and had the muscles to show for it.

"I don't know who," I said as I set my skates by the door and unzipped my jacket.

"Are you hurt?" Blake asked. His blue eyes spotted the bandage on my wrist, which I'd clumsily wrapped myself that morning. "I guess that answers my question."

"It's sprained, and I've got a few bruises, but I'm fine." I might have understated the part about the bruises. I was covered in them and some were quite spectacular. I didn't want to make my brother any more furious, though. I could already see anger burning in his hazel eyes.

"Haven't the police figured out who did it?" he asked. "Have you talked to Sawyer about it?"

"Sawyer was at the community center when it happened," I said. "But there's not much to go on. I didn't see who pushed me, and there weren't any witnesses. I have my suspicions, but no evidence."

How I could find evidence to back up my suspicions, I wasn't yet sure, but I planned to keep trying to figure that out.

"Whoever it was shouldn't be able to get away with it," Gareth grumbled.

"Maybe they won't," I said, hoping I could eventually pin the crime on Amber or Roman, or whoever was responsible. "Are you two here alone?"

"Yes," Gareth replied.

"We've been dealing with a delivery that came in this morning," Blake added.

"I don't want to keep you from that for long," I said, "but I was hoping to ask you about Roman."

"What about him?" Gareth asked.

"I'm not sure if Irma's death had anything to do with the baking competition, but since I don't know that it *wasn't* related, I can't help but look at the other competitors and wonder if they could have harmed her. I really don't know anything about Roman, but he's worked for you for a while now. Do you think he'd be capable of hurting someone?"

Blake shot an uneasy glance at my brother.

"What?" I asked, knowing there was some silent communication going on.

"Roman isn't the easiest person in the world to get along with," Gareth said. "He's got quite an ego, and he's not interested in making friends with anyone. When he first started working here, he tried to throw a hissy fit in the kitchen one day. He quickly found out that I wouldn't tolerate that, and he's been a decent employee ever since."

"But?" I prodded, knowing there was something more.

"But he did have a history with Irma," Blake said.

"What kind of history?"

Gareth was the one to reply. "He worked at her bakery a few years ago, before he went off to culinary school. I don't know what happened between the two of them, but I do know that Roman hated Irma."

Chapter Seventeen

I WAS ON MY WAY OUT OF THE GONDOLIER WHEN I received a text message from Dizzy, letting me know that Consuelo Diaz had arrived at the library. Dizzy was about to take charge of a parent and tot group when she sent the text, so she didn't have time to question Consuelo about Irma's notebook. I dashed off a quick response, telling Dizzy that I was on my way to the library, ready for sleuthing duty.

I skated quickly along the frozen canals. Now that midmorning had arrived, a few others were out skating as well, and I noticed a group of kids out on the lake, playing a game of hockey and making the most of the start of their vacation from school.

As I skated, I pondered what Gareth and Blake had told me. Although they didn't know why Roman hated Irma so much, they'd always assumed that it was simply because Irma wasn't an easy person to work for. If she'd treated Roman anything like she treated Eleanor, I couldn't exactly blame him for having a severe dislike for the woman. I wanted to know just how much he hated her, though. Maybe his animosity ran so deep that when he was faced with the prospect of competing against Irma, something inside of him snapped.

At this point, that theory wasn't based on much more than speculation, but it was worth looking into. After all, what Gareth had told me suggested that Roman had a temper. He'd obviously learned to control it in my brother's kitchen, but Irma could have somehow pushed him over the edge.

Thanks to my fast skating, it didn't take me long to reach the library, so I turned my thoughts from Roman to Consuelo. I waved to Dizzy when I entered the library. She was in the midst of reading a picture book to the parent and tot group, but she sent a smile my way. I headed straight for the romance section. As Dizzy had predicted, I found Consuelo there, browsing the shelves, three paperback historical romances already in hand.

"Hi, Consuelo," I greeted in a low voice, not wanting to disturb any other library patrons.

She smiled when she saw me. "Rebecca, congratulations! You did a great job in the finals of the competition. You're a very talented baker in addition to a talented chocolatier."

Her kind words helped chase away the chill still clinging to me from my trip to the library. "Thank you. I enjoyed being in the competition."

Her gaze traveled down to my wrist. "I heard you had some trouble before the finals started."

"That part wasn't so great, but the actual baking was fun." I unzipped my jacket now that I was warming up. "I don't want to take you away from your browsing for long, but I was hoping you could tell me a bit about Irma's notebook."

"Ah," she said. "The infamous notebook."

"I'd never heard of it until after her death."

"If you lived closer to Irma, you would have." Consuelo ran her finger along the spines of the books on the shelf before tugging one out to take a closer look at it. "I live two doors down from her cottage, you see."

"And the notebook was common knowledge in the neighborhood?"

Consuelo glanced up from reading the back cover of the book. "She paid too much attention to what her neighbors were doing. This is a small town, and you kind of have to accept that people are going to know your business, but most people know there's a line that should not be crossed."

"And I'm guessing Irma crossed it?"

"I'd say so. She liked to spy on people."

"Like hiding in the shadows and peering in windows?" I asked.

"Almost. She used binoculars from her windows and her back porch. She watched what was going on *inside* other people's homes."

"That's creepy."

"Exactly. Since there's a cottage between mine and hers, I didn't have to worry about that too much. But her immediate neighbors . . ." Consuelo shook her head. "They didn't appreciate it, as you can imagine."

"I can," I said. "What about the notebook?"

"Irma took notes on what she saw and she let people know about it."

That echoed what Dizzy had overheard at the baking competition. "Did she blackmail people?"

"I don't think she ever asked for money or anything like that. She just liked to lord it over people that she knew their secrets and intimate details of their lives." Consuelo added the paperback to the stack of books in her arms. "I won't be surprised if it turns out that's why she was killed."

"I wonder if the police have the notebook," I mused out loud.

"I heard from a reliable source that they haven't found it," Consuelo said. "The killer probably has it."

"Or had it and then destroyed it."

"Could be," Consuelo agreed.

A tall woman with red hair turned down the romance aisle.

"Sylvia!" Consuelo greeted. "I thought I might see you here."

The two women started chattering about romance books, so I gave a quick wave to Consuelo and left them to it. It sounded like all of Irma's neighbors belonged on my suspect list. I wondered if there was a way to find out who those people were, without knocking on their doors. I immediately thought of Lolly. She knew just about everyone in Larch Haven and she'd likely be able to provide me with the names of at least some of Irma's neighbors.

I decided to make my grandparents' cottage my next stop, but I didn't make it that far before getting distracted. As I passed by Hooked on Books, the store beneath Dizzy's apartment, I spotted a familiar, angular profile through the large front window. Roman Kafka was in the shop, browsing the shelves.

I hesitated out on the cobblestones, but not for long. Carrying my skates in my good hand, I entered Hooked on Books and wiped my boots on the mat inside the door. Roman had disappeared deeper into the store, but I found him when I peeked down the science fiction and fantasy aisle.

A few other customers browsed the shelves, and the owner of the store stood behind the sales counter, chatting with an older woman, but Roman and I had the aisle to ourselves.

"Hi, Roman," I said quietly. "Good job at the competition the other day."

He glanced my way before returning his attention to the books on the shelf in front of him. "Same to you," he mumbled, not sounding particularly sincere.

He shifted farther along the shelves and I wondered if he was trying to put some distance between us. I decided not to skate around my purpose for approaching him.

"It's terrible what happened to Irma. Do you think it had anything to do with the competition?"

He didn't bother to look at me when he responded. "Who would kill someone to win a baking competition?"

"You're right," I said, keeping my tone casual. "It probably wasn't the competition. After all, lots of people didn't like Irma. I hear you used to work for her. What was that like? Did she drive you crazy?"

Roman turned his blue eyes on me. They were icier than the wind outside.

"Keep your nose out of my business." His words held the same chill as his eyes.

He moved past me, jostling my shoulder on his way by, and strode out of the store.

So much for getting any information out of him. Was his reticence simply in his nature, or did he have something to hide?

I had no idea.

Perhaps Sawyer was right. Maybe sleuthing was best left to the professionals.

I picked a couple of new cozy mysteries off the shelf and took them to the counter to pay.

I might leave the store without any further clues, but at least I wouldn't be empty-handed.

LOLLY AND POPS WERE BOTH AT HOME WHEN I STOPPED by their cottage. I entered through the back door and found Lolly in the kitchen, baking a batch of gingerbread. After chatting with her for a minute, I carried on into the cozy living room, where Pops sat working on a jigsaw puzzle in front of a crackling fire. I joined him at the small table and helped him with the puzzle. As I snapped a piece into its proper place, I wished I could put the pieces of the real-life murder mystery together as easily in my head.

Lolly joined us a short while later, bringing us mugs of her homemade hot apple cider. I breathed in the aromatic steam rising from my mug. With gingerbread baking in the oven, the live tree in the corner, and the cider in front of me, Lolly and Pops's cottage smelled like Christmas.

"I talked to Consuelo Diaz at the library today," I said after we'd all made it partway through our cider. "She says Irma spied on her neighbors. Do you think one of them might have killed her?"

"I certainly hope not," Lolly said, aghast. "I hate to even think of it."

"*Somebody* killed her," Pops said as he fit another piece of the puzzle together. "And probably someone from our town."

Lolly shook her head sadly. "Unfortunately, that's likely true."

"Do you know who lives next to Irma's cottage?" I asked, hoping I sounded only mildly curious. If my grandparents caught on to the fact that I was looking into the murder, they wouldn't be impressed, if only because they wouldn't want me in any danger.

Lolly thought for a moment. "Consuelo's place is two doors down. The Rashids live on one side of Irma's cottage and the MacIntosh family on the other."

Neither of those names had come up in my investigation so far.

"And Gillian and Hank Dubois live in the cottage right behind Irma's," Lolly added. "Their garden backs onto hers."

"Dubois, as in Amber Dubois?" I asked.

"That's right," Lolly confirmed. "Amber's parents."

I let that information sink in. Could Amber have had a dual motive for killing Irma? First, to secure herself a spot in the Baking Spirits Bright finals and, second, to exact revenge on Irma for something she'd done to Amber's parents? Or maybe to protect her parents from some secret coming to light, thanks to Irma's spying.

There seemed to be an endless and dizzying whirl of possibilities spinning around inside my head. I had no problem adding people and motives to my mental list, but what I really needed to do was eliminate suspects. Alibis would be the best way to do that, I figured, but people didn't always take kindly to being asked where they were at the time the crime was committed. Juniper was a good example of that. Roman hadn't even allowed me to get that far in the conversation.

I attempted to put another piece of the jigsaw puzzle together, but it didn't fit where I thought it would. "I'm guessing Juniper doesn't live at Irma's cottage any longer."

"Heavens no," Lolly said. "She moved out as soon as she finished high school. She rents one of the town houses on Stockholm Lane."

That was well out of sight of Irma's cottage, so Irma likely hadn't been spying on her daughter. At least, not from home. Not that Juniper needed to be spied on to have a motive to kill her mother. She already had a double motive, as far as I was concerned. She was angry with Irma about her grandmother's jewelry and she stood to inherit everything from her mother.

So many motives. So few clues.

Now that I had an alibi and my name was clear, I considered giving up on sleuthing and instead focusing only on my work at True Confections and the upcoming holidays.

I stayed at my grandparents' cottage for lunch, helping Pops complete one corner of his puzzle. Then I set off into the cold, intending to head home for a quiet afternoon spent with my cats and one of the new books I'd purchased.

I decided to make one stop on the way, at the fudge and taffy shop, for a bag of saltwater taffy that I would give to Pops for Christmas. When I had a bag of the colorful confection in hand, I continued along the cobblestone walkway, heading for the nearest dock so I could skate home on the canals. Before I got to the dock, I stopped outside the local jewelry store, catching sight of Sawyer through the front window. He stood with the owner of the store, Graham Hughes, behind the sales counter, looking over Graham's shoulder at a computer screen.

I glanced at the town houses across the street. The same row of town houses where Juniper lived. I looked at the jewelry store, with its two outdoor security cameras. I quickly put two and two together in my head.

Pulling the shop's door open, I tried to enter as quietly as possible, but an electronic bell announced my arrival.

Sawyer glanced up, as did Graham, but while Graham quickly refocused on the computer screen, Sawyer's attention stayed on me.

"Looks like she arrived home a few minutes before nine p.m.," Graham said to Sawyer. "Is that helpful?"

"I'd like to get a copy of that footage, please," Sawyer said, all the while looking at me.

"Sure thing," Graham said, maneuvering the mouse.

I didn't miss the hint of suspicion in Sawyer's eyes as he rounded the counter and came toward me.

"Were you looking at surveillance footage of Juniper's town house?" I asked quietly.

"Becca." There was a hint of a warning in his voice.

"Because there's a three-hour gap of unaccounted time between when Juniper left Stephanie's place and when she arrived home. If that's who you were just talking about."

Sawyer put a hand to my lower back and steered me to the far corner of the store. "We've talked about this," he said in a low voice.

"We have, but I can't stop myself from being curious."

He heaved out a sigh. "It's not safe to go around talking about these things."

"I'm safe with you."

He stared into my eyes for a beat.

Warmth flooded my cheeks and I quickly averted my gaze and unzipped my jacket halfway. I told myself that it was the temperature of the store getting to me, even though I knew that was a lie.

Sawyer spoke again as if the heated pause hadn't happened. "And I'm the only person you've talked to about the murder today?" He didn't believe that for a second.

"Well, no," I admitted. "I talked to Dizzy, Gareth, and Blake. And Lolly and Pops."

"And?" He knew there was more.

"I might have had a brief word with Juniper and Roman. Oh, and Consuelo Diaz too."

Sawyer scrubbed a hand down his face. "Becca."

"Don't be mad," I pleaded, hoping he wasn't.

"I'm not mad. Frustrated, but not mad."

"I actually made up my mind to go home and have nothing more to do with the murder, but then I saw you in here."

"I like that decision," Sawyer said. "The one before you decided to come in here, that is."

"I've got a copy of the footage ready for you," Graham called out from across the store.

"Thank you," Sawyer said to him before turning back to me. "I can walk you home."

"Not necessary," I said, slipping past him. "I'm sure you have plenty of other things to do."

He was about to say something more to me, but I didn't give him a chance. With a cheery wave, I dashed out the door. Normally, I would have welcomed his company on my walk home, but I wasn't keen on him continuing his lecture.

On the one hand, I knew he was right and I should keep my nose out of the investigation. On the other hand, I knew that all the questions in my head would likely drive me crazy if I didn't try to find answers to them.

Nevertheless, I decided I would attempt to forget about

the murder, at least for a while. I skated home and got a fire going before curling up on the couch with Binx and Truffles and one of the cozy mysteries I bought at Hooked on Books.

I snapped a picture of the book open on my lap, with the two cats snuggled up on my blanket-covered legs. I sent the photo to Sawyer along with a message saying, Minding my own business.

When he responded later with a text saying, About time, I smiled and got back to my book.

Chapter Eighteen

MY NEW TREND OF STAYING OUT OF THE MURDER IN-
vestigation continued into the next day. That wasn't too difficult, since I was busy with work all morning. Still,
temptation arose when I overheard customers in the shop
chatting about Irma's death. It wasn't difficult to stay out of
their conversation, though, because they didn't say anything I hadn't already heard. As soon as I'd restocked the
display case, I returned to the kitchen and paid no further
attention to what any other customers might or might not
have to say on the subject.

I finished my day's work a bit earlier than usual, not
wanting to be late meeting up with Sawyer for our trip to
the Christmas tree farm. I hoped he wasn't still annoyed
with me. I loved visiting the Christmas tree farm and I
wanted us to have a good time together, not argue about my
predilection for sleuthing.

I met Sawyer in the parking lot at the edge of town,
where he kept his pickup truck.

"How's the wrist?" he asked as he opened the passenger-side door for me.

"A lot better," I said as I climbed into the truck.

The swelling had gone down, and I no longer bothered with the elastic bandage. I still had a few twinges when I moved my wrist in certain ways, but most of the time I forgot that I'd ever injured it.

"How are you doing?" I asked when Sawyer joined me in the truck.

"Not bad." Sawyer buckled up his seat belt. "I'm glad I've got the day off."

"I'm glad too." I watched him as he started the engine and backed out of the parking spot. "It must not be easy working on a murder investigation."

"It makes things more stressful than usual." He flicked on his turn signal before easing out onto the highway.

"Do you think it's close to being solved?" I asked, hopeful.

"Progress is being made, slowly."

"You know about Irma's notebook, right?"

"I've heard of it."

A thought struck me. "Do you know if the jewelry Juniper inherited from her grandmother was in Irma's cottage after her death? Because if Juniper killed Irma and then ransacked the cottage to find the jewelry, it would be missing, right?"

Sawyer didn't respond.

I sat back, feeling silly. "Of course you've already thought of that. But Juniper hasn't been arrested. Does that mean the jewelry wasn't taken from Irma's house?"

"Becca . . ."

I pressed on. "Has Juniper accounted for the gap of time between when she left Stephanie's place and when she got home?"

"Juniper's not being cooperative. And that's all I'm going to say on the subject."

"Do you think she's the killer?"

"Becca," he said again, this time with a stronger warning underscoring my name.

I rested my head against the back of the seat. "I know. I'm annoying you. Sorry."

"I'm not annoyed, but I worry. The fact that there's a killer out there is bad enough. Knowing you could end up in danger again . . ." He rubbed his jaw before replacing his hand on the steering wheel. "I want to keep you safe, but I need your help with that."

I hated knowing I was the source of the tension thrumming through him at the moment.

"Okay," I relented. "I solemnly swear not to question anyone I suspect of killing Irma for the next twenty-four hours."

Sawyer sent me an unimpressed, sidelong glance before returning his eyes to the road.

"Hey, it's a start," I said.

"I suppose," he grudgingly agreed.

"I'll even pinky swear." I held out my little finger.

"We don't need to pinky swear. Your word is good enough."

"We should still pinky swear," I said.

"I'm too old for that."

"There's no such thing as too old to pinky swear," I told him.

I'd pushed him to the edge of exasperation, but he hooked his finger around mine. He held on a beat longer than necessary and gave my finger a gentle squeeze before letting go.

I decided it was time to change the subject. "Did you get your invitation to the Christmas Eve open house at Lolly and Pops's place?"

"I saw the email this morning."

"Will you be able to make it?"

"I'll be working till seven that evening, but I could drop by after that if it's not too late."

"Definitely not too late," I assured him. "It's a come-when-you-can sort of thing."

"Then I'll be there."

"What about Christmas Day? We're having a big family dinner at Gareth and Blake's house. You're welcome to join us." I didn't like the thought of him being alone on Christmas.

"I'll be working that day too."

"Christmas Eve *and* Christmas Day?"

"By choice," he said. "A lot of my colleagues have families or at least significant others. With my mom not coming till the new year, I figured I'd step up to the plate."

"You could always come by after work for pumpkin pie."

"I'll probably be working late that night. But thank you. I appreciate the invitation."

"At least you'll get good food on Christmas Eve."

"I'm sure it'll be great, but the company will be even better."

My cheeks warm, I turned to look out the side window as Sawyer left the highway for the long driveway leading to the Christmas tree farm. We spent the next hour looking at trees, and not saying a word about the murder. It was nice to have some holiday-related fun, and I was pleased to see that Sawyer relaxed more and more as we walked around the farm, checking out all the trees, looking for the perfect two to take home.

I chose a Douglas fir, as was my tradition, and Sawyer picked out a blue spruce. By the time we had the trees loaded in the back of his truck, darkness had fallen over the farm and my fingers and toes had become painfully cold.

A small bonfire snapped and crackled not far from the parking lot. Several people had gathered around it, warming up while they chatted with one another, but my attention strayed to the small building used for a seasonal café that served hot drinks and sugar cookies.

"How about some hot chocolate?" I suggested to Sawyer.

"Sounds like a good idea," he said. "You look like you're about to turn into an icicle."

"I'm not far off," I admitted, huddled in my coat.

We headed into the café, where a wall of warm air hit me as soon as I stepped inside. I almost sighed with relief, even though it would take a while for me to shake off my chill.

Sawyer and I headed straight for the counter, where we ordered a large hot chocolate and a sugar cookie each. It wasn't until we turned around, ready to find ourselves a free table, when I noticed Daniel Hathaway in the far corner of the café. He shared a small table with a man I'd never seen before.

As if feeling my gaze on him, Daniel glanced up. It took only half a second for him to recognize me. I smiled at him, but he was so quick to avert his uneasy gaze that I wasn't sure if he noticed. His shoulders hunched forward in his black wool coat and he rested an arm on the table, leaning closer to his companion, as if trying to make their conversation more private.

Sawyer and I claimed a table by the window, well away from Daniel. I stared at the back of his head while I broke a piece off my cookie and munched on it. He'd seemed almost fearful that I'd seen him here. What was up with that? Why would I care if he was at the Christmas tree farm's café? Maybe his behavior had more to do with his companion. But I didn't recognize him, so again, why would I care that he was here with Daniel?

"What are you staring at?" Sawyer asked, taking a look over his shoulder.

"That man in the black wool coat," I whispered. "Have you seen him before?"

Sawyer continued looking over his shoulder until he caught a glimpse of Daniel's profile. "Not that I recall. Why?"

"I saw him at Victor's art gallery when I bought the painting that's over my fireplace. Then he was at the preliminary round of Baking Spirits Bright. I spoke to him that day, and he told me that his name is Daniel Hathaway."

"So he's a tourist?"

I shrugged. "I guess so. But I feel like he didn't want me seeing him here."

Sawyer checked over his shoulder again. "Are you sure you're not reading too much into it?"

"Maybe." I had to admit that Daniel didn't seem quite as tense now as he had moments before. "But seeing him again has reminded me of something. Don't get mad at me for bringing up the murder again, but this is something you should know. I saw Daniel Hathaway talking to Irma before the first round of the competition."

"What were they talking about?"

"I have no idea. All I know is that Daniel shook his head at something Irma said. Then, when Irma walked off, she didn't look happy."

"Irma never looked happy."

"Okay, true," I conceded. "But she *really* didn't look happy. At the time, there was a rumor going around that Daniel was the guy from *Bake It Right*. I wondered if Irma was trying to butter him up, but it turns out he wasn't with the magazine."

"But maybe Irma thought he was, and then found out he wasn't," Sawyer said. "That might have annoyed her."

"You're probably right." I took a sip of my delicious hot chocolate, topped with a generous swirl of whipped cream.

"Just to be clear, though," Sawyer said, "he's now on the list of people you shouldn't be talking to about the murder."

I grabbed a napkin and wiped whipped cream from my mouth. "So you're saying you think he's suspicious?"

"I'm saying better safe than sorry." He practically pinned me to my chair with his dark eyes. "And don't forget your promise."

I wiggled my pinky finger at him with a smile. "I won't."

Daniel and the other man left together a few minutes

later. Sawyer and I spent the rest of our time at the café chatting about things that had nothing to do with murder. When we got back to Larch Haven, Sawyer helped me set up my tree in its stand. Then he left to meet up with some friends for a hockey game on the frozen lake. I considered going out to watch the game, or maybe even join in, but I decided I'd had enough of being cold. My cottage was so nice and cozy, and Binx and Truffles wanted cuddles, so I parked myself on my couch instead.

Although I tried to lose myself in a holiday movie, my thoughts kept drifting back to Daniel Hathaway and his odd behavior at the tree farm café. As the movie played on in the background, I picked up my phone and did a quick Internet search. I might have promised Sawyer not to question anyone about the murder, but I hadn't said anything about poking around for information online.

Twenty minutes later, I gave up, feeling frustrated. While there were plenty of people named Daniel Hathaway with an online presence, I couldn't find a single speck of information about the Daniel Hathaway currently staying in Larch Haven.

That didn't necessarily mean anything. Not everyone used social media or had information about themselves scattered over the Internet.

Even so, the lack of information left me more curious than before.

Who was Daniel Hathaway, and did he have some connection to Irma that went beyond possible mistaken identity?

Although I didn't have the answers to those questions, I thought I might be able to find them. Without breaking my promise to Sawyer.

Chapter Nineteen

~~~~~~~~

ALTHOUGH SNOW WAS IN THE FORECAST FOR LATER in the day, the sky was clear when I walked to work the next morning. Stars twinkled overhead and I stopped on a stone bridge to look up and take in the sight of the constellations. Despite the beauty of the early morning sky, I didn't linger for long. As the clouds had disappeared the evening before, the temperature had done a nosedive. Plus, Sawyer had warned me against walking alone in the dark. I didn't have anyone to accompany me that morning, but I could at least not prolong my journey.

I tugged my scarf up over my nose, which felt like it was rapidly freezing from the inside out, and hurried onward to Venice Avenue. I slowed my pace, momentarily forgetting about the cold, when I noticed a faint light inside Irma's bakery. Normally, that wouldn't have caught my interest. Irma always arrived at work far earlier than I did. But Irma was dead and the bakery had been closed since her murder. So who had turned the light on?

I stopped outside the bakery's front window and realized that someone hadn't turned on an overhead light in the back of the building. The beam of light, previously steady, now bounced around. It was a flashlight, or a flashlight app on a phone. I peered through the shadows of the darkened storefront, trying to catch sight of who was in the back, but I couldn't see anything more than the moving light.

The killer had searched Irma's handbag and likely her cottage as well. If they hadn't found what they were looking for, maybe they'd come to search the bakery next.

My heart kicked into overdrive. I didn't want the burglar to spot me through the window, so I quickly dashed out of sight and fished my phone out of the depths of the pocket of my puffy coat. The icy air bit at my hands when I removed my gloves to use the phone. I called 9-1-1, and quickly explained about the intruder at the bakery. I hoped I wasn't raising a false alarm. Maybe Juniper was at the bakery for some legitimate reason. After all, she was Irma's heir. But if that was the case, she would have turned on the bakery's lights. She wouldn't be creeping around by the beam of a flashlight.

The 9-1-1 operator advised me to wait inside True Confections for the police to arrive. I gladly followed that advice. Despite my thick coat and many other layers, I was shivering and my fingers and toes had crossed the line from painful to numb.

I shut and locked the shop door behind me, but stayed by the front window, watching for the police to arrive. I hoped the burglar wouldn't escape before they showed up. There was a chance that the intruder could take off out the back door. The True Confections kitchen had a window that looked out onto the back alley, but if I wanted a view of the bakery's back door, I'd have to go out behind the shop. That wasn't something I was about to do in the circumstances.

Sawyer would be proud of how careful I was being.

Within minutes, red and blue light reflected off the snowbanks. I peeked out the shop door as a police cruiser crawled along the cobblestones, its siren silent. It pulled to a stop outside of Irma's bakery. As soon as I recognized Sawyer climbing out of the driver's seat, I hurried over his way. I didn't get far when he held out a hand to stop me.

"Wait inside, Becca," he said.

I turned around to do as requested, knowing he was trying to keep me safe. Who knew how the person inside the bakery would react when they realized they were about to get caught?

I had my hand on the shop's door, ready to go inside, when Sawyer spoke again.

"Never mind, Becca. It's fine."

"What do you mean?" I asked.

Sawyer hadn't even gone in the building yet.

"Nyberg caught the intruder climbing out the back window."

Tugging my scarf up over my chin, I joined him in front of the bakery. "Who is it?"

Instead of answering, Sawyer gestured at the building. Inside, an overhead light flicked on and Nyberg emerged from the back, a woman walking in front of him.

"Stephanie?!" I blurted out as soon as I recognized her.

Nyberg unlocked the front door and Sawyer joined them in the bakery. I followed close behind him, hoping he wouldn't kick me out.

I wanted to ask Stephanie what she was doing there, but I bit my tongue. I never seriously believed that Stephanie could have killed Irma, but the fact that she was sneaking around the bakery put her firmly on my suspect list, at least for the moment, and I had promised Sawyer not to question any of my suspects for the next while. It wasn't necessary for me to ask the question, anyway. All I had to do was listen.

"Becca, I swear I didn't kill Irma," Stephanie burst out when she saw me. "I came here to look for something. That's all."

"The notebook." I didn't need to phrase it as a question. I couldn't think of anything else she might be searching for in the bakery.

She nodded as a tear ran down her cheek.

"Ms. Kang," Sawyer cautioned, "you might not want to say anything more at this point."

Sawyer nodded at Nyberg, who proceeded to read Stephanie her rights as he snapped handcuffs around her wrists.

Stephanie's eyes widened. "You're arresting me?" She turned her pleading eyes to me. "Irma told me she saw Rob leaving my place in the middle of the night. She thinks we were having an affair, but that's not what happened. We're still good friends and he needed someone to talk to after a fight with his wife. But if that rumor got out, it could hurt his marriage. I just wanted to find the notebook so no one would get the wrong idea. Becca, please tell Juniper I didn't kill her mother. I swear I didn't."

"Stephanie," I said, "don't say anything more until you've spoken to a lawyer, okay?"

With fear shining in her tear-filled eyes, she nodded.

"We'll go out the back to my cruiser," Nyberg said, before leading Stephanie in that direction.

"Was she talking about Rob Myers?" Sawyer asked me once they were gone.

"She must have been," I replied.

Stephanie and Rob had been high school sweethearts, but they broke up when they went their separate ways to different colleges. Rob had since married someone else, but I knew that he and Stephanie had remained good friends over the years, like she'd said.

I looked around the bakery. Stephanie hadn't made a mess during her search, but there were a couple of drawers left partway open.

"I'm guessing there was an official search of this place after Irma's death," I said.

"We searched it from top to bottom," Sawyer confirmed.

"And the notebook was never found?"

"I shouldn't answer that question."

"That's all right," I said. "I'm pretty sure the police don't have it."

If the cops hadn't found Irma's infamous notebook, then in all likelihood the killer had found it when they'd searched Irma's cottage. Most of the town assumed that was what had happened and yet Stephanie was still looking. Either she'd acted on a desperate hope that no one had found the notebook, or she knew the killer didn't yet have it because *she* was the killer.

As much as I didn't want Stephanie to be the murderer, I couldn't discount her simply because I liked her. If the police hadn't considered her a serious suspect before, they probably would now. I hoped that Stephanie would turn out to be innocent, but I couldn't help but wonder how desperately she'd wanted to keep any rumors about her relationship with Rob from circulating through town.

Lois had left her kitchen shortly before eight on the night of the murder. Stephanie could have left her apartment just after that and gone straight to the town hall. The timeline was tight, but she still could have killed Irma.

I glanced around the bakery once more. "I guess I should get back to True Confections."

"Good idea," Sawyer said. "I can practically see the wheels turning in your head and it's a lot safer to think about chocolates than what you're thinking about right now."

"But did you notice that I didn't ask Stephanie any questions?"

"It's a good practice," he said. "Keep it up."

I rolled my eyes, but I had a hint of a smile on my face.

"Becca," Sawyer said as I was on my way out the door, "thanks for making the call."

I nodded, and then left him there in the bakery.

Although I worried about how Stephanie was faring at the police station and whether someone I liked so much could be a murderer, focusing on work helped keep my thoughts from whirling around too crazily in my head. When I eventually stopped for a break, I had a fresh batch of gingerbread decorated, as well as plenty of eggnog truffles, candy cane bonbons, almond creams, and ice wine truffles ready to sell.

I drank down a glass of water and then ventured out into the front of the shop to see how things were going. I stopped in my tracks when I saw Daniel Hathaway in the store, browsing the shelves. Clearly, he hadn't yet left town. Maybe this was my chance to find out more about him.

I took a step in his direction, but Angela appeared in front of me.

"Becca, perfect timing," she said. "Could you bring out some more ice wine truffles and eggnog truffles, please? They've been flying off the shelves this morning."

"Sure. I'll do that right away," I told her.

After one last glance at Daniel, who had his back to me, I retreated to the kitchen. I set aside a few dozen of the freshly made chocolates to be boxed up and carried a tray of the remaining ones out front to refill the display case. Even though I'd been gone for only a couple of minutes, Daniel Hathaway had already left the shop.

Disappointed, I transferred the truffles to the display case and then tucked the empty tray under my arm.

"That man in the long dark coat who was in here a few minutes ago," I said quietly to Angela so the other customers wouldn't overhear. "Did he give you his name?"

"No," Angie replied. "We barely talked at all. He paid for a box of chocolates and left."

"Did he happen to pay with a credit card?" I asked, hopeful.

"Cash." Angie looked at me more closely. "Why the interest in him?"

"It's not important," I said as two customers approached the sales counter.

I left Angie to look after them and headed into the office, where I grabbed my coat. Daniel Hathaway's appearance at True Confections hadn't answered any questions for me, so it seemed I needed to stick with the plan I'd devised the night before. I got bundled up and passed through the shop on my way out to Venice Avenue, heading for Victor's art gallery.

Daniel had purchased an expensive Gregor Marriott painting at the gallery and I figured he most likely would have done so with a credit card. And his credit card would have his real name on it. Maybe I was on a wild-goose chase and Daniel Hathaway was exactly who he claimed to be—a tourist—and simply lived a low-profile life without an online presence. But considering everything else that had been going on in town lately, I wasn't ready to accept that explanation. Not until I'd looked at other possibilities. One such possibility was that he'd given me a false name when we'd introduced ourselves to each other.

When I entered the gallery, the place was deserted. I wiped my feet on the welcome mat and made my way farther inside, my eyes scanning the paintings and photographs on the wall as I went. When I got closer to the sales counter, I heard a low murmur of voices coming from somewhere in the back. Victor appeared from that direction a second later and smiled when he saw me.

"Morning, Rebecca," he greeted. "How are you liking your new painting?"

"I love it," I said with sincerity. "It looks amazing above my fireplace."

"Glad to hear it. How can I help you today?"

"Remember the man who purchased the Gregor Marriott painting on the day I was here with my friend?"

"The tourist in the expensive suit?" he asked.

"That's him," I confirmed before launching into the

story I'd rehearsed in my head. "There's something I need to talk to him about, but I don't know how to track him down. Do you happen to know his name?"

"He did introduce himself." Victor rubbed his chin as he thought. "I think his name was Daniel something."

"I've been having trouble finding a way to contact him," I said. "Would you be able to check what name was on his credit card?"

"He didn't use a credit card to pay," Victor said. "He paid in cash."

My eyebrows hitched up in surprise. "For such an expensive painting?"

"It's somewhat unusual, but not unheard of. I got the feeling he was looking specifically for Marriott works, so he probably came prepared to buy one."

"I see," I said, disappointed.

"Sorry I can't be of any more help," Victor said. "He told me he was a tourist, so he might not even be in town anymore."

"You might be right." I didn't bother to mention that I'd seen him earlier in the day. "Thanks, Victor."

I was about to turn to go when Juniper appeared from the back hallway, taking me by surprise. I didn't think I imagined the chill in her gaze when she sent the briefest of glances my way.

"I left all the information on your desk, Victor," she said. "I'll have more pieces ready in a week or so."

"I'm looking forward to seeing them," Victor told her.

Juniper wrapped a scarf around her neck and left the gallery.

"Juniper's an artist, right?" I said, remembering that she'd said as much during her argument with Irma at the town hall.

"A painter, yes," Victor replied. "Oils, mostly. I sell some of her work here."

Two women entered the gallery at that moment, so I

quickly thanked Victor and got on my way. I was ready to give up on sleuthing. I couldn't seem to fit any puzzle pieces together in my head, whether for the murder or the mystery surrounding Daniel Hathaway.

Sawyer was right—I'd be better off thinking about chocolates instead of crimes and mysteries. I decided to give that my best shot.

Chapter Twenty

FOR THE NEXT FEW HOURS, I SUCCEEDED AT THINK-
ing of nothing other than chocolate truffles, chocolate bonbons, chocolate lollipops, and chocolate figurines in the
shapes of snowmen and Santa Claus. After wrapping up for
the day and cleaning the kitchen, I got bundled up and set
off to meet Dizzy so we could attend the Christmas craft
fair together. Outside, snow fell from low clouds that hid
the surrounding mountains from view. Although the snow
had started falling less than an hour ago, it was already ac-
cumulating on rooftops and the cobblestone roadways.

When I reached the eastern end of Venice Avenue,
Dizzy was waiting for me, huddled under the shelter of a
shop's awning. She waved a gloved hand when she saw me,
and I picked up my pace.

"Sorry to keep you waiting," I apologized as she fell into
step with me.

"I haven't even been here a full minute," she said. "And
I was admiring the snow. It's really coming down."

"According to the forecast, we could get more than a foot overnight."

"Sounds good to me," Dizzy said. "But I don't have to do much shoveling."

"I have to do some, but I don't mind either." In fact, I loved snow, at least when I didn't have to drive anywhere. I hoped I could hit the slopes soon. I hadn't done enough snowboarding yet this winter.

"We should go snowboarding soon," Dizzy said as if she'd read my mind. "And snowshoeing."

"How about snowshoeing tomorrow?" I suggested. "And snowboarding on your next day off."

"Deal."

I glanced her way before changing the subject. "How are things with your parents? Did you talk to them yet?"

Dizzy's face fell. "I tried. I asked outright what they were keeping from me."

"And?"

"Then they got a video call from my aunt and that was it. They chatted away until after I went to bed."

"You need to try again."

She sighed. "I will."

I put an arm around her shoulders. "Everything will be okay, Diz."

Please let that be the truth, I silently begged of the universe.

She gave me a grateful smile as we climbed the steps to the front door of the community center. Inside the building, we pulled off our hats and stomped the snow from our boots. Then we headed into the gymnasium, the site of the Christmas craft fair.

Folding tables had been set up all around the perimeter of the gym and a decent crowd of shoppers had already gathered, browsing the goods on display. Right away I could see that there was plenty to choose from. People were selling baked goods, handmade Christmas decorations, stained-glass panels and ornaments, small paintings, jewelry, and hand-knitted socks, scarves, and hats. Dizzy and I started at the table to our left and worked our way around the room from there.

As I stopped to admire a stained-glass panel featuring a bright red cardinal surrounded by holly, I caught sight of a flash of bright color out of the corner of my eye. Amber, wearing a winter jacket in bright magenta, was entering the gymnasium, Paisley Hooper following one step behind her.

Although I kept moving along the tables, pretending to check out the items on display, my thoughts drifted away from the craft fair. The threatening note Amber had received still bothered me. If the threat, my fall down the stairs, and Irma's murder were all the work of someone hoping to increase their chances of winning the baking competition, how come Roman and Stephanie hadn't received any threats or come to any harm?

Perhaps Roman thought he would be a shoo-in if he whittled the competition down. But that didn't make sense to me. Stephanie owned the local cake shop and I thought Roman would have known that she'd be stiff competition. So wouldn't he have targeted Stephanie next after Irma?

If Stephanie was behind all the incidents, then why didn't she try to get Roman, a professional pastry chef, out of the competition?

My gaze strayed away from the goods in front of me to where Amber and Paisley were admiring some handmade jewelry. Dizzy had already moved to the next table ahead of me, so I joined her there as she looked at a display of Christmas tree ornaments.

"Dizzy, I need to talk to you," I whispered in her ear. "Out in the hall."

She followed me to the door, without any hesitation.

"What's up?" she asked as soon as we stepped out of the gymnasium.

We were alone in the hallway, but I still kept my voice

at a whisper. "I want to find out if Amber or Paisley pushed me down the stairs on the day of the finals."

"You think it was definitely one of them?"

"I really don't know," I admitted. "But if nothing else, I could eliminate them from the pool of suspects. For that incident, at least."

If I could find out if Amber was involved in Irma's death, so much the better. Technically, I'd kept my promise to Sawyer because twenty-four hours had passed since our conversation in his truck. Still, a nugget of guilt settled in my stomach. I knew he wouldn't like what I was about to get up to.

"I take it you have a plan," Dizzy said.

"I'm forming one, but I need to take a look around upstairs. Will you come with me?"

It was probably silly, but I wasn't keen on wandering around the second floor of the community center on my own, not after what had happened the last time.

"You know I'm on board," Dizzy said, making me smile.

We hurried up the stairs to the second floor, where all was quiet. Feeling too warm now, I shrugged out of my jacket and draped it over my arm, and Dizzy did the same with hers. I stood in the middle of the hallway, looking around. I spotted an air vent in the wall, up near the ceiling, almost directly across the hall from the stairway.

"We're going to need a place to hide," I said, trying the door to the left of the stairwell. It was locked.

I tried the door on the other side of the stairwell, while Dizzy tested the ones across the hall. All were locked.

"Darn." Maybe I needed to come up with another idea.

"It's okay," Dizzy assured me. "Janelle Roper was at the front desk when we came in. She volunteers at the library sometimes and we get along great. I bet she'll lend us a key to one of these rooms, especially if we tell her why we want it."

"It's worth a try."

We returned to the main floor and made a beeline for the front desk. Janelle wanted to help us, but she was hesitant about letting her keys out of her sight. Luckily, she came up with a compromise—she would unlock one of the doors on the second floor for us. That way she could keep her keys in her possession.

Dizzy and I thanked her profusely before returning to the gymnasium. In our absence, Amber and Paisley had moved from one display of handmade jewelry to another. We headed over their way, sauntering so it wouldn't appear as though we'd zeroed in on them.

We edged up to the table where Amber and Paisley were looking at earrings, and I lifted up a necklace with a heart-shaped pendant, pretending to admire it.

"At least we'll know who pushed me down the stairs soon," I said to Dizzy, as if continuing a conversation we'd already started.

"Thank goodness there's that security camera in the air vent on the second floor," Dizzy added, playing her part. "Whoever pushed you obviously didn't know about the camera. Too bad the police didn't find out about it earlier."

"At least they know now," I said. "An officer is coming to pick up a copy of the footage later today."

I set down the necklace, not allowing myself to look Amber and Paisley's way until I turned to walk off, with Dizzy at my side. Then I sent the most subtle of glances their way.

Amber and Paisley huddled together, with worried expressions on their faces.

"It must have been one of them," Dizzy whispered to me as we walked out of the gymnasium, trying our best to remain casual. "Did you see how guilty they looked?"

"Maybe they were in on it together," I said. "They both seemed worried about the camera."

As soon as Dizzy and I got out into the hallway, we burst into a run, charging up the stairs to the second floor. As Janelle had promised, the door to the classroom to the left of the stairwell stood open. Dizzy and I slipped into the room and closed the door all but a crack, leaving the lights turned off. Then we waited.

It didn't take long for hurried footsteps to sound in the stairwell. Seconds later, I heard hushed female voices.

"You were supposed to check for security cameras!"

I was sure that was Amber's voice. I peeked through the crack in the door. Amber and Paisley emerged from the stairwell and stopped in the middle of the hallway.

"I did check!" Paisley insisted. "How was I supposed to know that there was one hidden in an air vent?"

Amber spotted the vent near the ceiling. She planted her hands on her hips. "How are we going to get the camera out of there?"

"Maybe there's no point in trying," Paisley said. "The camera might send the footage to a computer wirelessly. If that's the case, stealing the camera won't help."

Amber turned on Paisley. "And if that's the case, you're going down with me. I'll make sure of it, just like I sent Rebecca Ransom crashing down those stairs."

I glanced at Dizzy, who was listening as intently as I was, though she couldn't see out the door. She met my eyes and nodded. I opened the door and stepped out into the hall, Dizzy right behind me.

Amber and Paisley spun around, their eyes widening when they saw us.

I stared hard at Amber. "So it was you who pushed me down the stairs."

Amber's mouth gaped open, but not for long. She snapped it shut, her blue eyes hardening, and then she finally spoke. "Good luck proving it."

"That won't be a problem," Dizzy said as she picked up my phone from the floor.

Before hiding in the classroom, I'd set the device there, leaning against the wall, the voice recording app activated. It was still recording, a fact that Amber didn't miss.

She lunged forward, making a grab for the phone.

Dizzy spun on her heel, turning her back to Amber and holding my phone out of her reach. Amber grabbed Dizzy's arm in a vicious grip.

"Let go of her!" I clamped my hand around Amber's wrist and squeezed hard.

She released Dizzy with a growl of pain and anger, and I stepped in front of my best friend, hoping to shield her from any further violence. Amber was breathing heavily, her nostrils flared, and I could almost feel anger radiating off of her in searing hot waves. I couldn't trust her to keep herself under control.

"Give it up, Amber," I said. "You've been caught and now you have to deal with the consequences."

"Are you going to tell the police?" Paisley asked with trepidation.

I'd almost forgotten about her. I glanced her way, just long enough to notice that her face had gone pale. Then I returned my attention to Amber, not wanting to let my guard down.

"Maybe," I said.

Dizzy stepped up beside me. "Why shouldn't she? She could have been badly hurt!"

"She just wanted to scare you," Paisley said to me. "Right, Amber?"

"Shut up, Paisley," her friend snapped.

I watched Amber closely. "I find that hard to believe. After all, if you were willing to kill Irma to get a place in the finals of the baking competition, why would you stop at simply trying to scare me? You probably wanted me in the hospital, at the very least."

"I didn't kill Irma!" Amber fumed. Her gaze darted to my phone, still held in Dizzy's hand.

I tensed, thinking Amber was going to lunge at my friend again.

"Stop recording," Amber demanded.

"Why should we?" Dizzy asked, not moving.

"I didn't kill Irma and if you want to know anything more, stop recording." Amber was practically seething now.

Dizzy looked to me for a decision. I gave her a grudging nod. At least we had proof that Amber had pushed me down the stairs. I knew we wouldn't get anything else from her if we didn't shut off the recording app and I still had questions I wanted answered.

Dizzy stopped the app from recording and handed me the phone. I tucked it into the back pocket of my jeans, where I hoped it would be safe from Amber's clutches.

"Okay, talk," I said.

Paisley beat her to it. "Amber wanted to win the competition."

Amber glared at her friend and spoke through clenched teeth. "Seriously, Paisley. Shut. Up."

Paisley pressed her lips together, her eyes downcast.

"I needed the win to take my blog to the next level," Amber said as if it were the most obvious thing ever.

"And you figured Becca was your biggest competition," Dizzy guessed.

Amber shot her a disparaging look. "No. That would have been the two *professionals*. Duh."

Dizzy sent a death glare Amber's way, but kept quiet.

"So why push me down the stairs and not do something to Stephanie or Roman?" I asked.

"Opportunity," Amber said to me like I was stupid. "Believe me, if I'd had a chance to push one of them down the stairs, I would have done it. But you were the only one I had a chance to spill coffee on. I got Paisley to put a sign on the door of the main floor restroom so you'd have to go upstairs. You walked right into my trap." A smug smile appeared on her face before fading away. "I was hoping the threatening note would scare off at least one of the others."

"So you did write the note yourself," Dizzy said before I could. "We figured as much."

"Congratulations, Sherlock," Amber said, her voice full of scorn.

Dizzy looked ready to throttle Amber, and I couldn't blame her. I wasn't far off from that myself.

"If you were willing to do all that to win a competition, why should we believe that you wouldn't kill Irma to get a spot in the finals?" I asked.

"I don't care what you believe. I didn't kill Irma and that's the truth." Amber turned her icy eyes on Paisley. "And if you'd actually done what you were supposed to do, we wouldn't be in this mess right now."

"I couldn't have known there was a camera hidden in the vent!" Paisley said in her own defense.

"There is no camera in the vent," I told them.

Amber's glare landed on me. "You set us up."

"That's the least you deserve," Dizzy said.

Amber whirled on Paisley. "If you'd kept your mouth shut, none of this would have happened!"

"How is it my fault?" Paisley asked, her eyes shining with tears.

"You're my assistant! You're supposed to take care of things. You're supposed to make sure things don't end up in a mess."

Paisley sniffled and started to cry. "You always blame me for everything. And I'm not just your assistant. I'm supposed to be your *friend*."

Amber scoffed, and that only made Paisley cry harder. Blood trickled out of her nose.

Amber's face paled. She took a step away from Paisley. "You're bleeding. I can't—"

She took another step back and then collapsed to the ground.

Chapter Twenty-One

"AMBER!" PAISLEY CRIED.

Dizzy and I crouched down next to Amber's crumpled form. She stirred and groaned as her eyelids fluttered before opening.

"Amber, are you okay?" I asked, resting a hand on her shoulder.

Out of the corner of my eye, I saw Paisley dash into the women's restroom.

Amber groaned again and then looked at Dizzy and me with dazed eyes. "What happened?"

"You fainted," Dizzy said.

"We should call an ambulance." I tugged my phone out of my pocket.

Amber grabbed my wrist with surprising strength, considering she'd regained consciousness mere seconds ago. "Don't you dare."

"You passed out cold," Dizzy told her.

Amber released her death grip on my wrist. She'd probably given me a fresh set of bruises.

She sat up slowly and Dizzy put an arm around her back to help her.

"I don't need an ambulance." She pressed a hand to her forehead. "I'm fine. I only passed out because Paisley was bleeding."

As Amber finished speaking, Paisley emerged from the washroom. Her nose had stopped bleeding and she'd cleaned all the blood from her face.

She hurried over to Amber's side. "I'm so sorry about that, Amber."

Amber glared at her. "You know what happens when I see blood."

"I didn't know I was going to have a nosebleed!"

"Let's not fight," Dizzy said in her stern librarian voice. "We're calling an ambulance."

I thought she'd made the right decision. Despite Amber's strong grip on my wrist moments ago, she seemed a bit woozy. She didn't even protest as Dizzy and I helped her scoot across the floor so she could lean against the wall.

I made the phone call while Dizzy ran downstairs to let the community center's staff know that an ambulance would be arriving soon, and why.

Amber sent one of her death glares my way after I ended the phone call. "You'd better not spread any rumors about this. It's not funny, you know."

"Nobody's laughing," I said. "Did you get hurt when you fell?"

She combed out her hair with her fingers. "No. Like I said, I'm fine."

"Has this happened before?" I aimed the question equally at Amber and Paisley.

"Many times," Paisley replied.

Amber let out a huff. "Not *that* many."

"She faints whenever she sees blood," Paisley explained.

"Only other people's blood," Amber clarified, sounding annoyed by the conversation. Or maybe it was the whole situation that had her aggravated. I got the feeling she didn't like to show any signs of weakness in front of others.

We fell quiet and waited in an awkward silence for several minutes until Dizzy returned, two paramedics on her heels. While Amber got checked over, Dizzy, Paisley, and I retreated farther down the hallway.

"Apparently Amber faints whenever she sees someone else's blood," I said, bringing Dizzy up to speed.

"She's always been like that," Paisley added. "And she hates fainting in front of people."

"Then you must be thinking what I'm thinking," Dizzy said to me.

I nodded.

"What's that?" Paisley asked, not on the same wavelength as us.

I lowered my voice to a whisper. "There was a lot of blood at the murder scene. I don't think Amber would have killed someone in a way that caused a lot of bleeding."

"Of course she didn't kill Irma!" Paisley said, also keeping her voice low. "I know she's not the nicest person in the world, but she's not a killer."

"Why do you stick with her?" Dizzy asked. "She treats you horribly. You deserve better than that."

Paisley clasped her hands together and looked down at them. "I'm beginning to realize that. I've always admired her, you know? She was so popular in school and I really wasn't. I thought it was amazing that someone like her would be friends with me. But she never treated me very well. And ever since she hired me as her assistant, it's been much worse." She let out a heavy sigh. "She only started food blogging after I got interested in baking and discovered that I was really good at it. It was like she couldn't stand me being better at something than she was. I didn't enter Baking Spirits Bright because I knew she'd have a fit and fire me." Paisley shrugged. "Still, she's not all bad."

"Maybe not," I said, although I hadn't seen any evidence of that myself. "But you really do deserve better."

Paisley nodded but didn't say anything. The paramedics were done and left without taking Amber with them. She'd refused to go to the hospital and the paramedics had declared her to be unharmed.

Amber got to her feet and dusted off the back of her jeans. "Let's get out of here, Paisley."

Paisley hooked her arm through Amber's and they headed for the stairs.

"Are you sure you'll be okay?" Dizzy asked with a hint of worry.

Amber ignored her.

Paisley glanced back at us as they started down the stairs. "I'll make sure she gets home safely."

Dizzy and I were happy enough to leave that task with her. We waited until the two of them were out of sight and earshot.

"So, I think that's one suspect we can cross off our list," Dizzy said. "If Amber had wanted to kill Irma, even in the heat of the moment, she would have grabbed a rolling pin or something like that. She wouldn't have stabbed anyone."

"My thinking exactly," I agreed. "And even if she did, she would have passed out right next to Irma and likely would have ended up covered in blood. Plus, the blood around Irma would have been disturbed. I didn't see any signs of that. Whoever killed Irma must have got out of the way quickly after stabbing her, otherwise they probably would have left more of a blood trail when they left the murder scene."

"Ugh. That's gruesome to even think about. I'm sorry you had to see Irma like that."

"Me too." I could feel my mood sinking and didn't want to continue that trend. "How about we go back to the craft fair?" I suggested. "We haven't seen everything yet."

"Shouldn't we call the police about Amber?" Dizzy asked. "You could have broken your neck when she pushed you."

"I'll talk to Sawyer about it later. I don't think Amber will be going anywhere."

Dizzy agreed with my plan, so we returned to the floor below and spent the next hour browsing all the goods on offer. I picked out a few presents, making some headway with the list of names on my Christmas shopping list.

With our purchases tucked safely in reusable bags, we left the community center to find the snow falling harder than ever.

Dizzy looked up at the sky. "I hope my parents stayed in Larch Haven today. It's not a great day for being on the highway."

"Speaking of your parents," I said as we walked along the snowy cobblestones, "you really need to try talking to them again."

Dizzy's shoulders sagged. "I know. I can't let them dodge the subject anymore."

We rounded a corner and Dizzy's apartment came into view.

"Perfect timing," I said as I spotted Mr. and Mrs. Bautista up ahead.

They stood out front of Hooked on Books, speaking with the store's owner, Tassie Johnson, who was sweeping snow from the walkway in front of her shop. As we drew closer, Dizzy's parents finished their conversation with Tassie and turned our way. They smiled and waved when they saw us.

"I think you should get it over with right now," I said to Dizzy.

She nodded with determination. "You're right." Her resolve wavered. "Will you stay while I talk to them?"

"If you want me to, of course."

"I really do," she said, worry clear in her voice.

My heart ached for her. I desperately hoped that her parents weren't hiding anything terrible.

The four of us met up in the middle of the road and decided to head into Dizzy's apartment for hot drinks. Dizzy and I prepared a pot of tea in the kitchen before joining her parents in her cozy living room. Once everyone had their cup filled, Dizzy looked my way, her eyes full of dread.

I gave her what I hoped was an encouraging nod.

She drew in a deep breath and set her cup and saucer on the coffee table. "Mom, Dad, I know there's something you've been hiding from me. Please don't deny it, because I know it's true. And you've got me really scared. Is it something terrible? Is one of you sick?"

Her parents appeared taken aback, but for only a brief moment.

"You've been worried that one of us is sick?" her mom said with regret. "I'm so sorry, sweetie. It's nothing like that."

"Your mother and I are both fine," her dad added.

"What about Lola?" Dizzy asked in a panic. Her one remaining grandmother still lived in the Philippines.

"She's fine," her mom rushed to assure her. "Her arthritis bothers her, of course, but aside from that she's doing quite well."

"Then why have you been so secretive?" Dizzy asked. "Please tell me."

Her parents glanced at each other and her dad nodded.

"We didn't want to get your hopes up in case our plans fall through," her mom said.

"What plans?" Dizzy asked.

Her dad was the one to answer. "We're hoping to move back to Vermont, and we want to bring your grandmother with us."

Dizzy stared at them for a second, and then all her worry vanished and a smile appeared on her face. "All three of you might move here?"

"That's what we want to happen," her mom said. "But all the pieces have to fall in place."

"We've been looking around, seeing where we might like to live if things work out," her dad added.

Bits of information clicked together in my head at the same time as they did so for Dizzy.

"When we saw you by the hospital up in Snowflake Canyon," she said, "you were looking at the town houses, not meeting up with a friend."

"We were looking at the town houses," her mom admitted. "But we didn't lie. The real estate agent, Evelyn, is an old friend."

"You could have told me all this from the beginning," Dizzy said. "That would have saved me a lot of worry."

"We were trying to protect you from potential disappointment." Her dad glanced at his wife. "Clearly, that was the wrong move."

"You two really aren't that good at keeping secrets," Dizzy said.

Her mom smiled. "I suppose that's a good thing."

Dizzy jumped up from the couch and hugged each of her parents in turn. "I'm so glad there's nothing wrong."

When she dropped back onto the couch next to me, she gave me a hug. "Thanks for staying, Becca."

"I'm happy for you," I said as I hugged her back.

I ended up staying for a delicious dinner cooked by Mrs. Bautista, and the four of us had a great time eating and chatting.

When Dizzy saw me out of her apartment that evening, I said, "That's two mysteries solved. You know what's up with your parents and I know who pushed me down the stairs at the community center."

"Just one mystery left to go," Dizzy said.

Unfortunately, it was the most complicated and most dangerous one of all.

Chapter Twenty-Two

THAT NIGHT, AFTER CLIMBING INTO BED WITH BINX and Truffles curled up beside me, I sent a text message to Sawyer. I let him know that Amber had admitted to pushing me down the stairs at the community center and why she'd done so. I was too sleepy to wait for a response, so I set my phone on the bedside table, snuggled down beneath the covers, and drifted off to sleep.

DURING MY LUNCH BREAK THE NEXT DAY, I DECIDED to walk over to Love at First Bite to pick up some cupcakes for Dizzy and me to enjoy after snowshoeing that afternoon. Okay, so that wasn't the only reason I decided to visit the cake shop. I also wanted to know if Stephanie was still in police custody.

I didn't get my answer right away. When I entered the shop, Stephanie's assistant, Donna, was the only person behind the counter. A woman and a little girl who couldn't have been more than five years old stood by the display case, the little girl contemplating which cupcakes to choose.

I caught Donna's eye and said quietly, "Is Stephanie in today?"

Donna hesitated before replying. "She's in the office. She's not feeling great."

I figured that probably had more to do with her predicament than any physical ailment.

The little girl came to a decision and Donna grabbed a box for her selections. While everyone in the front of the shop had their attention fixed on the cake slices and cupcakes, I edged around the end of the sales counter and slipped into the back hallway. I half expected Donna to call out to me and tell me I couldn't go back there, but instead she kept chattering with the customers.

The door to the office stood open and I peeked inside to find Stephanie seated at the room's lone desk, her arms folded on its surface and her head resting on top. Her shoulders shook as she cried.

I tapped on the doorframe. "Stephanie?"

Her head jerked up and she looked at me with wide, red-rimmed eyes. She hurried to wipe tears from her cheeks with her sleeve. "Becca. Hey."

I moved farther into the office and pulled a chair up to the desk. "I came by to see how you're doing, but I think I've got my answer."

Stephanie sniffed and gave me a watery smile. "Sorry I'm such a mess."

"You don't have to apologize." I unzipped my coat and sat down. "How much trouble are you in with the police?"

"I'm not. Not anymore." She grabbed a tissue from the box on her desk and carefully wiped beneath her eyes. "Juniper came to my defense. She told the police that I had her permission to be at the bakery and that she didn't care that

I'd climbed through the unlocked window when I realized I'd misplaced the key she gave me."

"She gave you a key?" I said with surprise.

"Well," Stephanie hedged, "let's just say that's what she told the police."

"I see." I tugged my hat off my head and ran a hand over my hair to tamp down any staticky strands. "So, the police aren't pressing charges?"

"No, thank goodness. I thought I'd ruined my entire life there for a moment, all because I was afraid of rumors spreading." She opened the top drawer of her desk and pulled out a small compact. When she checked her reflection in the compact's small mirror, she made a face. "Ugh. I'm a disaster. Thank goodness for waterproof mascara, though." With a sigh, she shut the compact without bothering to touch up her makeup.

"So, how come you're crying?" I asked. "From relief?"

I wasn't sure that was the case. For someone who was off the hook with the police now, she didn't look particularly relieved. In fact, she struck me as still quite stressed.

"I might be in the clear with the cops, but things are still such a mess and I don't know what to do." She drew in a shaky breath and looked toward the ceiling, tears welling in her eyes again. She blinked a few times and they receded.

"What's such a mess?" I asked. "Do you mean the fact that Irma's murder is still unsolved?"

Stephanie got up from her chair and eased the office door shut before returning to her seat.

"Can I tell you something in confidence, Becca? I know you're good friends with Sawyer, but I don't want this getting back to the police. I could really use someone to talk to, though."

"Are you going to tell me that you killed Irma?" I asked with apprehension.

Her eyes widened. "No! Of course not! I told you before that I didn't kill her, and that's the truth. The thing is . . ." She stared down at her lap for a moment. "I'm worried that Juniper might have done it."

While it came as no surprise to me that Juniper could be suspected of the murder, I was taken aback that Stephanie would say as much.

"Why do you think that?" I asked.

"You know how Juniper was really mad at Irma for keeping some jewelry from her? Jewelry that Juniper inherited from her grandmother?"

"I remember."

"The thing is . . . I was over at Juniper's place after the police released me yesterday and I saw the jewelry."

"The jewelry Juniper and Irma fought about? How can you be certain it was the same jewelry?"

"Juniper showed me photos of it in the past. They were some of her grandmother's favorite pieces and she has a portrait of her grandmother wearing the necklace and ring. I swear I saw the same ones in Juniper's apartment yesterday."

I sat back in my chair as I absorbed that information. "Irma's handbag was dumped out and her cottage was ransacked on the night of her death. So, you think Juniper killed her and when she didn't find the jewelry in her mother's bag, she tossed the cottage, found the jewelry, and took it home?"

"That's about the size of it."

"But Juniper's your friend," I said. "Do you really think she's capable of murdering her mother?"

Stephanie's tears made a comeback. A fat one rolled down her cheek and she wiped it away with one finger. "I really don't *want* to believe it," she said, her voice trembling with emotion. "But I can't deny the fact that Juniper has a temper. And the fights she got into with Irma . . . they could be seriously intense. I'm scared that Juniper couldn't take it anymore and snapped. She wouldn't have planned to hurt Irma, but in the heat of the moment . . ."

"She might have struck out at her," I finished for her.

Stephanie nodded and wiped away another escaped tear. "It's terrible of me to even think that, right?"

"Given the circumstances, it's probably only natural," I said.

The fact that Stephanie could even consider the possibility that her close friend had killed Irma made Juniper a stronger suspect in my mind than she already had been. I could never suspect Dizzy of murder. I knew she didn't have it in her to do something so terrible.

"You need to tell this to the police," I said.

Stephanie's eyes widened again. "No! I can't! And you can't either. Please."

"Stephanie, we're talking about murder here," I reminded her.

"I know, but maybe I'm completely wrong. And Juniper saved me from getting charged with breaking and entering. My life as I know it could have been over yesterday, but thanks to Juniper it's not. Please, Becca. Don't tell anyone what I just told you."

"I don't want to break your confidence, Stephanie," I said, "but I really don't think we should be keeping this to ourselves."

"Maybe Juniper got the jewelry back before Irma was killed," she said with desperation. "That's possible, right?"

"Sure, it's possible," I conceded. "But it's also possible that she killed Irma and then ransacked the cottage until she found the jewelry."

Stephanie seemed to shrink in on herself. "Maybe I can find out how she got the jewelry."

"Is she already aware that you know she has it?"

"No. I saw it when she was out of the room. When she came back, I pretended I hadn't noticed."

"If you change that, and she is the killer, you could put yourself in danger," I pointed out.

"Juniper would never hurt me."

"If she really did kill her mother, you can't be sure of that."

Stephanie buried her face in her hands. "I don't know what to do."

"Why don't you let me talk to Sawyer?" I suggested. "That way you're not the one betraying her to the police."

She dropped her hands. "No, not yet. Please, Becca. Give me some time to think?"

"Okay," I said with reluctance. "But I don't know how long I can keep this from Sawyer."

"I understand. I just need a chance to get my thoughts together."

I got to my feet and zipped up my jacket. "I'll leave you alone so you can do that."

Even though what Stephanie had told me had my mind spinning, I remembered to stop and purchase a box of cupcakes on my way out of the shop. I meant to head home from there, but as soon as I stepped outside, I spotted Eleanor Tiedemann going into the pharmacy two doors down. I quickly changed my plans.

With one arm tucked around the box of cupcakes, I followed Eleanor into the pharmacy. As the door drifted shut behind me, I spotted Eleanor disappearing down one of the aisles. I peeked between the rows of shelves and saw with relief that she was the only person in sight. She stood halfway down the aisle, perusing the selection of pain relievers. I sidled up next to her and pretended to do the same.

"Hey, Eleanor," I said as I feigned interest in the display of ibuprofen. "How are you doing?"

She sent me a sidelong glance before selecting a bottle of acetaminophen. "Fine, thanks."

"I hear you're thinking of buying Irma's bakery. Is that right?"

"How did you hear that?" she asked with surprise and a touch of suspicion.

"Your son mentioned it the other day."

She relaxed at that. "I'm looking into the possibility."

"That's great. I hope it all works out for you." Before Eleanor could turn away, I quickly added, "Have you heard the rumors about Irma's notebook?"

The blood drained from Eleanor's already pale face. "Notebook?" The word came out faint and shaky.

"The one where she wrote about everyone's secrets." I picked up a bottle of ibuprofen, still pretending I was there to shop. "I think a lot of people would like to get their hands on it." I put the ibuprofen back on the shelf and turned my full attention on her. "Is that what you were looking for when you went through Irma's handbag?"

I didn't think it was possible for Eleanor's face to get any paler, but it did. She looked like a ghost. A ghost who was ready to pass out.

"Are you all right?" I asked with alarm. I didn't want her fainting in the middle of the pharmacy.

She pressed a hand to her chest. "I'm fine." Her gaze flicked around. "I wasn't looking for the notebook. I wasn't . . ."

Clutching her bottle of acetaminophen, she spun away from me and hurried down the aisle. She almost collided with her son as he came around the corner.

"There you are, sweetie," she said to Cameron in a breathless voice. "I'll pay for this and we can get on our way."

She hurried past her son and over to the sales counter. Cameron, however, didn't move. He stood there at the end of the aisle, glaring at me. I had the distinct impression that he'd overheard my conversation with his mother.

I pretended that his angry glare didn't faze me in the least. Sending a smile his way, I headed in the opposite direction and left the pharmacy.

Once outside, I paused for a moment to gather my thoughts.

Eleanor had denied searching Irma's handbag for the notebook, but I didn't doubt for a second that she'd lied to me.

Chapter Twenty-Three

EARLIER IN THE DAY, I'D RECEIVED A TEXT MESSAGE from Sawyer, telling me he wanted to talk about Amber confessing to pushing me down the stairs. As I walked away from the pharmacy, I received another message from him, asking if I could stop by the police station. I set my box of cupcakes on a bench so I could type out a quick response, letting him know I was on the way. Then I gathered up my cupcakes again and walked over to the police station at the edge of town. Hopefully, our chat wouldn't take too long. I was supposed to meet Dizzy at my cottage in an hour so we could go snowshoeing.

When I arrived at the police station, Sawyer met me in the reception area and led the way back to a large room with several desks in it. Two of the desks were occupied by police officers, one working on a computer and the other speaking quietly to someone on the phone. Sawyer's desk was located at the back of the room, near a window that looked out onto the frozen canal.

I set my box of cupcakes down next to his computer and

wriggled out of my coat before sitting down across the desk from him.

Sawyer eyed the box. "I see you were at Love at First Bite."

I didn't miss the hint of suspicion in his voice. "What's wrong with that?"

His gaze shifted from the box to me. "Stephanie owns Love at First Bite. And Stephanie's mixed up in the murder investigation. The investigation that you're supposed to be staying out of."

"As you can see," I said as I opened the bakery box, "I was there to purchase cupcakes." I nudged the box closer to him. "Would you like one?"

He kept his eyes fixed on me. "Are you trying to distract me?"

I closed the box again. "If you don't want one . . ."

He placed a hand on the box so I couldn't move it away from him. "I haven't eaten since breakfast."

With a smile, I opened the box again. He checked out the selection and picked out a chocolate cupcake with peanut butter frosting. I knew all along that he'd want that one.

"Thank you," he said as he pushed the box back my way.

"You're welcome." I sat up taller in my seat. "And for the record, I kept my promise. I didn't question any of my suspects for a full twenty-four hours."

"I think we should extend that deal."

"Didn't you want to talk about Amber?" I asked in an attempt to avoid further promises. "Dizzy and I recorded part of our conversation with her. And what she said before she knew we were there."

Sawyer stared at me for a long moment, knowing full well why I'd changed the subject. "I'm going to want to listen to that," he said eventually.

I pulled out my phone. "I'll send you the file right now."

A second later his phone lit up on his desk as he received the file. We listened to the recording together. Then, while he peeled the wrapper off his cupcake and devoured it in a few bites, I told him how Dizzy and I had set up Amber and Paisley, and what had transpired after we shut off the recording app.

When I finished giving him the details, we sat in silence as three seconds ticked by.

"You're mad," I said, noting the tension in his jaw and the storminess in his dark eyes. "At me?" I hoped that wasn't the case.

"At Amber, for pushing you down the stairs," he said. "You could have broken your neck."

"I'm pretty ticked off at her myself," I admitted. "So, you're not mad at me?"

"A little frustrated, maybe, but not mad. You don't know that Amber's not Irma's killer. Confronting her like that could have triggered her to react violently again."

"I didn't do it alone."

"And Dizzy's supposed to be your bodyguard?" He didn't think much of that, which wasn't surprising. At five feet, two inches, Dizzy stood a good six inches shorter than me.

"She can be pretty fierce," I said.

He pinned me with his dark gaze. "Seriously, Becks."

I sighed. "Okay, I guess it was risky. But it's unlikely that Amber's the killer, right? She would have passed out at the murder scene and most likely would have smeared blood all over the place."

"Her fainting issue makes her less likely to be the killer," Sawyer conceded, although somewhat begrudgingly. "But it doesn't rule her out entirely. And you didn't know about her problem with blood when you confronted her."

"True," I admitted. "But it all worked out in the end. Are you going to talk to her?"

"As soon as I can track her down."

"Will you arrest her?" I asked.

"I'll talk to the chief first, but most likely."

That was one case pretty much wrapped up.

I almost told him what Stephanie had shared with me about Juniper and the jewelry, but I stopped myself. Maybe I could give her a chance to come forward with the information herself. I wouldn't be able to wait too long, though. I already felt guilty about not telling Sawyer.

I jumped up from my seat, trying to ignore my guilt. "I won't keep you any longer."

Sawyer got to his feet. "Becca."

I knew full well what he'd left unsaid. "Okay, no more confronting people about any possible crimes. I promise."

"Where are you off to now?" he asked, as if he didn't quite believe what I'd said.

"Home and then snowshoeing with Dizzy." I flashed him my most innocent smile. "There's nothing dangerous about that, is there?"

"HOW ARE YOU FEELING NOW THAT YOU KNOW WHAT your parents were keeping from you?" I asked Dizzy as we set off along the shore of Shadow Lake on our snowshoes.

"So much better," Dizzy said, her smile saying even more than her words. "I know I shouldn't get my hopes up too much in case things don't fall into place, but I can't help it. I'm really excited about my grandma coming to live in Vermont. It's been hard seeing her only once a year."

Dizzy made an annual trip to the Philippines to visit her extended family. Since her grandmother didn't travel much anymore, that was the only time Dizzy got to see her.

"I'm so glad they weren't hiding anything bad from you," I said. "Now you can enjoy Christmas without any worries."

"It's such a load off my shoulders. Thank you for giving me the push I needed to confront them."

"What are friends for?" I said with a smile.

"Friends are for helping to solve mysteries."

"We've done that too. Now I know who pushed me down the stairs and why. Sawyer knows too." I quickly brought her up to speed on the conversation I'd had with him at the police station.

"Do you think Amber will get arrested?" Dizzy asked. "She deserves to."

"Probably. But I'm kind of hoping she won't go to jail."

"She could have killed you, Becca!"

"I know, but I hope that getting arrested will be enough for her to learn her lesson."

"She's so full of herself that she probably doesn't think she did anything wrong," Dizzy said.

"You might be right about that."

I decided to leave Amber's fate to the justice system and not worry too much about it.

We let the subject drop and focused on cutting a trail through the powdery snow along the lakeshore. Other people snowshoed along this route on a regular basis, but no one had gone this way since the last snowfall. I was glad of the cold temperature. Snowshoeing along an ungroomed trail was hard work and aside from my nose and cheeks, which were stinging from the bite of the icy air, the rest of me was already warming up.

We reached a trail that led off into the forest, away from the lake.

"Do you want to head this way for a bit?" I asked Dizzy, pointing at the trail.

"Sure."

We veered away from the lake and into the forest. The trail soon intersected with a perpendicular one. A snowmobile had recently traveled along that pathway, leaving tracks behind. Dizzy and I decided to turn that way. As soon as we did, we picked up our pace. It was so much easier snowshoeing along the snowmobile's path than through the fresh, untouched powder.

I stopped short a moment later and held my breath.

Dizzy came to a stop next to me, her attention on the same thing as mine. A male cardinal had landed on a tree branch a few feet ahead of us. His bright red feathers stood out beautifully against the white snow.

"That could be a Christmas card," Dizzy whispered as we admired the bird.

Carefully, so as not to startle the bird, I retrieved my phone from the pocket of my jacket and raised it up. The bird hopped along the branch, but didn't fly away. I snapped a photo in the nick of time. The cardinal spread his wings and took off, disappearing up into the air and over the trees.

"Did you get a good one?" Dizzy asked.

I showed her the photo I'd taken. It really did look like the front of a Christmas card.

Once I had my phone tucked away again, we continued on our journey.

"We should be talking suspects," Dizzy said as we made our way through the forest.

"We should, although Sawyer would disagree."

"Sawyer doesn't appreciate our help."

"I don't think he'd even call it help," I said. "Meddling, maybe."

"Or something that would get bleeped out on television."

I laughed at that, but then refocused and told Dizzy about my encounter with Eleanor at the pharmacy.

"She was definitely looking for the notebook," Dizzy said once I'd finished.

"I don't doubt it for a second," I agreed.

"But how are we going to figure out which suspect actually committed the crime?" Dizzy asked.

"I wish I knew. It's all so complicated. I wish I could solve mysteries as easily as Jessica Fletcher."

"Hey, we haven't done so badly in the past."

"I'm not sure Sawyer would agree." The last time I figured out who had committed a murder in our town, I'd almost become the killer's next victim.

The distant roar of a snowmobile engine reached my ears, disturbing the peace of the forest.

"Speaking of Sawyer," Dizzy said, "I bumped into him yesterday and he mentioned that Mrs. Lawrence tried to set you up with her nephew."

"I totally forgot about that. I'm not sure why everyone thinks my love life is their business."

Dizzy laughed. "Have you forgotten where we live? At least the Gossip Grannies aren't involved. Yet."

I rolled my eyes heavenward. "That's something I definitely don't need."

I had to raise my voice to say those last words. The snowmobile was drawing closer, the persistent, droning roar of its engine growing louder by the second.

When I glanced over my shoulder, I spotted the black machine come around a bend in the trail, heading our way. The driver leaned toward the handlebars. The mirrored visor on the black helmet hid the driver's face.

"Careful, Dizzy," I warned. "I don't think this person is going to slow down."

We shuffled over to the side of the wide pathway. I expected the snowmobiler to zoom past us, but instead the machine veered in our direction.

"What are they doing?" Dizzy asked with alarm.

The driver didn't slow down. If anything, the snowmobile sped up.

I gripped Dizzy's arm. "Get out of the way!"

We scrambled through the deep snow at the edge of the pathway and in among the trees. Branches grabbed at my hat and hair and scratched my cheeks, but I barely noticed.

The snowmobile zoomed past, straightening out on the path at the very last second, spraying Dizzy and me with snow as it roared by. Within seconds, the machine sped around a bend and the sound of its engine died away.

"Jerk!" Dizzy yelled after the snowmobiler.

I smacked a spindly branch that was poking me in the

face. "Whoever that was, they shouldn't be allowed on a snowmobile."

"Seriously," Dizzy grumbled. "They could have killed us!"

The incident had left me feeling as aggravated as Dizzy sounded.

We made our way back out onto the path.

"Maybe we should turn back and stick to the lakeshore trail," I suggested. "Whoever that was, I don't want to run into them again."

"I'm with you there."

We headed back the way we'd come, but we hadn't made it far when my stomach sank like an anchor in the ocean. I could hear the snowmobile's engine again, growing louder and louder.

"Are you kidding me?" Dizzy looked over her shoulder at the same time as I glanced over mine.

The snowmobile roared into view from around a bend.

Dizzy waved her arms at the driver. "Hello! How about sharing the trail?!"

"Dizzy!" My voice sounded strangled.

The snowmobiler had sped up again.

"Run!" I yelled.

Dizzy was already on the move when I got the word out. We scurried off the trail again. The trees grew sparsely here, so we kept going, trying to put more distance between us and the trail.

To my relief, the snowmobile slowed down as it got closer. Dizzy and I paused, breathing heavily, halfway up a small hill.

My relief evaporated when the driver maneuvered the snowmobile off the path, aiming it directly at us. The trees growing in this spot weren't dense enough to protect us and I didn't think the incline would hold off the driver either.

"Keep going, Dizzy!" I urged, my voice edged with panic.

We scrambled to the top of the hill as the driver moved in among the trees.

"They must be crazy!" Dizzy yelled over the rumble of the engine as we reached the top of the slope. "Becca!"

We both drew to an abrupt stop as she said my name. Ahead of us, the snow-covered ground dropped away. It wasn't quite a cliff, but the way forward was perilously steep.

I glanced back. The snowmobiler guided the machine around a tree, giving it a clear path to us.

"Hurry!" I said to Dizzy as I undid the bindings on my snowshoes.

She did the same.

As the snowmobile's engine revved louder, we plunged forward. We tried running down the slope but we both fell and tumbled down the rest of the way. I thought the snow would stop us at the bottom, but we overshot the shoreline and slid out onto the frozen lake.

When I finally came to a stop twenty feet from the shore, I looked back toward the forest. The snowmobile was perched at the top of the steep embankment. As I watched, it backed up and turned around. The engine roared and the machine shot off, heading away from us. The noise of the engine died off into the distance.

I let out a breath of relief and sat up.

We're safe, I thought.

Then the ice cracked.

Chapter Twenty-Four

I DROPPED FLAT ON MY STOMACH, LISTENING TO THE terrifying sound of a crack forming in the ice beneath me.

"Becca!" Dizzy cried out with alarm.

"Are you okay?" I yelled back.

She was off to my right, a few feet closer to shore.

"I'm fine," she replied, still sounding worried. "How bad is the ice?"

"I can't tell."

Unlike closer to town, where the snow had been cleared from the ice to create a skating area, the fresh powder had been undisturbed here until we'd tumbled across it. The thick layer of snow hid the crack from my view. Not knowing exactly what I was dealing with made me all the more nervous. Luckily, having grown up next to the lake, Dizzy and I knew what to do.

Slowly, I started logrolling my body closer to shore.

"Careful," Dizzy cautioned.

I froze at the sound of another crack running through the ice beneath the snow.

"Becca?"

"I'm okay," I called out, without moving anything other than my mouth. "How are you doing?" I didn't dare raise my head to see how much progress she'd made.

"I'm almost to shore. I'll call for help as soon as I get there."

My heart pounded so hard that I worried its beating would cause the ice to crack even more. I drew in a steadying breath and let it out slowly. I started rolling again, my muscles tense. Every second, I expected to hear a thunderous crack, to plunge into the freezing water. I rolled over once, then again. The ice held firm. My panic eased ever so slightly, and I picked up my pace.

"I'm off the ice!" Dizzy yelled.

That eased some of the tension in my chest.

"You're almost here." Dizzy sounded much closer.

I kept rolling through the snow. Seconds later, Dizzy grabbed my arm.

"You're safe now." She helped me to my feet.

As soon as I was standing, I dropped back down into the snow on the shore. My legs didn't want to hold my weight. Dizzy knelt down beside me.

"You're okay?" she asked.

I nodded, still short of breath from the fear that had gripped me.

Dizzy wrapped her arms around me and gave me a hug. "That was terrifying."

"Seriously," I agreed.

"I haven't called for help yet," she said. "Even though we're off the ice, I think I should still report what happened."

"Good idea." As my residual fear faded away, I focused more on how we'd ended up out on the frozen lake. "We definitely need to report the snowmobiler."

"What a maniac!" Dizzy dug her phone out of her pocket. "They could have killed us!"

"Maybe that's exactly what they were trying to do."

Dizzy's eyes widened. "Do you think the snowmobiler is the same person who killed Irma?"

"I think it's definitely a possibility."

"A terrifying one."

We both looked toward the forest. All was quiet, without even a distant hum of a snowmobile's engine, but my unease refused to disappear completely.

Dizzy tugged off her gloves so she could use her phone. I was glad she was making the call. With the way my hands were trembling, I wasn't sure that I could have managed anything requiring manual dexterity.

By the time Dizzy ended the call, I felt steady enough to get to my feet. We climbed the steep, snow-covered slope we'd tumbled down earlier and retrieved our snowshoes before returning to the lakeshore to wait for the police. I hoped Sawyer would be the one to show up, but a female officer arrived and introduced herself as Officer McNally.

Dizzy and I were in the middle of telling McNally what had happened when we heard someone approaching from the trail that led into the forest. I almost smiled when I saw that it was Sawyer. Having him around took the edge off of the fear that hadn't quite faded away completely.

When Sawyer joined us, Dizzy and I started the story over again from the beginning.

"Can you describe the snowmobile or the driver?" Sawyer asked after we'd finished.

Dizzy and I shook our heads.

"The driver wore all black and one of those visored helmets," I said. "The snowmobile was black but I didn't notice any other details."

"Everything happened so fast," Dizzy added, "and we were focused on getting out of the way."

Sawyer had a neutral expression in place, but for a second I thought I saw a flicker of emotion in his eyes.

"It was probably some young guy thinking he was being funny," McNally said.

Dizzy and I exchanged a glance. When I looked Sawyer's way a second later, I knew he hadn't missed it.

"I'll talk with some of the owners of the lakeshore properties," Officer McNally continued. "Maybe someone saw the snowmobile and knows who was driving it."

I didn't think she'd have much luck with that, but Dizzy and I thanked her.

"I'll give you two a ride back to town," Sawyer said.

We didn't protest. The fun had fizzled out of our snow-shoeing outing and I was on the brink of shivering from the cold. Dizzy had already started shivering and was huddled inside her jacket. She and I put our snowshoes back on and followed the officers along the trail into the forest. When we reached the wider, perpendicular trail, McNally climbed onto an ATV and sped off ahead of us.

When we reached the lakeshore property that was located the farthest from town, the trail widened into an un-paved roadway. Someone had plowed the road at some point, but not since the most recent snowfall. Vehicles had cut dirty tire tracks in the snow, most of which turned into the driveway of the nearest home. The road provided access to the lakeshore properties and curved out around the edge of town before meeting up with the highway.

Sawyer had left a police SUV parked at the end of the road. Dizzy and I removed our snowshoes and piled into the back seat.

"Is there anything else you want to tell me?" Sawyer asked once he was settled in the driver's seat.

I met his eyes in the rearview mirror. "I don't think it was a random prankster."

"Me either," Dizzy said.

Sawyer started the engine. "Then you've probably got Irma's killer worried."

"That's what I figured." I sat back in the seat, wishing I knew who it was I'd worried so much that they wanted to harm me, or at the very least give me a good fright.

As we drove slowly along the forest road, Sawyer glanced at us in the rearview mirror again. "Dizzy, your parents are staying with you, right?"

"Yes." She picked up on the reason for his question. "Do you think the snowmobile driver might try to hurt us again?"

"It's a possibility. Becca might have been the sole intended target, but not necessarily. I'm guessing you've been egging her on."

"Assisting her," Dizzy corrected. "I'm the Dr. Hazlitt to her Jessica Fletcher. Except I'm a librarian, not a doctor."

"Please tell me that doesn't make me Sheriff Tupper," Sawyer said.

"Nope." Dizzy smiled. "You're more Metzger than Tupper, for sure."

Thanks to the rearview mirror, I didn't miss Sawyer's eyes flicking heavenward before returning to the road.

"I'm not interested in lecturing you two again," he said.

"And you don't need to," I assured him.

I didn't think I had him convinced, but he didn't argue that point.

"You should stay with your family, Becca," he said as he turned the SUV onto the highway.

His obvious concern sent fresh fear skittering through me.

"I'll be fine at my cottage," I said, as much to convince myself as Sawyer.

"Becca, what if someone tries to kill you again?" Dizzy asked, worry edging its way into her voice.

"Maybe the snowmobiler wasn't trying to kill me," I said, wanting that to be the truth. "Maybe they simply wanted to scare me. I mean, if you want to kill someone, running them down with a snowmobile probably isn't the easiest way to go about it."

"Dizzy and I would both feel better if you stayed with family," Sawyer said.

Dizzy nodded her agreement. "Way better."

"I'll think about it." That was all I was willing to commit to.

I appreciated their concern, and I probably would feel more at ease if I weren't on my own that night, but Dizzy's parents occupied her spare room and if I showed up at my grandparents' cottage or at my brother's place, they'd want to know why I wasn't staying at home. I wasn't eager to admit to them that I'd poked my nose into the murder investigation. They probably wouldn't want to let me out of their sight if they knew about that.

Sawyer pulled off the highway and into the small parking lot beside the police station.

"At the very least, don't go anywhere alone after dark," he said. "I'll check in with you later."

I thanked him, and then walked Dizzy home. She wasn't happy about me walking to my cottage alone, but it wasn't dark yet, although it would be soon. Reluctantly, she let me set off on my own, and I texted her as soon as I arrived home safely, hoping that would put her mind at ease.

I didn't tell her that I wasn't staying home for long. Despite the fact that I didn't want to spend the night with family and explain why, I didn't feel like being home alone either, even with my cats to keep me company. So instead, I decided to go to the Gondolier for a while, so I could have plenty of people around me.

I hurried along the canals to Giethoorn Avenue, determined to make it to the restaurant before darkness shrouded the town. The sun had already disappeared behind the mountains, and the last of the daylight was fading quickly. Fortunately, several tourists and locals still wandered around town, making me feel safer. Still, it came as a relief to reach the Gondolier.

I bypassed the host stand and headed for the bar, where

I spotted my brother-in-law, Blake, mixing cocktails. Two women in their twenties sat at one end of the bar, but the rest of the stools were unoccupied. I perched on the one farthest from the women.

"Hey, Becca," Blake greeted. "I'll be with you in a second."

He finished mixing the drinks and set them on a tray that a server picked up. Blake exchanged a few words with the two women at the far end of the bar and then came over my way.

"What's up?" he asked. "Are you hungry?"

"Definitely." My stomach rumbled in agreement.

Snowshoeing was hard work. So was getting chased by a rogue snowmobiler.

"How about the seafood linguine?" Blake suggested. "Without the mussels."

"Sounds perfect." He knew I refused to eat the mussels that were typically included in the dish. "How come you're behind the bar tonight?"

"Trevor's off sick. Gia can cover most of his shift, but she can't make it in for another hour." He grabbed a clean glass. "Want something to drink while I get your food?"

"Just water, please."

Blake added ice to the glass and filled it with water before setting it on a coaster in front of me. "I'll go get your linguine."

While I waited, I turned on my stool so my back was to the bar, giving me a good view of the dining room. The restaurant was about one-quarter full, but it was the middle of winter and still early in the evening. During the tourist season, the place was almost always packed.

I noticed a few familiar faces in the room, including at one of the larger tables. The party of eight included the three judges from the Baking Spirits Bright competition—Victor, Consuelo, and Natalia—as well as event organizer Jaspreet. I recognized the four other individuals at the table, but I didn't know their names. I'd seen them at the baking competition and figured they were probably involved with organizing the event too.

I faced the bar again when Blake returned with a plate of seafood linguine in hand, minus the mussels. He slid the plate onto the bar along with a set of cutlery wrapped in a cloth napkin.

"There you go." He leaned his muscular forearms on the bar. "So, have you been staying out of trouble?"

"Ha ha," was the only response I gave him as I unrolled the napkin.

Blake and I were close and he was a good listener, but if I told him about the incident with the snowmobiler, he would tell Gareth. My brother would then switch into his overprotective mode, which could be seriously annoying. He probably wouldn't want me going anywhere or doing anything alone. Not that I wanted to be alone after what had happened, but I didn't want a babysitter either.

I did, however, tell him that Amber was the one who'd pushed me down the stairs. I left out the part about confronting her and Paisley at the community center, though. Fortunately, he was just glad the culprit had been caught and didn't ask too many questions.

One of the servers stopped by the bar and requested two pints of beer and a margarita, so I concentrated on eating my dinner while Blake worked. As I enjoyed the delicious seafood linguine, I realized I could do more than eat while I was at the Gondolier. Maybe I could get some valuable information too.

"Is Roman working?" I asked once Blake had passed off the beer and margarita to the server who'd brought him the order.

"He's here," Blake confirmed.

"When did his shift start?"

"A few minutes before you got here. Why?"

I shrugged. "Just curious."

"Right."

I didn't need to see the skepticism in his blue eyes to know he didn't believe me.

He lowered his voice. "Are you still thinking he's a suspect?"

I nodded and didn't add that I now suspected him of trying to run me down with a snowmobile as well as killing Irma. Now that I knew when Roman had arrived at the Gondolier for his shift as a pastry chef, I also knew that he could have been the person driving the snowmobile. He would have had enough time to get home, ditch his snow-mobiling gear, and get to the restaurant before I arrived.

He definitely hadn't liked it when I'd tried asking him how he felt about Irma. Was that brief conversation at Hooked on Books enough to clue him in to the fact that I'd poked my nose into the murder case?

"I sure hope he's not the murderer," Blake said so quietly that I almost couldn't hear him. "I don't like to think of a killer being right in our midst."

I didn't like to think about that either, but even if Roman wasn't the murderer, Irma's killer was most likely some-body we knew.

Chapter Twenty-Five

AFTER I'D FINISHED EATING AND GIA HAD SHOWN UP
to take over bartending duties, Blake offered to walk me
home and I took him up on that. I had planned to ask him
to walk with me, but I was glad that he'd offered first. This
way, I didn't run the risk of him asking me why I was uneasy about making the short trip on my own.

On our way out of the restaurant, I waved at the table of
Baking Spirits Bright judges and event organizers. It looked
as though they were enjoying the alcoholic drinks as much
as the food. They were laughing—a couple of them a little
too loudly—and Victor's face was flushed.

Seeing Victor reminded me of Daniel Hathaway, whom
I'd first seen at Victor's art gallery. I wondered if Sawyer
had looked into the mystery man at all. There was probably
a straightforward and uninteresting explanation for why I
couldn't find anything about Daniel Hathaway online, but
with an unsolved murder case hanging over the town, my
unanswered questions about the man left me feeling uneasy.

It was still fairly early in the evening when I arrived

home. Blake waited until I was safely inside and then set off back to the restaurant, with me waving to him through the front window. Truffles and Binx came to greet me as I shrugged out of my coat and hung it up in the closet. They wound around my ankles and I crouched down to greet them. Binx bumped his head against my knee and Truffles placed her front paws up on my leg, stretching up until I touched my nose against hers and stroked her fur.

"How about some dinner?" I suggested.

Binx gave a loud meow and charged off toward the kitchen. I laughed and followed, with Truffles keeping pace with me. Once the cats were happily eating, I got a fire going in the fireplace and stood back to admire my Christmas tree. The Douglas fir had full branches and stood about six feet tall. It filled the room with its scent, and the smell brought back memories of happy Christmases in the past.

I turned on some Christmas music and headed upstairs to get my decorations for the tree down from the attic. I was halfway to the second floor when someone knocked on the front door. I hesitated, worried that the snowmobiler now stood on my doorstep, waiting for another chance to scare me or to do something worse.

Giving myself a mental kick, I descended the stairs and peeked through the sidelight.

Sawyer stood on the front step, illuminated by the porch light, wearing jeans and a winter jacket. Relief eased the tension in my shoulders as I unlocked and opened the door.

"Hey." I moved back so he could come into the cottage. "Off work for the night?"

"Finally." He stepped inside. "It felt like a long day."

I shut the door behind him. "I'm sorry I added to your workload."

"It wasn't your fault. I'm just glad you're okay after what happened this afternoon. And I'm glad you knew what to do when you ended up out on the ice."

"My dad drilled ice safety into our heads when Gareth and I were growing up," I said. "I've never been more glad of that." I studied Sawyer's face for some clue as to why he'd shown up at my cottage. "What brings you by?"

"I wanted to see how you're doing."

"I'm fine," I assured him. "Can you stay awhile? I've got eggnog and those cupcakes from Love at First Bite." After the way our snowshoeing excursion had ended, Dizzy and I never got a chance to enjoy the desserts. "I was about to start decorating my tree."

"I can give you a hand with that if you like." He took off his jacket. "And I won't say no to the food."

"And I won't say no to your help," I said, smiling, as I hung his jacket in the closet. "Especially since I need to lug the decorations down from the attic."

"I'm happy to volunteer my muscles."

Binx and Truffles had wandered into the foyer to see who'd arrived. When they realized I was heading for the stairs, they dashed up ahead of me. Sawyer followed in my wake.

"Did you ever have a chance to talk to Amber?" I asked as I led the way up to the second floor. I hadn't thought to ask him the last time I'd seen him. The snowmobile incident had left me too distracted.

"We had a chat this afternoon. She admitted to pushing you down the stairs. Not that she had much choice, thanks to that recording you made."

Up on the second floor, I tugged the string to lower the steps to the attic. "Did you charge her with anything?"

"Simple assault." Sawyer helped me guide the stairs down until they reached the floor.

I stayed standing at the base of the steps while Binx and Truffles scampered up to the attic. "Do you think she'll be sent to jail?" Maybe it was crazy of me, but I hoped that wouldn't happen. I wanted to believe that a lesser punishment would be enough to deter her from hurting anyone else in the future.

"It's possible, but it's her first offense, so it's also possible that she won't," Sawyer said. "How is your wrist, anyway?"

"Aside from the occasional twinge, it's fine now." A thought occurred to me. "When did you speak to her?"

"I finished up with her right before the call came in from Dizzy about the snowmobiler."

I started up the steep steps to the attic. "So there's no way that Amber was the one chasing us on the snowmobile."

That further confirmed my theory that she didn't kill Irma. We didn't know for certain that the snowmobiler and Irma's killer were one and the same, but I would have bet the five cupcakes in my kitchen that they were.

"Still, whoever did chase you isn't happy with you."

I paused and looked down at Sawyer where he stood at the base of the steps. "Is that why you're here? To keep an eye on me?"

"Only partly."

Something about the way he looked at me made my cheeks warm. I climbed the rest of the way up to the attic, hoping he hadn't noticed my flushed face. When I reached the top step, I pulled the string that switched on the light-bulb overhead.

I saw a flash of black as Binx zoomed behind a stack of boxes. Truffles hopped up onto an old trunk and surveyed the attic. I didn't have a whole lot of stuff stored up here among the rafters. That made it easy to find the two cardboard boxes of Christmas decorations. They were stacked one on top of the other, with a small plastic storage tub perched on top.

Truffles hopped to the floor and set off to explore the attic, so I took the plastic storage tub and set it on the trunk.

"Do you want both of these downstairs?" Sawyer asked, resting a hand on the top box.

"Yes. I think that one's pretty light. The one underneath is a little heavier."

Sawyer grabbed the top box as Binx streaked out from a dark corner and took a flying leap, landing on the plastic tub. The tub slid across the top of the trunk, with Binx on top like a feline surfer. Startled, Binx took another leap, and then disappeared into the shadows. I laughed, even as the storage tub crashed to the ground and the lid popped off, spilling papers all over the floor.

"Thank you, Binx," I called out sarcastically, though I wasn't really mad.

I crouched down to gather up the spilled papers.

Sawyer joined me. "Let me help you with that."

He scooped up a pile of papers while I did the same. I righted the plastic tub and dropped the papers I'd collected into it.

"What's this?" Sawyer was reading one of the pages he'd picked up.

The piece of paper was flattened out but was creased in several places from having been folded numerous times. I noticed two different types of handwriting on the page, both of which I recognized right away. I leaned in for a better look and my eyes widened when I started reading what was written in blue ink.

"Oh my gosh! You can't read that!" I tried to snatch the paper away from him, but he turned his back on me. "Sawyer!"

I darted around him and made another grab for the paper. This time he held it over his head. His eyes almost twinkled with a mischievous light.

"What's got you so worried?" he asked, still holding the paper aloft. "Is this a page from your diary or something?"

"I've never kept a diary." I jumped, trying again to grab the paper, but Sawyer easily kept it out of my reach.

I silently cursed the several inches of height that he had on me. He held the paper up near the attic's lone lightbulb.

"'I can't believe you're crushing on him,'" he read. He glanced at me before turning his attention back to the paper. "That's not your handwriting. Wait, is it Dizzy's?"

I planted my hands on my hips and glared at him. "Seriously, Sawyer. If you don't give that to me right now, I'm keeping all the cupcakes for myself."

"I'm not sure I'm hungry," he said with a grin. "When is this from and who did you have a crush on?"

"Middle school. Dizzy and I used to pass notes to each other. I kept a bunch of them, which I'm currently regretting." I held out a hand, ignoring his other question. "Paper or no cupcakes."

"Like I said, I'm not that hungry."

As he went back to reading, I hopped onto the trunk and jumped off, snatching the paper out of his hand. When I landed, I stumbled into him. He put an arm around me to steady me, but as soon as I had my balance back, I darted out of his reach.

One corner had ripped off the page when I grabbed it. Sawyer flicked the torn scrap at me and I caught it as it flitted toward the floor. I carefully folded the page of notes and tucked it and the small scrap safely into the pocket of my jeans. Then I scooped the rest of the papers up from the floor and dumped them into the plastic tub.

"That's top secret information in there," I said, securing the lid on the tub. "You don't have high enough security clearance to be reading it."

"That's okay. I saw enough."

"Enough for what?"

"To guess who you were crushing on in middle school."

"You didn't get enough details for that." At least, I hoped that was the case.

"Not from the notes. But the fact that you didn't want me reading them tells me you'd be embarrassed if I knew."

Keeping my gaze averted from his, I picked up the top

box of Christmas decorations. "Maybe I just don't want to dig up the past."

"Was it Tanner Gibson?"

I almost dropped the box. "Tanner? Are you kidding me? He was the most obnoxious guy in our year!"

"Which would explain your embarrassment."

"It wasn't Tanner Gibson. And that's all I'm saying."

"That's all right." He picked up the other box, an infuriating grin on his face. "I know who it was."

"No, you don't."

"I'm pretty sure I do."

"I'm pretty sure you don't."

"I'm a police officer. I'm good at figuring things out. I'm also good at reading people. Especially you."

I set my box down near the top of the stairs. "Are you here to tease me or to help me decorate my tree?"

"Can't I do both?" he asked.

"I can show you the door."

He laughed. "You know, he probably liked you back."

My stomach did a funny flip-flop. "I don't think so."

"I bet he did." He caught my gaze with his own. "Maybe he still does."

I suddenly couldn't feel the floor beneath my feet. My pulse quickened and a tingling energy rushed across my skin. I wondered if there was some strange electrical phenomenon happening in the air around us. Maybe ball lightning was about to appear in my attic. Dizzy would be so disappointed to miss it.

Then Sawyer grinned and set his box down next to mine, breaking our eye contact.

The tingling energy slowly dissipated and I knew without a doubt that it was something Sawyer and I had created between the two of us.

He patted one of the boxes. "I'll go down first and you can pass these to me."

He climbed partway down the steep stairs and reached up for the boxes as I passed them to him one at a time. My pulse was slow to settle down, but eventually it did.

After I coaxed Binx and Truffles out of the attic, Sawyer and I carried the boxes down to the main floor and set them near the tree. My cats followed, Binx with cobwebs and dust bunnies tangled up in his whiskers.

I picked him up off the floor and cleaned him off. "Goofball," I said with affection as I set him back down.

He immediately darted behind the Christmas tree. Truffles hopped up on the couch and started grooming herself.

Sawyer and I set to work, untangling strings of multicolored lights and wrapping them around the tree. At first, I worried that I'd be nervous around him after the moment we'd shared in the attic, but we settled back into our easy camaraderie without a hitch.

"There's something I need to tell you," I said once we'd finished putting up the lights and had started adding baubles and other decorations to the branches.

"It's okay," he said. "I get it. I was irresistible back then. Still am."

I grabbed a cushion from the couch and threw it at him. He caught it easily.

"I'm talking about the murder, not . . . other things that aren't any of your business." There was no way I was going to admit that he'd guessed right about my middle school crush.

He tossed the cushion onto a nearby armchair, his face growing more serious. "All right. Spill. What have you been up to now?"

"Nothing."

He raised his eyebrows as he hung a red bauble on the tree.

"Seriously," I said. "When I stopped by Love at First Bite—"

"I knew you'd been there for more than just cupcakes."

I quieted him with a withering glare. "I *innocently* went to say hi to Stephanie in her office and found her upset." I paused while I hung a wooden reindeer on a branch. "She didn't want me to tell you this, but I don't feel right keeping it from you."

I hesitated, remembering how upset Stephanie had been. "Becca?" Sawyer prodded.

I sighed, knowing I couldn't keep the secret any longer. "Stephanie's afraid that Juniper might have killed Irma."

Chapter Twenty-Six

I EXPLAINED ABOUT THE JEWELRY THAT JUNIPER NOW had in her possession and the fact that Stephanie was worried that Juniper had broken into her mother's cottage to get it, possibly after murdering Irma in a fit of rage. Sawyer listened carefully to every word.

"You were right to tell me, Becca," he said once I finished.

"Do you think Juniper really could have killed her own mother?" I didn't want to believe it, but she was certainly a strong suspect and the information Stephanie had provided only made Irma's daughter look more guilty.

"It's possible," Sawyer said. "It's also possible that she didn't."

"Do you know if the jewelry was already missing from Irma's cottage when it was officially searched the morning after her death?"

"We didn't have a description of those particular pieces at the time, so I don't know."

I sighed as I hung another ornament on the tree. "I know

murder investigations take time, but all this wondering about who might be the guilty party is wearing at my nerves. Especially after what happened this afternoon."

"We'll figure it out, Becca," Sawyer said. "And by 'we,' I mean me and my colleagues, not you and me."

"I hear you."

Sawyer didn't look entirely convinced, but he didn't argue with me. "In the meantime, look out for yourself. You need to be extra careful until the killer is caught."

I promised him that I would be.

I stepped back to admire our work. We'd done a good job, and seeing the fully decorated tree brought a smile to my face.

"Thanks for helping me," I said. "You definitely earned another cupcake."

"Even after what happened in the attic?"

Warmth touched my cheeks and I hoped they hadn't turned bright pink. "Even so," I said, doing my best to sound casual.

Since it was getting late, I ended up sending one of the cupcakes home with Sawyer. He waited on the front step until I'd locked the door behind him and then I watched through the sidelight as he set off through the softly falling snow. I made sure every window and door was locked before I went to bed. Fortunately, the events of the day caught up with me, sending me off to sleep before I had time to worry about the possibility of the snowmobiler creeping around my cottage during the night.

I STARTED OFF THE NEXT MORNING WITH A COMBINA-
tion of yoga and Pilates, something I liked to do whenever I wasn't in a rush to leave the cottage first thing. It helped ground me and put me in a good frame of mind before tackling the day. It was also a practice that had helped me regain my strength after suffering a ruptured appendix the

previous winter. Once my workout was complete, I had to spend a few minutes shoveling my front walkway. Binx and Truffles watched from the warmth of the cottage, seated on one of the front windowsills. They didn't show any interest in venturing outdoors this morning.

After a quick shower and an equally quick breakfast, I walked to True Confections and spent the next couple of hours baking gingerbread and making chocolates. When I took a break, I peeked out the front and saw that Angela had her hands full with a crowd of customers. I jumped in to help her and soon the rush trickled off. I was about to return to the kitchen when Paisley showed up.

"Last time I was buying for myself," she said after we'd exchanged cautious greetings. "This time I'm here for Christmas gifts."

I didn't fail to notice that she was speaking more to Angie than to me. Every time her gaze met mine, it darted away again. I decided there wasn't much point in me hanging around, but when I headed for the back hallway, Paisley addressed me directly.

"Becca, wait."

When I turned around, she gave me a brief, tremulous smile.

"I wanted to apologize for my part in the whole stairway incident," she said, her words tentative. "I'm sorry you got hurt and I'm really glad your injuries weren't any worse."

"I appreciate that." I was going to end the conversation there, but instead said what was on my mind. "Why would you want to hang around with someone like Amber? She doesn't seem like much of a friend."

Paisley sighed. "I know. And I'm not working for her anymore. I quit yesterday."

"She must have taken that well," I said with a hint of sarcasm.

A faint smile appeared on Paisley's face and then faded away. "She had one of her tantrums, but she'll get over it.

As for our friendship . . . I don't know. I think I might focus on trying to make some new friends."

"That sounds like a good idea," I said.

The phone rang in the office, so I took the opportunity to excuse myself and answer it. When I returned to the front of the shop a few minutes later, Paisley had gone.

"It's nice to see she's growing a bit of a backbone," Angie remarked.

"Hopefully she won't get sucked back into Amber's vortex of drama and negativity," I said.

"Only time will tell."

I agreed with Angie and then told her I was heading out for a while. Dizzy wasn't working at the library until the afternoon, so I'd arranged to meet up with her at Gathering Grounds midmorning. I arrived at the coffee shop first, so I claimed a booth for us, and Dizzy showed up soon after. Once we had hot drinks in front of us, we settled in for a chat.

Quietly, so none of the other customers would overhear, I filled her in on what Stephanie had told me. She agreed that the information made Juniper look even guiltier than before.

Once we'd finished discussing the murder case, I told her about Sawyer reading the notes we'd passed to each other one day in middle school. She laughed as I relayed the story.

"It's not funny, Diz," I said as she was almost overcome by a fit of giggles.

"I'm sorry, Becca," she said, still laughing, "but it kind of is."

"Thanks a lot." I glared at her but without effect.

I took a long drink of my chai tea, waiting for her laughter to subside.

When it finally did, she asked, "Does he know that he's the one you had a crush on back then?"

My cheeks grew warm. They were doing that all too often for my liking.

"I think he guessed."

I almost told Dizzy what else he'd said, but nervousness shimmied around in my stomach and I couldn't bring myself to share that detail.

I knew that things had been different between Sawyer and me since I'd moved back from Los Angeles. We still had the ease of our lifelong friendship, but the air between us was often charged with an electricity that hadn't been present before, even back when I'd had a crush on him. I hadn't let myself think about that much, though. The thought of disturbing the status quo stirred up anxious butterflies in my stomach.

"Don't look so worried, Becca," Dizzy said. "I'm sure he won't tease you about it forever."

I shook my head. "Why did I keep those notes?"

"I kept a bunch of them too, but I don't think there's anything in them that would embarrass me."

"Are you sure about that?" I asked. "Because I remember you having a crush on Mr. Kepler."

"Oh my gosh! I forgot all about that!" She lowered her voice. "Let's never speak about it again."

Now it was my turn to laugh. "I bet everyone has embarrassing memories from middle school."

"Suddenly more of mine are flooding back." Dizzy grimaced. "Maybe we should destroy those notes."

The bell above the door jingled and a blast of cold air rushed into the coffee shop.

"Look who's here," Dizzy said, waving to the newcomer.

I checked over my shoulder. Sawyer pulled his beanie off his head and raised a hand in greeting before heading for the counter.

I turned back to Dizzy and noticed a mischievous glint in her eyes.

"Don't you dare," I whispered. "You are not bringing up middle school notes or crushes in front of Sawyer."

She pretended to zip her lips shut.

Sawyer bought himself a coffee and a piece of pie, and then headed over our way. I scooted along the bench seat so he could sit next to me.

"I'm guessing I don't want to know what kind of scheming you two have been doing," he said as he sat down.

"Scheming?" I said with feigned innocence. "Us?"

"Where would you get such an idea?" Dizzy asked.

Sawyer shook his head. "The two of you whispering together always means trouble."

"Nobody's cooking up any trouble this morning." I took the fork from his plate and scooped up a bit of his blueberry pie. I managed to slip it into my mouth before he grabbed his fork back.

"This is my breakfast, thank you very much." He dug his fork into the pie and took a big bite.

"Pie for breakfast?"

"I wholeheartedly approve." Dizzy reached toward his plate.

He quickly moved it out of her reach. "Get your own."

Dizzy contented herself with a sip of her latte.

"There's something I forgot to ask you yesterday," I said to Sawyer. "Have you learned anything about Daniel Hathaway?"

"That's the guy we first saw at the art gallery, right?" Dizzy asked.

I nodded. "I haven't been able to find out anything about him."

"I haven't talked to him yet," Sawyer said. "He's staying at the Larch Haven Hotel. I left a message for him there, but I haven't had a response."

"I take it you're not working today," I said, knowing that he usually started his shift early in the day.

"Nope. But I'm going to stop in at the station for a few minutes. I need to talk to Detective Ishimoto about what you told me last night. I'll check my messages while I'm there, in case Hathaway's been in touch since yesterday."

"When you do talk to him, will you let me know what he has to say?" I requested.

"Becca . . ."

"I know, I know. But I can't help but be curious."

"Curiosity can be hazardous."

"Speaking of hazardous," Dizzy jumped in, "any leads on our snowmobiling maniac?"

"No," Sawyer replied before taking a drink of his coffee. "Officer McNally spoke with some of the owners of the lakefront properties, but nobody saw the snowmobiler yesterday afternoon. And a lot of people around these parts own black snowmobiles."

The lack of leads didn't surprise me and I didn't think we could count on identifying the snowmobiler as a way to catch Irma's killer. I was about to say as much when I spotted Mrs. Lawrence getting up from a table near the back of the coffee shop. She was with another gray-haired woman whose name I didn't know, although I recognized her from around town.

As Mrs. Lawrence buttoned up her coat, her companion headed for the door. When Mrs. Lawrence started to follow her, I tried to burrow between Sawyer and the back of the bench seat.

"Hide me," I said, trying to make myself as small as possible.

"What are you doing?" Sawyer asked, twisting around to try to get a look at me.

I realized my attempt to hide wasn't going to work. I considered sliding beneath the table, but decided that would be a little too extreme. Reluctantly, I sat up straight as Mrs. Lawrence got closer. She stopped by our table when she noticed me. My stomach sank at the gleam that appeared in her eyes.

"Oh, Rebecca," she said. "Good morning. Have you spoken to my nephew yet?"

That was exactly the subject I was hoping to avoid.

"I haven't," I said, wondering how I could politely put an end to her matchmaking attempts. "Thank you for your concern, but I'm not looking to be set up with anyone."

"You really mustn't let that Hollywood fiasco hold you back."

"It has nothing to do with my past relationship," I assured her. It especially didn't have anything to do with the fictional Hollywood drama that the Gossip Grannies had concocted and which Mrs. Lawrence apparently had bought into completely. "And I'm happy as I am."

Sawyer's hand tightened around the handle of his coffee mug. Across from us, Dizzy was struggling to contain the laughter that was threatening to bubble out of her, but as soon as Mrs. Lawrence turned her way, Dizzy's mirth was replaced by apprehension.

"How about you, Desiree?" Mrs. Lawrence said to her. "My nephew, Brian, is a very successful lawyer. He takes after his father more than his mother when it comes to looks, but looks aren't everything, you know."

"Thank you, but I'm in a committed relationship." Somehow, Dizzy managed to keep a straight face while saying that. She almost had me believing her words.

"Oh," Mrs. Lawrence said with surprise. "I wasn't aware."

"Are you coming, Agnes?" Mrs. Lawrence's companion called out from over by the door.

Mrs. Lawrence looked as though she wanted to say something to Sawyer next, but instead she hurried off to follow her friend out of the coffee shop.

"Phew." Dizzy drank her latte like the conversation with Mrs. Lawrence had left her parched.

I nudged Sawyer with my elbow. "You dodged a bullet there. She had her matchmaking sights set on you next."

"I don't think Brian's my type," he said.

Dizzy laughed. "I'm sure Mrs. Lawrence has a niece or granddaughter for you."

"What is it with this town's senior citizens and meddling?" he asked.

"It's like a sport for them," I said.

"They should take up carpet bowling instead," he grumbled as he got back to eating his pie.

I turned my attention to Dizzy. "I think you owe us some details. You're in a committed relationship?"

She grinned. "With the library."

"It's not healthy to be married to your work."

"We're not married," she said, still smiling. "More like living in sin."

Sawyer shook his head. "You two are nuts. Not as nutty as Mrs. Lawrence, but still . . ."

I rested my head on his shoulder. "But you love us anyway."

He didn't deny it.

As I straightened up again, I caught the way he was looking at me. The intensity in his dark eyes sent heat spreading along my skin. I averted my gaze to find Dizzy watching us.

She rested her arms on the table and leaned forward. "Sawyer, do you believe in aliens?"

"Wait," I cut in. "You mean, you've never asked him that before?"

That was the question she usually asked when sizing a person up.

Dizzy shrugged. "I never needed to before." She turned her attention back to Sawyer.

He finished off the last bite of his pie and set down his fork. "Sure. It's a vast universe. We're probably not the only intelligent life form around—if you can call humans intelligent, because sometimes I really wonder about that—but that doesn't mean I believe every story about alien abductions or sightings of flying saucers. I believe in crackpots and people seeing what they want to see far more than I do in aliens."

Dizzy nodded with satisfaction. "Fair enough."

I caught Dizzy's eye, silently asking her why she'd brought up the subject. I knew she caught my drift, but she just gave me an enigmatic smile and finished off her latte.

"I should get going," she said, setting down her cup. "I need to run a few errands before going to work."

Sawyer got up at the same time as she did. "I should be heading out too."

I downed the remains of my chai tea and pulled on my jacket as I slid off the bench seat.

Dizzy and I said goodbye to Sawyer outside the coffee shop and he set off to the east.

"I didn't want to say this with Sawyer around," Dizzy said, "but if you want, I can put my research skills to work and see if I can dig up anything on Daniel Hathaway."

"Please do. I don't know if he's got anything to do with the murder, but there's something mysterious about him."

"I'll let you know what I find out."

"Thanks, Dizzy."

She set off in one direction and I walked off in the other. I'd almost reached True Confections when I passed Juniper. She was bundled up against the cold and had her shoulders hunched against the wind. I caught her eye and she glared at me for a second before looking away and picking up her pace.

I wondered once again if she'd killed her mother.

I shivered as I entered True Confections, and I didn't think it was because of the cold.

Chapter Twenty-Seven

LATER THAT DAY, AS I SLID MY KEY INTO THE LOCK ON the front door of my cottage, I remembered that I had a stack of library books I'd been meaning to return. I decided I should take care of that right away, so I kicked off my boots when I stepped inside and then ran up the stairs to my bedroom. After grabbing the five books from my bedside table, I returned to the main floor. I was about to put my boots back on when I paused, noting the conspicuous absence of my cats. At least one of them usually came to greet me whenever I arrived home.

"Binx? Truffles?" I called out.

Nothing but silence followed.

A hint of concern crept into my thoughts, along with a sprinkling of suspicion.

I set the library books on the hall table and quietly made my way toward the back of the cottage. When I reached the family room, I stopped short.

The Christmas tree lay on the floor, it's top pointed my way. The silver star was on the rug at my feet and the remains of a shiny, red bauble were scattered across the hearth.

Truffles sat on the windowsill, pointedly ignoring me and the scene of destruction. I couldn't see Binx anywhere.

"Truffles, did you have anything to do with this?"

She finally looked my way, but then licked a paw and started grooming her face. She wasn't about to admit to anything. I suspected a certain black cat more than her anyway.

"Where's your brother?" I rested my hands on my hips. "Binx?"

He peeked around the corner of the couch and blinked his green eyes before sauntering my way and brushing up against my legs.

"Look at my poor tree." I picked him up and turned so he had a good view of the toppled Christmas tree.

He gave a quiet meow and bumped his face against my chin, purring.

My heart melted.

"I guess I can't blame you. As far as you're concerned, trees are for climbing. I'm sure this was too much of a temptation to resist."

I kissed the top of his head and set him down. I tugged my phone from my pocket and snapped a photo of the scene to share with friends and family. Then I shrugged out of my jacket and got to work.

It took me a couple of minutes to wrestle the tree upright and get it steady in its stand again. I lost another ornament in the process, but it was a plain silver bauble, from the same set as the smashed red one, and nothing I was upset about. All my more treasured ornaments were still intact.

I checked the floor beneath the tree and was relieved to find that the water from the stand had spilled onto the tree skirt and not the hardwood floors. All in all, there wasn't much damage done.

After hanging the tree skirt over a chair to dry, I stood

back to check my repair job. A black blur zoomed past me and up into the tree. The branches shook, causing baubles and other ornaments to jingle together.

"Binx!" I exclaimed.

His furry black head poked out from between the branches, his green eyes wide and comical.

I burst out laughing and quickly snapped another photo.

"Get down from there, you scallywag," I scolded.

Binx ignored me and climbed higher.

I rescued one of my favorite glass ornaments before it slid from its branch. I set it on the mantel for the time being and called for Binx to come down out of the tree again, but he was having far too much fun to pay any attention to me.

Eventually, I coaxed him down by rattling the package of his favorite treats.

"I should have predicted that this would happen," I said as I poured some of the chicken-flavored treats into his dish.

I added some tuna ones to another dish for Truffles. She hopped down from the windowsill and came over to eat her snack daintily while Binx scarfed his down.

"I guess I have to come up with some sort of solution so you don't end up destroying all my ornaments," I said to Binx. "But first, I need to get to the library before it closes. Try not to wreak too much havoc while I'm gone."

The cats ignored me and continued eating. I wouldn't be getting any promises from them.

I returned to the tree and removed a few more of my favorite ornaments—just in case—before posting the photos I'd taken on social media. Once I finished doing that, I pulled on my boots and jacket, slid the library books into a cloth bag, and set out into the chilly afternoon.

When I was about halfway to the library, my phone chimed, letting me know that I'd received a text message. It turned out to be from Blake. He'd seen the pictures I'd posted online and asked if I wanted help to secure my

Christmas tree so Binx couldn't knock it over again. I quickly replied in the affirmative and told him I'd stop by to see him shortly.

My hands were freezing by then, so I put my phone away and tugged my gloves back on. Minutes later, I arrived at the library and hurried inside, eager for a break from the icy air, which was growing colder as the afternoon progressed.

As much as I would have liked to browse the shelves and check out a few more books, I decided to keep my visit brief. Darkness would soon settle over the town, and I didn't want to get caught walking on my own without daylight to offer me some protection. I hoped the crazy snowmobiler no longer had any intention to harm or frighten me, but I couldn't count on that.

After returning my books, I waved to Dizzy. She was on the phone, dealing with library business, but she gestured to me to come her way. I waited by the circulation desk as she finished up her phone call. After hanging up, she leaned over the counter and lowered her voice.

"I tried to see what I could find out about Daniel Hathaway."

"And?" I asked with interest.

Dizzy frowned. "I struck out. I found lots of people with that name, but none of them seemed to be the right guy."

My shoulders sagged with disappointment. "That's the same problem I had."

"I can usually find *something* about a person," Dizzy said. "It's a bit strange."

I agreed, but we didn't get to chat any further. A woman arrived at the circulation desk with her three children, each of them carrying a small stack of books. With a wave, I left Dizzy to her work.

When I turned around, I noticed Mrs. Lawrence heading in my direction. Luckily, she hadn't seen me yet. I ducked into the nonfiction section and stayed hidden behind a shelf of biographies until she disappeared down the romance aisle. I didn't dislike the woman, but I didn't want to get into another matchmaking discussion, and I had no confidence that she'd decided to let the subject drop since our last encounter.

With the coast clear, I made my escape and set off in the direction of the Gondolier, knowing that was where I'd find Blake and Gareth. Even though I'd kept my stop at the library short, the outside world had grown darker while I was indoors. I picked up my pace and scanned my surroundings as I walked. Nobody appeared to be paying any attention to me, but I nevertheless stayed on high alert as I followed the cobblestone walkways along the frozen canals.

As I walked, I thought about what Dizzy had told me. Now more than ever, I wanted to find out something about Daniel Hathaway, but I was out of ideas. Hopefully, Sawyer would have more success than Dizzy and I had.

As I approached Giethoorn Avenue, I spotted a familiar figure up ahead of me. Roman was probably heading to the Gondolier to start his shift. I hoped my brother didn't have a killer working in his kitchen, but I hadn't been able to rule out Roman as a suspect. Unfortunately, that was true of most people who'd made it onto my suspect list.

As much as I'd tried to unravel the mystery of who'd killed Irma, it didn't feel like I'd made much progress. I now knew that Amber had pushed me down the stairs, and I doubted that she was the murderer, but beyond that I didn't seem to know much at all. For every question I'd managed to answer, new ones popped up. At least, that's how it seemed.

Sawyer was right. I should leave the investigating to the professionals. He and his colleagues were far better equipped to untangle this knot of a case.

I had reached the brink of deciding to wash my hands of the murder investigation and have nothing more to do with it when Roman caught my attention again. He glanced over his shoulder before skirting around the shop at the eastern end of Giethoorn Avenue. When he reached the back corner of the building, he looked over his shoulder again before darting out of sight.

I was far enough back that he didn't see me, but I certainly noticed him and his behavior. The fact that he was going around to the back of the row of businesses wasn't unusual. Many of Gareth and Blake's employees entered the restaurant through the back door. In this case, however, there was something decidedly shifty about the way Roman was acting. If he was simply heading to work, why was he so concerned about being seen?

It took me all of two seconds to make up my mind about what I should do. I broke into a run, hoping the treads on the bottom of my boots would keep me from slipping on the cobblestones. I followed in Roman's footsteps, sticking close to the side of the building where someone had shoveled a path through the snow. When I reached the back corner, I peeked around it with caution. Roman had almost reached the Gondolier.

I crept along the narrow alleyway that provided access to the back of the row of buildings, all of which housed businesses on the main floor and apartments above. I ducked into a recessed doorway when Roman slowed his pace. When I chanced a quick peek out of my hiding spot, I was glad I'd moved so quickly. Roman shot another nervous glance over his shoulder, but didn't see me lurking in the doorway.

Instead of entering the restaurant through the back door, Roman reached inside his coat and withdrew what looked like a book. After yet another quick look around, he opened the Gondolier's dumpster and tossed the book inside. He shut the lid without making more than the slightest noise and then he hurried into the restaurant like he couldn't wait to get to work.

I darted out of my hiding place and made a beeline for

the dumpster. So much for turning in my amateur sleuth card. My curiosity was running full throttle now and I had to know what Roman had discarded. Maybe it had nothing to do with the murder, but his shifty behavior had set off alarm bells in my head, and I certainly hadn't forgotten about Irma's infamous notebook, which seemed to be missing since her death.

As Roman had done moments before, I glanced around to make sure I didn't have an audience. Satisfied that I was alone, with no lookie-loos in any of the windows, I dragged an empty wooden crate closer to the dumpster and climbed up on it, hoping it wouldn't break beneath my weight.

I pushed up the lid and wrinkled my nose at the smell that greeted me. Gareth and Blake did their best to cut down on waste by composting and by donating leftover food to the local food bank, but there was inevitably still some garbage to go out each day, and the smell threatened to turn my stomach. I held my breath and peered over the edge.

On top of a grease-stained piece of torn cardboard was a brown leather notebook, its cover worn by much handling. I pushed the dumpster's lid fully open so it wouldn't fall shut on me when I leaned forward. I braved the smell to draw in a deep breath of air, and then leaned over the edge, desperately hoping I wasn't getting anything disgusting on my jacket. I had to stretch my arm out as far as I could, but I managed to close my gloved fingers around the notebook.

I snatched it up and rocked my weight backward so I could tip myself up and out of the dumpster. My feet hit the crate with a great crack of splintering wood. The crate crumbled beneath me and I tumbled to the ground. I rolled over and up to my feet, relieved to find myself no worse for wear. I was even more glad to find that I still held the notebook safely in my hands.

Leaving my gloves on, I opened the book. Cramped handwriting filled the pages. I let the notebook fall open to a page somewhere in the middle, and focused on the writing. There were several notations, each with a date above it. I read one of the entries.

Saw Grace Elroy looking overly cozy with Harold Frodsham this morning. Affair? I'll keep an eye on them.

My pulse picked up. This had to be Irma's notebook.

I flipped to the front. The owner hadn't written their name anywhere that I could see, but I was still convinced that this was the notebook I'd heard rumors about. I flipped to the back and found the last entry. To my disappointment, it was dated nearly three weeks before Irma's death.

Sylvia Baldini ordered another custom cake today, no doubt to pass off as her own at her next bridge club meeting.

I'd hoped that Irma had written something shortly before her murder, something that would have told me why she was killed and who had carried out the terrible deed. But unless Sylvia Baldini had waited three weeks to kill Irma to keep her from spilling the cake secret, that wasn't the case.

Maybe it didn't matter, though.

The fact that Roman had the notebook in his possession and had tried to dispose of it surreptitiously told me that there was a good chance that the pastry chef was Irma's killer.

Standing alone in the deserted alleyway made me feel uneasy. Roman could open the back door of the restaurant at any moment and find me with the notebook. The police probably wouldn't be thrilled that I'd picked it out of the dumpster, but I couldn't undo my actions and I didn't want to put it back in with the garbage and leave it there unsupervised. So I tucked the book safely inside my jacket and hurried out of the alley before pulling out my phone and calling Sawyer.

Chapter Twenty-Eight

SINCE SAWYER WASN'T ON DUTY, HE CALLED DETEC-
tive Ishimoto and the two of them met me on Giethoorn
Avenue, where I was pacing back and forth in an effort to
keep myself from freezing. Although I found the detective
a tad intimidating, I was glad to see her, if only because it
meant I might soon be able to get myself out of the cold.
Sawyer's presence brought the intimidation factor down a
notch or two and I appreciated that he'd come along, especially since it was his day off.

I handed the notebook to the detective right away and
she flipped through it briefly with gloved hands before slipping it into a plastic evidence bag. I'd taken a few more
peeks at the notebook while I waited for Detective Ishimoto and Sawyer to arrive and had found that it confirmed
Stephanie's story about Irma seeing her with her now-
married ex and misinterpreting their relationship. I'd also
noticed that a page had been torn out near the beginning of
the book. The entries on the surrounding pages dated back
a few years, but that didn't mean the missing page wasn't

significant. I really wanted to know if Roman had torn it out or if that was done long ago, perhaps by Irma herself.

By the time Detective Ishimoto had bagged the notebook, Officer McNally had joined us. She arrived in time to hear me explain how I'd come into possession of the notebook. When I'd finished recounting the short tale, Detective Ishimoto asked me to show her exactly where I'd picked it up.

"Once I knew what it was, I wasn't sure if I should put it back in the dumpster," I said as I led the way down the alley toward the Gondolier. "I was wearing gloves the whole time I handled it."

While Detective Ishimoto peeked into the dumpster, I glanced Sawyer's way, feeling nervous about what his colleagues might think about my actions. The detective wasn't giving much away, and I hoped I wouldn't end up in any trouble.

Sawyer gave me a reassuring nod behind Detective Ishimoto's back and that eased some of my anxiety, allowing me to breathe more easily.

The detective shut the dumpster and addressed me. "I'll need you to come by the station and give a statement about what you saw this afternoon."

"Sure. Are you going to arrest Roman?"

"I'm going to speak with him before I do anything else," she replied. "He's inside?"

"He should be," I said. "I didn't see him leave. He's probably at work in the kitchen."

She held up the plastic-encased notebook. "Thanks for reporting this. If you can provide your statement today, that would be great."

"Of course."

By the time I got the words out, Officer McNally had opened the restaurant's back door. She held it for the detective and then followed her inside.

As the door drifted shut behind them, I wondered if I

should text my brother and let him know that his pastry chef was about to get grilled by the detective. I decided not to bother. By the time I got the text written, Gareth would probably already know what was going down.

"Do you want to head over to the station right now?" Sawyer asked once we were alone in the alley.

I stuffed my gloved hands into my jacket's pockets. "I might as well. Best to get it over with."

"I'll walk with you." He looked my way as we set off along the alley. "You look like you could use a hot drink."

"Could I ever," I said, wiggling my fingers inside my pockets. "I'm about to turn into a block of ice."

"Why don't we stop and get some hot chocolate on the way. I know you don't like coffee, and the stuff at the station is more like tar anyway."

I grimaced at that description. "Hot chocolate definitely sounds good. I'm buying, though. It's the least I can do after interrupting your afternoon off."

"I'm glad you did. The notebook could be important."

"I hope it helps close the case. I don't like to think that Gareth and Blake might have had a murderer working in their restaurant all this time, but this really makes Roman look guilty."

"It definitely doesn't look good." Sawyer sent a glance my way. "I don't suppose you read the notebook and found anything about Roman."

"I took a quick peek or two," I admitted.

"I figured as much," he said with a wry note to his voice.

"Always with my gloves on," I reiterated, hoping I hadn't accidentally smeared any important fingerprints. "But I didn't see Roman's name anywhere. That doesn't mean it's not in there, though, and there was a page missing."

"Torn out?"

"That's what it looked like."

We stopped at a hot chocolate stand by the town's main dock, where the vendor was selling drinks to pedestrians as well as skaters on the canal. As we continued on our way, I held my take-out cup in both of my hands, trying to get some of the heat from the drink to seep into my numb fingers. It didn't help much in that respect, but the hot chocolate felt good going down every time I took a sip.

At the station, Sawyer led me to a small room with a table and four chairs. I waited there while he went in search of one of his fellow officers. He returned a minute later, accompanied by an officer named Jared Tuffin. Sawyer stayed with me while I recounted the events of the afternoon for Officer Tuffin, starting with Roman's suspicious behavior and ending with me calling Sawyer about what I'd found.

It didn't take long to get my statement over with, but by then it was completely dark out, and had been for some time.

"I'll walk you home," Sawyer said as I zipped up my jacket.

"Thank you."

I didn't even consider protesting. Even though the police now had Roman in their sights, and possibly even in their custody, I wasn't keen on walking home alone, just in case he wasn't the rogue snowmobiler.

I shivered when we left the warmth of the station for the icy, swirling wind, which now carried a few fine flakes of snow with it. I'd finished my hot chocolate while giving my statement and now I longed for another.

"Were you in the middle of anything when I called you earlier?" I asked as we set off along the cobblestone walkway.

"Shoveling snow, but I was just finishing up."

"No snowboarding today?"

"Hopefully on my next day off." He shoved his hands into his pockets. "Today was for catching up on things around the house."

"I hope I didn't throw you off track too much."

"Nope. The only thing I've got left to do is grab a few groceries."

I realized I'd never gone inside the restaurant to see Blake as planned. I considered texting him while I walked, but I didn't want to remove my gloves. The text message could wait.

I told Sawyer about Binx's escapades with my Christmas tree.

He laughed at the story. "He probably thinks you brought the tree inside especially for him."

"I think you're right about that. Blake's going to help me rig something up to hopefully prevent any further disasters." I dug my key out of my pocket as we reached my cottage. "Do you want to come in?"

"I need to get to the grocery store before it closes, but if Binx has struck again, I'll help you get the tree upright."

He waited in the foyer while I kicked off my boots and hurried to the back of my cottage. Binx and Truffles met me in the hall, but didn't give me any clue as to what they'd been up to in my absence. I peeked into the family room with apprehension. A couple of nonbreakable ornaments lay on the floor, but at least the tree was still standing.

I returned to the foyer. "There are signs of troublemaking, but the tree is still upright."

"Better try harder next time," Sawyer said to Binx, who'd followed me to the foyer.

"Don't encourage him or you'll have to clean up the mess next time."

Sawyer laughed and picked up Binx. "You be good, buddy."

Binx bumped his head against Sawyer's chin and then settled in against his chest.

"Sorry, but I can't stay," Sawyer said before setting Binx down on the floor.

With a swish of his tail, Binx sauntered back down the hall.

As I stood there, looking at Sawyer before me, a rush of warm feelings nearly overwhelmed me. I stepped into him and gave him a hug. His arms came around me and I soaked in his warmth and solidity for a moment before making myself step back. His hands slid along my arms until his fingers intertwined with mine.

"What was that for?" he asked.

"For putting up with me."

He gave my hands a squeeze. "That's not exactly hard, Becks."

"Even when I send your blood pressure skyrocketing?"

Still holding my hands, he stepped closer, causing my heart rate to spike.

He kissed my forehead and then grinned. "Most of the time you're actually good for my blood pressure."

I didn't know about my own blood pressure, but my pulse was cantering along much faster than it should have been.

I stepped back and slid my hands out of his, even though I didn't really want to.

I wrapped my arms around my middle so I wouldn't reach for him again. "Remember that the next time you're exasperated with me," I said.

"You say that like it's guaranteed to happen."

"Isn't it?"

"With the things you and Dizzy get up to? Yes."

We shared a smile.

"I guess I should let you go," I said, suddenly conscious of time ticking by.

He set a hand on the doorknob. "This time."

He looked me straight in the eye and grinned before opening the door and stepping outside. I locked up behind him and returned to the family room, trying to ignore my racing heart.

I texted Blake to explain why I hadn't dropped in on him at the restaurant and then I dished out dinner for Binx and Truffles while they rubbed up against my legs.

"You're such sweethearts," I said, giving them both a pat on the head once I'd set their dishes on the floor.

They purred as they dug into their food.

Standing in the middle of the kitchen, I considered what I should make myself for dinner. My phone chimed while I was thinking and I opened the new text message. Blake was on his way over, and he was bringing me some dinner.

Perfect timing. I happily gave up on my cooking plans and instead simply poured myself a glass of eggnog. While I waited for Blake to arrive, I switched on the lights on the Christmas tree and got a fire going in the fireplace.

The wind rattled at the windows, but I was safe and warm. Here in my cozy cottage, it was hard to believe that someone had been murdered recently, and that a snowmobiler with ill intent had chased me and my best friend. Still, I couldn't push those events from my mind, especially not after what I'd witnessed that afternoon.

Blake showed up with a paper bag of food for me and a few items he'd grabbed from home to help secure my poor Christmas tree against any further shenanigans on the part of a certain black cat with green eyes.

"Thank you for this," I said, accepting the bag of food from him while he kicked off his boots.

"Tell me more about what you saw Roman doing in the alley," he requested even before he had his jacket off.

My text message had been short and vague, so I wasn't surprised that he wanted more details.

As I led the way toward the kitchen, I recounted the story again, as I had for the police.

Blake appeared troubled when I finished and I couldn't blame him.

"I really hope he's not guilty," he said. "If we've had a murderer working for us, putting our other employees in danger . . ."

"You couldn't have known," I said, hoping to ease his worries. "And I doubt anyone at the restaurant was in danger.

If Roman is the killer, I don't think he's some maniac out to kill at random."

I didn't add that he might have chased Dizzy and me on a snowmobile.

Instead, I refocused on what had transpired at the Gondolier earlier. "Did the police arrest Roman?"

"Not at the restaurant. They escorted him to the police station for questioning."

"He went willingly?"

"I'm not sure about willingly, but he went, protesting his innocence."

"What exactly did he say?" I asked, hoping for details.

"That he didn't kill anyone. He claims he found the notebook lying in a snowbank. He said he picked it up and took a look and thought it was nothing, so he tossed it in the dumpster on his way to work."

"But he was acting shifty about it."

"Probably because that was all a lie," Blake said. "The detective fished a crumpled piece of paper out of the garbage when she was in the kitchen, after asking my permission. When Roman saw her do that, he went so pale I thought he was going to pass out."

"The missing page from the notebook!" I exclaimed. "But whatever was on that page must have been written years ago."

"Maybe Irma had been holding something over his head for a long time and he finally couldn't take it any longer," Blake suggested.

"You could be right about that," I said.

I decided to be optimistic and believe that the police had the right guy and would soon arrest him for Irma's murder. I still had some unanswered questions, but hopefully those would get answered in time. For now, I decided to do my best to focus on other things, starting with dinner.

I practically inhaled the toasted shrimp sandwich that Blake had brought. While I ate, he installed a couple of discreet wall anchors. When I'd finished the sandwich, I helped him wrap fishing line around the trunk of the Christmas tree and then we secured each end to one of the anchors.

Blake tested the system by tipping the tree this way and that. It rocked a bit, but wouldn't move more than a few inches in any direction.

"That should do it," he said. "But you could try wrapping some tinfoil around the bottom of the trunk too. That deters some cats."

"You seem to have experience with this kind of thing."

"I had a cat growing up that was crazy about Christmas trees."

"Well, thanks for sharing your wisdom. I'll try the tinfoil too."

Blake stayed long enough to have a glass of eggnog, and then he returned to the restaurant. I curled up on the couch with my cats and watched Christmas movies for the rest of the evening while trying my best not to think about Irma's murder.

Chapter Twenty-Nine

AFTER WORKING IN THE KITCHEN AT TRUE CONFEC-
tions for three hours the next morning, I was about ready to
burst from curiosity. I took a break to send a text message
to Sawyer, asking if Roman had been arrested. He didn't
reply right away, so I ventured out to the front of the shop,
hoping the town grapevine might prove to be a better
source of information.

Jaspreet Joshi entered through the front door as I emerged
from the back hallway. She was bundled up against the cold
and carried a large tote bag with her.

She smiled when she saw me. "Rebecca! Exactly the
person I wanted to talk to."

"What can I help you with?" I asked.

She dug through her bag. "I've got something for you.
Bake It Right sent copies of the holiday issue for each of the
competition finalists." She produced two copies of the magazine from her tote bag and held them aloft. "These are yours."

Angie hurried out from behind the counter, almost bub-
bling with excitement. "Let's see!"

I accepted the copies from Jaspreet with thanks and passed one to Angie.

"The feature starts on page ten," Jaspreet said as we flipped through the magazine.

"Here it is!" Angie exclaimed at the same moment as I found the right page. "That's a great picture of you, Becca!"

I glanced briefly at the photo of me busy at my baking station, but then turned my attention elsewhere. Each finalist had an entire page devoted to them and their creation. The page about me had three small photos in addition to the one of me in the midst of baking: one of my completed edible model of Larch Haven, one of the True Confections storefront, and one of the interior of the shop. The latter featured me and Angie in our True Confections aprons, smiling for the camera.

"Your picture is in here too," I said, nudging Angie's arm with my elbow.

"Oh my gosh!" She beamed. "I've never been in a magazine before!"

I smiled, glad she was happy.

"Thanks so much for bringing these by," I said to Jaspreet. "And for all you did for the event."

"My pleasure," she said. "I'm glad it went well after the tragedy. Well, except for your tumble down the stairs. I hope you're feeling better now."

"All healed," I assured her.

"I heard about Amber's confession. If we'd known right away that she had pushed you, we would have kicked her out of the competition."

"At least she didn't win," Angie said. "It would have been terrible if she did."

Jaspreet agreed.

"Did they mention the murder in the magazine?" Angie asked, skimming the article.

"No, thank goodness," Jaspreet replied. "The murder was reported on by some news outlets, of course, but I'm glad *Bake It Right* kept the story positive."

Two customers entered the store, so Angie reluctantly closed her copy of the magazine and got back to work, greeting the newcomers.

"Would you like to sample some chocolate?" I offered Jaspreet as Angie held out the sample tray to the other customers.

"I won't say no to that," Jaspreet said, "but I also came here to buy a few boxes of chocolates. They're going to be thank-you gifts for all the Baking Spirits Bright volunteers."

"That's a nice gesture."

"We had a dinner for everyone at the Gondolier, and that was paid for with funds from the event, but we had a bit of room left over in the budget, so I thought I'd do a little something more for them."

"Do you have anything in particular in mind?" I asked.

"I was thinking boxes of assorted chocolates."

Once Jaspreet had sampled some chocolate from Angie's tray, I led her over to a nearby shelf and helped her choose the gifts for the volunteers. I was carrying the stack of boxes she'd chosen over to the counter when the bell above the door announced the arrival of more customers. I had to hold back a groan when I saw that the Gossip Grannies had arrived.

"Hi, Delphi, Luella," I said in a cheery voice, not letting any of my true feelings show.

Sometimes an acting background came in handy even when I wasn't onstage or in front of a camera.

The two women returned my greeting, but said nothing more to me for the moment. The customer Angie had just finished serving left the store and the Gossip Grannies wandered over to one of the display tables, chatting with each other. I did my best to tune them out and stay focused on Jaspreet.

"Would you like these gift wrapped?" I asked as I set the boxes on the counter.

"Yes, please," Jaspreet said. "That would be great. Then I can deliver them right away. Or some of them, anyway. I just saw Victor at his gallery, and Consuelo should be at her café. The other volunteers might be harder to track down."

Angie came over to join me. "I'll give you a hand with that."

While the two of us got to work gift wrapping the boxes in purple True Confections wrapping paper, Jaspreet wandered along the display case, checking out the different types of chocolates.

"Did you hear the news?" Delphi said to her, drawing her away from the chocolates.

"About what?" Jaspreet asked.

"It turns out you had not only a murder victim in your competition, but the murderer as well," Luella announced with glee.

Jaspreet's eyes widened. "Who's the killer?"

"Roman Kafka," Delphi said with authority.

"Has he been arrested?" I asked before I could think better of joining their conversation.

"Not without plenty of resistance," Luella said. "It took four officers and a Taser to subdue him."

I glanced Angie's way, not sure how much of that I should believe. My cousin appeared to share my skepticism.

Luella continued her story, not noticing the look that passed between Angie and me. "Then, once he was on the ground, subdued and cuffed, one of the officers gave him a few good kicks to the head."

"After that, he confessed to everything," Delphi added. "The murder and a slew of other crimes."

"Are you sure about that?" I asked. "Because making up stories about the police using excessive force isn't something you should be doing lightly."

"Making up stories!" Delphi harrumphed.

She and Luella shot daggers at me with their eyes before turning away. Jaspreet appeared uncomfortable now. She left the Grannies and migrated back over to the counter, where Angie and I were wrapping the last two boxes.

While I rang up the sale for Jaspreet, Delphi and Luella browsed the shop, whispering to each other. I wondered if they were now making up spiteful stories about me as revenge for daring to question them. If they were, so be it. Sometimes the ridiculous rumors they started crossed the line. I didn't regret speaking up.

Still, I wondered if there was any truth to their latest tale. I doubted most—if not all—the details, but Roman really could have been arrested after the police questioned him yesterday.

When Jaspreet left the store a minute later, I retreated to the office, leaving Angie with Delphi and Luella. I checked my phone, but Sawyer still hadn't replied to my text message.

I decided I needed a bit of exercise before getting back to making more chocolates. A brisk walk out in the cold air would do me good.

And if my path happened to take me by the police station, so much the better.

Chapter Thirty

~~~~~~~~~~

I GOT BUNDLED UP AND GRABBED A SMALL PAPER bag filled with an assortment of misfit chocolates. I tucked it safely in my pocket and passed through the front of the shop on my way out, relieved to find that the Gossip Grannies had gone. Angie was busy with two new customers, but she had everything under control, so I waved to her and got on my way.

When the cold wind blasted me in the face, I second-guessed my decision to head outdoors, but I wanted answers, so I wasn't about to let the winter weather deter me. I tugged my beanie farther down over my ears and set off along the cobblestone walkway. By the time I reached the police station at the edge of town, I was shivering and looking forward to getting indoors, but I didn't even make it up the front steps.

As I put one foot on the first stair, the station door opened and Sawyer emerged, wearing his police jacket and winter hat. He spotted me right away, and lifted a hand in greeting before tugging on some gloves and jogging down to meet me.

"Are you heading out on a call?" I asked.

"No, but there's someone I need to talk to."

I eyed the front door of the police station with longing. It wasn't exactly an ideal place to hang out, but it would have provided me with some respite from the biting wind.

"Is it okay if I walk with you?" I asked, giving up on the idea of getting out of the cold.

"Let me guess," Sawyer said as he started walking, "you want to ask about Roman."

I hurried to keep up with his long strides. "The Gossip Grannies stopped by True Confections with quite a story. I wanted to find out if any of it is true."

Sawyer rolled his eyes toward the cloudy sky. "What have they come up with this time? Aliens? No, wait. That's more Dizzy's thing. The Gossip Grannies probably think Roman is a cannibalistic serial killer."

"Actually, I heard them say before that Irma had ties to the mob, so maybe they think Roman is a professional hit man. But that's not what they were talking about this time. They said he'd been arrested."

"Not true."

"Really? But the notebook . . ."

"Roman swears he found it in a snowbank shortly before he tossed it in the dumpster," Sawyer said, confirming what Blake had told me. "There's no other evidence tying him to the crime, so we're trying to see if we can verify his story. In the meantime, we're keeping a close eye on him. Please don't mention that to anyone, though. We don't need it getting back to him that he's being watched."

"My lips are sealed," I promised. "If he wasn't arrested, then I guess it's safe to assume that the part about the Taser and four officers taking Roman down was a complete lie."

Sawyer shook his head with disbelief. "Those ladies seriously need a hobby."

"Seriously," I agreed. I waited until we'd walked a few more paces before saying, "So, the page Roman tore out of the notebook and tossed in the trash in the Gondolier's kitchen must not have clinched the case against him."

"I'm guessing you heard about that from your brother," Sawyer said.

"Blake, actually."

"Right, he was at your place last night. How's the tree doing?"

"Standing tall and unharmed, last I checked. I think Blake's system will work." I realized he'd succeeded at distracting me for a brief moment. "What about that torn page?"

"It wasn't the only one missing from the book."

"Really?" I said with interest.

"A later page—probably the last one Irma had written on—had been carefully cut out. Likely with the help of a knife."

"Suggesting that two different people removed the pages." I considered another possibility. "Or the same person at different times. Maybe Roman cut out the one page and then at the last minute realized there was an earlier incriminating page that he needed to get rid of too." I looked to Sawyer. "What was on the page Detective Ishimoto retrieved from the trash?"

He shook his head again. "Like a dog with a bone."

"Can't you at least give me a hint about what was on it?" I pleaded.

"Nope."

"Sawyer . . ."

"Becca . . ."

I decided to try a different angle. "So, the place you're going now . . . does it have anything to do with the murder investigation?"

Sawyer sent a sidelong glance my way. "Maybe."

I dug the bag of chocolates out of my coat pocket. "I brought you some misfits."

"Do I need to arrest you for attempting to bribe a police officer?"

"No bribe. I'll give these to you even if you tell me to get lost."

For a second, I worried he might do exactly that, but instead he let out an exasperated sigh before speaking.

"I'm going to talk to someone who had ties to Irma."

I handed him the bag of chocolates. "You don't think Roman's guilty?"

"Thank you," he said as he tucked the chocolates into the pocket of his police jacket. "He's our prime suspect at the moment."

"But you want to cover all angles?" I guessed.

"Something like that."

"What kind of angles, exactly?"

"After reading Irma's notebook, I want to check into a couple of things."

That didn't tell me much, but it did make me even more curious. I wished I'd had a chance to read the entire notebook.

"What kind of things?" I pressed.

"You never give up, do you?" Sawyer said instead of answering my question.

We turned a corner into a residential neighborhood. Cute timber-frame cottages lined the frozen canal. Not too far ahead, in front of one of the cottages, Eleanor Tiedemann was shoveling snow from the walkway.

A lightbulb went off in my head. "It's Eleanor you want to talk to."

"Don't you need to get back to the shop?" Sawyer asked as we drew closer to Eleanor.

"Not really," I said.

"Mrs. Tiedemann," Sawyer called out as we approached Eleanor. "Can I have a moment of your time?"

As she stopped shoveling and stuck the blade of the shovel into the snow, she regarded Sawyer with wary eyes. "I suppose."

"'Bye, Becca," Sawyer said, quietly enough that only I could hear.

Getting the message loud and clear, I stopped and let him meet up with Eleanor alone. I stayed put, though, hoping to overhear something before I walked away.

"What's this about?" Eleanor asked. She tugged at the sleeves of her coat and then adjusted the hat on her head. She was definitely nervous.

"I'd like to talk to you about Irma Jones's notebook," Sawyer said.

Eleanor's already pale face turned pasty white. "What about it?" She grabbed onto the handle of the shovel, and I suspected she was using it for support.

"It contains information about your son, Cameron," Sawyer told her. "Information I'm sure you wouldn't want getting out."

Before I had a chance to fully absorb what Sawyer had said, Eleanor burst into tears.

"Please don't arrest my son," she begged as she sobbed.

I gave up on staying on the sidelines and hurried closer. "What did Cameron do?" I asked Eleanor.

I sensed more than saw the annoyed look Sawyer shot my way, but I pretended not to notice at all.

Eleanor managed to stop sobbing and wiped at her tears. "Nothing terrible."

"The colleges he applied for might disagree," Sawyer said.

Eleanor stood up taller. "He only lied on one application. I found out about it and made sure he was honest with all the others. He's not going to the college he lied to. He's attending one of the places he applied to honestly."

"How did Irma find out about it?" Sawyer asked.

Her shoulders slumped. "She overheard me at the bakery, talking to Cameron on my phone. I was scolding him for lying. When I hung up the phone and turned around, Irma was there, smirking at me. Then she made a big show of writing something in her notebook. I knew it was about me and Cameron." Her face transformed with bitterness. "That woman was an evil witch. She didn't have a single kind bone in her body."

"That's why you rummaged through Irma's bag at the town hall," I said. "You were trying to find the notebook."

"I wanted to get rid of it. I knew that wouldn't change the fact that she knew about Cameron's lie, but she'd been writing terrible things about people in this town for years. I wanted to get my hands on it and burn it."

"But you didn't find the notebook in her bag," I said. "Or, I interrupted you before you had a chance."

Eleanor frowned. "I got enough of a look to see that it wasn't there."

"So after you killed her, you ransacked her cottage," I guessed.

Her eyes widened. "No!"

Sawyer put a warning hand on my arm. "Becca."

I held back the other questions I wanted to ask.

"I didn't kill Irma!" Eleanor looked from me to Sawyer, her eyes full of fear. "I swear! And I can prove it, remember?"

Sawyer nodded. "Your alibi checked out."

"Alibi?" I echoed with surprise.

They both ignored me, and I couldn't blame them. My role in the conversation wasn't exactly legitimate, but I wished I'd known about her alibi sooner.

"Mrs. Tiedemann, is your son at home?" Sawyer asked.

She gulped, realizing the implication of the question. "Cameron didn't hurt anyone."

"Is he at home?" Sawyer repeated.

"No," Eleanor replied. "But I can call him and get him to come home."

"Please do that."

"My phone's inside." She headed for the front door of her cottage.

Sawyer turned to me. "Becca, I'll take it from here."

"Do you think Cameron killed Irma?" I whispered.

"Becca . . ."

I held up my hands in surrender. "Okay, okay. I'm going."

As he followed Eleanor, I walked off, disappointed that I wouldn't get to listen in on what happened next. I was distracted from that disappointment when I spotted Daniel Hathaway up ahead, strolling along the canal.

I picked up my pace, hoping to catch up with him.

"Mr. Hathaway!" I called out before he could turn a corner out of my sight.

He stopped and turned around. As I jogged toward him, recognition registered on his face, a hint of wariness following right behind it.

I wasn't exactly sure what I wanted to say to him, but I didn't want to let him slip away. At the very least, maybe I could find out how long he'd be in town. That way I'd know how soon Sawyer needed to have a chat with him and make sure he wasn't somehow connected to the murder.

I'd almost reached him when a black-clad figure darted out from between two cottages. For a second, I thought the figure was trying to embrace Daniel.

Then Daniel staggered backward, his eyes wide with shock.

I barely had a chance to register the knife protruding from his chest before he toppled over and tumbled down the bank of the canal.

Chapter Thirty-One

"SAWYER!" I YELLED.

The black-clothed figure fled, disappearing between the cottages before I could get a good look at them.

I scrambled down the bank to the frozen canal. I was only partially aware of screams and shouts nearby as I slipped and slid along the ice to Daniel. He was splayed out on his back, his eyes closed.

My mind felt numb from shock. I could hardly believe that he'd been stabbed, even though it had happened right in front of me and I could see the knife still in his chest. A pool of blood slowly bloomed on the ice around him. I knelt beside him, trying to avoid the blood, and took his hand in mine.

"Daniel?" My voice broke on his name and I choked back a sob. "Can you hear me?"

He didn't so much as flutter his eyelids.

I heard pounding footsteps and glanced over my shoulder in time to see Sawyer slide down the bank toward me.

I shuffled to the side to make room for him next to Daniel.

"He's been stabbed." I could hear the disbelief in my voice.

Sawyer put a hand to my face and looked me right in the eye. "Are you hurt?"

"No."

He released me. "Did you see who did it?" he asked as he leaned over Daniel.

"Not his face. He came out of nowhere and then took off between two of the cottages."

Sawyer spoke into his radio in a terse voice while administering first aid to Daniel. I wiped a tear from my cheek and sat on the ice, feeling helpless.

Two police officers navigated their way down the snowy bank to the frozen canal and joined Sawyer. I stood up on trembling legs and retreated to a spot beneath a nearby bridge so I wouldn't be in the way. After a word with Sawyer, one of the officers climbed the bank again and disappeared. Maybe he'd gone in search of Daniel's attacker. Whoever the assailant was, they were probably long gone.

I drew in a deep, shaky breath, and wiped away my remaining tears. I caught sight of the growing puddle of blood around Daniel and averted my gaze. I didn't want him to die. The location of the injury had me worried. I hoped the knife hadn't penetrated his heart.

Sirens cut through the air, along with shouts from various directions. Paramedics arrived on the scene and clambered down the bank, carrying a stretcher.

I tried to block everything out and hugged my knees as I stared at the other side of the canal. Some of my shock wore off and I became more aware of the details around me. A black item sat on the ice on the far side of the canal, partially hidden by the shadows beneath the bridge. After pushing myself to my feet, I slid across the canal and picked up the black object.

It was a wallet. Daniel's, maybe. It could have fallen from his pocket when he tumbled down the bank. I opened it with fumbling, gloved fingers and slid out a driver's license. It was Daniel's photo on the card.

I checked the name. No wonder I hadn't found anything about him online. Daniel Hathaway wasn't his name. Not exactly, anyway. The driver's license identified him as Philip Daniel Hathaway-Marriott.

Marriott.

As in Gregor Marriott, the famous Vermont artist?

"Becca!"

I turned to see Sawyer approaching. He pulled me into his arms and I leaned against him, but I couldn't give him a proper hug with his vest and duty belt in the way. I stepped back and realized I had tears on my cheeks again.

Sawyer rested his hands on my shoulders. "Are you sure you're okay?"

"I'm fine." I tried to keep my voice steady. "What about Daniel? Is he still alive?"

"At the moment. The paramedics are going to take him to Cherry Park to meet the air ambulance."

I hoped he'd get to the hospital in time for the doctors to save him.

"It happened right in front of me, Sawyer." My voice trembled despite my attempt to stay calm and collected. "He was fine one second, and then . . ."

"I know. I'm sorry you had to see that." He squeezed my shoulders before letting go.

I tried to regain my composure. "I hope he's going to be okay. What about the person who stabbed him?"

"Gone, but we've still got people looking. You said it was a man?"

"I . . . I'm not sure." That was my initial impression, but now doubts crept in, making me second-guess myself. "It all happened so fast. All I really saw was someone in dark clothes. I didn't see their face at all." I wished I had more to tell him.

"That's okay." Sawyer glanced back toward Daniel. The paramedics were carefully loading him onto the stretcher. "I want to get you out of here," he said, returning his attention to me. "Are you okay with going to the station to give a statement?"

"Yes." I would have been happy to go almost anywhere simply to get away from the scene of the attack and the disturbing pool of blood on the ice. "But one second." I showed him the wallet. "I found this on the ice. It must have fallen from Daniel's pocket. Check out the name on his driver's license." I handed him the card as well.

Sawyer studied the license. "That explains why you couldn't find any information about him online."

"Why do you think he lied about his name?" I asked.

"Maybe he didn't." Sawyer tucked the license back into the wallet. "Maybe he goes by Daniel Hathaway in informal situations."

I wasn't sure I bought that.

"Come on." Sawyer took my arm and helped me up the bank to the cobblestone walkway. He turned the wallet over to another officer, who passed him the keys for one of the police cruisers parked nearby.

Curious but cautious onlookers peeked out of cottage windows. I avoided making eye contact with them.

Sawyer and I climbed into the cruiser and he waited until the ambulance had pulled away with Daniel inside before starting the engine. It didn't take long to get to the police station and Sawyer soon got me settled in the same room where I'd given my statement about Roman and seeing him toss Irma's notebook into the Gondolier's dumpster. Sawyer took my statement, and then he had to move on and do the same with other witnesses, but not before he arranged for my brother to come pick me up.

I sat on a hard chair in the lobby, waiting for Gareth. When he burst in through the front door of the building, I jumped to my feet. He pulled me into a hug, giving me a squeeze before letting me go.

"You're okay?" he asked, looking at me closely.

"Fine," I said. "A little shaken up, but that's all. Is Roman at the restaurant?"

"Yes. Why?" Understanding dawned on his face. "So he wasn't behind the stabbing. And that could mean he also didn't kill Irma."

"It could," I agreed, although I knew we couldn't be completely certain of that. The two crimes might not be related.

"Let's get you home. You can pack some things and come stay with me and Blake."

"But I don't want to leave Truffles and Binx," I protested.

"You can bring them too," Gareth said as he ushered me out to the golf cart he'd parked in front of the police station.

As we climbed aboard, I managed to convince him to let me stay at my cottage, on the condition that he and Blake would stay over with me. Considering everything that had happened recently, I was glad I'd have company. And this way, I didn't have to disrupt Truffles and Binx's routine.

Gareth had to go back to the restaurant for a few hours, so we stopped and picked up Dizzy on the way to my cottage so I would have company until the restaurant closed for the night. Dizzy sat in the back seat of the golf cart, leaning forward between me and Gareth as my brother drove and I relayed everything that had happened.

After Gareth dropped us off at my cottage, Dizzy sat me down at the kitchen table and made me a mug of hot chocolate.

"I can't believe Daniel got stabbed in broad daylight! Right in front of you!" She set the mug on the table and then gave me a hug. "I'm so glad you didn't get hurt."

"Me too. I wish I knew how Daniel was doing."

"Sawyer might be able to update you in the morning."

"I hope so." I eyed my laptop, where it sat on the coffee table across the room. "Maybe I can find out more about Daniel aka Philip."

I'd filled Dizzy in on what I'd found out from the driver's license.

"Tomorrow," Dizzy said in a voice that left no room for argument. "Tonight, you need to look after yourself. We're going to sit on the couch with warm blankets and watch feel-good Christmas movies."

That sounded like the perfect idea to me.

Chapter Thirty-Two

DIZZY ENDED UP STAYING THE NIGHT AT MY COTTAGE
as well as Gareth and Blake. Having so many people under
the same roof with me made me feel safe and allowed me to
fall asleep without much trouble. I had one nightmare that
jolted me awake shortly before midnight, but after that I slept
soundly. When I made my way downstairs in the morning
with my phone in hand, I found Dizzy sitting on the floor
near the Christmas tree, playing with Binx and Truffles. Gareth sat at the kitchen table, eating breakfast, while Blake
stood by the counter, pouring orange juice into a glass.

"Morning, sleepyhead," Blake said when he saw me. He
held up the carton of juice. "OJ?"

"Please." I set my phone on the table and peeked over
Gareth's shoulder. "What are you eating?"

"Cottage cheese."

I made a face. "Gross."

"You're gross," my brother shot back.

I was tempted to stick my tongue out at him, but managed to restrain myself.

"The level of maturity here is astounding," Blake said as he handed me a glass of orange juice.

Dizzy got to her feet and came over our way. "Some things never change." She put an arm around me and rested her head on my shoulder. "Did you sleep?"

"I did." I didn't bother to mention the nightmare. I gave her a hug with my free arm. "Thank you all for staying. It really did help."

"Glad to hear it," Gareth said as he finished off his breakfast.

"Do you think the latest stabbing is somehow related to Irma's murder?" Dizzy asked.

"I've been wondering that myself." I set down my glass and got busy feeding Binx and Truffles while they purred and rubbed against my legs.

"Did the victim even know Irma?" Blake asked.

"He spoke to her at least once," I said. "I saw them together at the town hall. I don't know if he really knew her or not, though."

Once the cats were busy eating, I took my orange juice over to the coffee table, then grabbed my laptop and sank down on the couch.

Blake put his empty glass in the dishwasher. "If you're okay, we'll get going."

"I'm good," I assured him. "Thanks again for staying over."

Blake stopped by the couch to kiss me on the top of my head before heading out. Gareth came over my way too, but all he did was ruffle my hair into a mess.

"Hey!" I tried to lean out of his reach.

He laughed and carried on his way.

"Brothers," I grumbled under my breath.

"Do you still want to go to the snowmobile parade in Snowflake Canyon tonight?" Dizzy asked as she flopped onto the couch beside me.

"Definitely."

"You won't be too scared to go out?"

I thought about that before responding. "I think it'll be good for me to get out and do something."

Dizzy watched as I opened the Internet browser on my laptop. "Are you looking for information on Daniel Hathaway? Or the man we know as Daniel?"

"Yes. I'm hoping there's something to find, now that we know his real name."

Dizzy tucked one leg beneath her and got more comfortable on the couch. "If the latest incident wasn't related to Irma's murder, don't you think it's strange that Daniel—a visitor—would get attacked here in Larch Haven?"

"I guess it depends on whether or not he knew somebody here who had a beef with him."

"Or how desperate someone was to get to him?" Dizzy said.

I considered that line of thought. "Because someone could have followed him from out of town? That's a possibility too."

I typed the name Philip Hathaway-Marriott into the search bar and added the name Gregor Marriott. Dizzy shifted closer to me so she had a better view of the screen.

The results that popped up confirmed my suspicions.

"He's Gregor Marriott's great-grandson," I said as I skimmed an article about an exhibit of Gregor Marriott's artwork that Philip had organized two years earlier.

"Why do you think Philip bought that Marriott painting at Victor's gallery?" Dizzy asked. "Is he trying to get his great-grandfather's artwork back in the family?"

"Maybe," I said.

"If that's the case," she continued, "that would explain why he came to Larch Haven. He could have been on the hunt for the Marriott artwork being sold by the estate of that private collector Victor mentioned, and he tracked that autumn landscape to the gallery here in town. But that doesn't explain why anyone would want to try to kill him."

She grabbed my arm, her eyes wide. "Becca, what if you were the intended target?"

"I wasn't. The assailant easily could have come at me instead of Daniel, but they didn't."

Dizzy relaxed with relief and let go of my arm. "Thank goodness."

I thought back to the day when Dizzy and I had first seen Daniel aka Philip. I pictured the events in my mind, from our arrival at the gallery to the time we left. I felt like I had most of the puzzle pieces required to figure out what was going on, but I needed a couple more to make everything fit together.

I did another search on the Internet, testing out the theory that was taking shape in my head.

"You're onto something," Dizzy said as she watched me. "I can tell from the look on your face."

"Maybe."

I scanned a couple of articles, my excitement building.

Dizzy leaned closer and read along with me. "Not maybe," she said. "Definitely."

She was right. I passed her the laptop and jumped up so I could grab my phone.

"We need to talk to Sawyer."

Chapter Thirty-Three

SAWYER WANTED ME TO STAY HOME, OUT OF AN abundance of caution, while he followed up on the information Dizzy and I had given him. I decided to take his advice, at least for the time being. Dizzy stayed at my place until noon, and we baked batches of gingerbread and mandelhörnchen while listening to Christmas music. After Dizzy left to meet her parents for lunch, I wrapped all the Christmas presents I'd purchased and tucked them under the tree.

Binx had considered climbing the tree while Dizzy and I were baking, but the tinfoil I'd wrapped around the trunk deterred him, at least for the moment. I suspected he hadn't given up for good, but at least I didn't have to worry about the tree falling over anymore, thanks to Blake.

With all the presents wrapped, I settled on the couch with a book and read for a while. Even though I was interested in the story, I found it hard to focus. I kept checking my phone to see if Sawyer had texted me, but the only messages I received were from Dizzy, Blake, Angie, and Lolly, all of whom were checking in to see how I was doing. I'd spoken to Lolly and Pops on the phone the night before to make sure they heard an accurate version of the latest incident and to assure them that I was fine. They'd then passed the story on to Angie.

By the time the sun sank behind the western mountains, I was going stir crazy. I wanted to know how Daniel was doing and if the new leads had panned out. I sent a text message to Sawyer for the third time that day, but I didn't receive a response. I knew he was busy, but the waiting was wearing at my nerves.

When Dizzy texted to ask once again if I still wanted to go to the parade, I answered in the affirmative. I'd stayed home all day to ease Sawyer's worries, but I didn't think I was at risk of coming to any harm. Like I'd told Dizzy, the knife-wielding attacker easily could have stabbed me, but had instead gone after Daniel.

Nevertheless, when Dizzy requested that I not wander through town after dark by myself, I agreed. She and her parents walked over to my cottage and then Mr. and Mrs. Bautista accompanied us to the parking lot, where Dizzy and I climbed into my car. We waved at her parents as we drove out of the lot and onto the highway. We headed up the mountain to Snowflake Canyon and found that plenty of people had the same plan for the evening as we did. We had to park about half a mile from the parade route, but we'd arrived early enough that we could walk there and still have some time to spare before the event began.

"I'd forgotten how popular the parade is," I said as we wandered along the main street of the town, which was more like an alpine village.

I hadn't been home for Christmas for several years, but before going away to college, I'd attended the parade with friends and family each December.

We moved with the flow of pedestrians heading to the edge of town, where the parade would take place along a snow-covered path.

"Good thing we didn't get here any later," Dizzy said as the marked route came into view. "I think we can still find a good spot, but we should hurry."

We picked up our pace as we followed the parade route to the west, searching for a thinning of the crowd. Old-fashioned streetlamps, similar to those found in Larch Haven, lined a nearby road and provided some light to see by, but the parade route was intentionally left fairly dark. That allowed the snowmobiles to have more impact. I knew from years past that each of more than one hundred snowmobiles would have colorful headlights that would illuminate the snowy trail in a magical way. There would also be twinkle lights on the machines, and sometimes on the riders' costumes as well. As per tradition, Santa Claus would bring up the rear on his sleigh, towed by one of the snowmobiles.

Briefly, I wondered if the snowmobiler who'd chased Dizzy and me would be among those in the parade. I pushed that thought aside. There was no way I could know if that was the case, and even if they were present, I doubted they could pick us out of the crowd.

Here and there along the route, snack vendors sold hot drinks and sweet treats. My stomach growled when I caught a whiff of caramel corn, but I decided a snack would have to wait until we'd staked out our viewing spot.

As we got farther along the parade route, the crowd thinned out. We spotted some free spaces across the trail, so we climbed over the barrier and dashed across before any officials could object.

"Perfect," Dizzy said with satisfaction as we took up our spot behind the barrier on the other side.

We had no one in front of us, so we'd have an unobstructed view of all the snowmobiles as they passed by.

The space around us quickly filled in with other spectators, many of whom held hot drinks either brought from home or purchased from one of the nearby vendors. As the cold night air seeped its way through my layers, strains of distant music reached my ears.

"The parade's starting!" a young boy piped up.

He stood next to us, with his parents stationed behind him. He leaned forward, trying to see the snowmobiles.

"It'll be a few minutes before we see anything," his mother told him.

I knew she was right, so that meant I had time to go grab some hot chocolate. I was already on the verge of shivering and I wanted something to help ward off the chill.

"Do you want some hot chocolate?" I asked Dizzy. "I'm going to make a quick run to the nearest vendor."

"Please," she said. "A peppermint one, if they have it."

"I'll be right back."

I threaded my way through the crowd that had gathered behind our viewing spot and then picked up my pace when I broke free of the press of bodies. The music was getting louder, but it was still a fair way off. I didn't think I'd have any trouble getting the drinks and making it back to Dizzy in time to see all the snowmobiles.

I'd almost made it to the nearest hot chocolate vendor when a man bumped into me as he walked in the opposite direction. I was about to apologize—even though he'd veered into me—when a hand gripped my arm and something hard pressed into my back through my winter jacket.

"Don't say a word," Victor's voice growled in my ear. "Keep walking like nothing's wrong."

In that moment I knew two things: Victor Barnabas had killed Irma, and he had a gun pointed at my back.

Chapter Thirty-Four

MY HEART POUNDED OUT A THUNDEROUS BEAT, SO loud in my own ears that it was hard to think. Even though I felt light-headed from fear, I did as commanded and continued walking, right past the hot chocolate vendor, and farther away from the crowd lining the parade route.

Victor kept the butt of the gun pressed into my back and gripped my arm with his other hand. He walked so close to me that I doubted anyone around us would notice the weapon. My expression probably showed my fear because I hadn't bothered to school it, but now all the other people were behind us.

We walked around a high snowbank and out into the parking lot near the ice slide that Dizzy and I had passed earlier in the week. Although security lights lit up the full lot, the place was still and silent, except for the distant parade music. Everyone had left their cars to take in the show, and the ice slide was closed for the night, shrouded in darkness, much of it out of reach of the parking lot's security lights.

As we crossed the lot, my gaze darted left and right in a frantic search for help in any shape or form. Setting off a car alarm might draw attention our way, but I couldn't tell which cars had alarms and which didn't. Even if I could tell, Victor might shoot me before I had a chance to do anything.

We left the parking lot, rounding another snowbank, before Victor marched me toward the forest. My mind whirred in a desperate attempt to come up with a plan to save myself. Once we were in among the trees I'd probably be done for. I needed to save myself before we reached the forest.

I wondered how much time had passed since I'd left Dizzy. Had she realized something was wrong? Probably not. Even though it felt like Victor had first pointed his gun at me half an hour ago, I knew it was more likely that mere minutes had passed.

My phone was tucked in the pocket of my coat, but I wasn't sure if I could slip it out without Victor noticing. I decided I had to at least try. It was either that or let him take me into the woods and shoot me.

We left the plowed walkway for deeper snow and I stumbled, nearly falling to my knees. My breath caught in my throat. I worried that my sudden movement would make Victor pull the trigger, but instead he yanked me upright again, his grip on my arm painful despite the padding of my winter jacket.

"Keep moving," he ordered.

Our progress slowed as we slogged through the deep snow toward the forest's edge.

"Why are you doing this?" I asked, hoping to keep him distracted as I tugged off my left glove.

"You know why," he snarled.

"No, I really don't," I lied, glad to hear I sounded convincing.

"Then you're not as smart as I thought. But you were asking questions. Poking around. Sooner or later you might have figured things out. I couldn't let that happen."

With the crunch of our steps in the snow masking the sound, I slowly unzipped the left pocket of my jacket.

I tried to keep him talking. "So you killed Irma and stabbed Daniel Hathaway?"

"I should have got a gun sooner. Then I could have taken you out at the same time as Hathaway. I would have tried to deal with you with the knife, but I didn't know there was a cop so close by. He came running, so I had to get out of there."

I suppressed a shudder. I'd been wrong about Daniel's attacker having no interest in harming me. If Sawyer hadn't been a few cottages away at the time, I might already be dead, or at least in the hospital like Daniel.

I slid my phone from my pocket, hoping I could wake it up, unlock it, and call 9-1-1 with one hand.

As soon as the screen lit up, Victor's head jerked toward the device in my hand.

The next thing I knew, he'd shoved me hard to the ground. As I lay in the snow, he snatched up my phone and hurled it off to the side. Then he grabbed my arm and yanked me back to my feet. This time he held the gun to the side of my head. I held my breath, my legs trembling beneath me.

"Don't try anything like that again." He returned the gun to my back and prodded me with it. "Get moving."

Tears blurred my vision, but I blinked them away. I couldn't give in to the feeling of helplessness that was threatening to overwhelm me.

"It was all about the paintings, wasn't it?" I asked, keeping my voice steady, even though I felt anything but.

"See. I knew you were trouble."

I pressed on. "You stole Gregor Marriott paintings and then sold them out of your gallery."

"I didn't steal anything," he said, his voice full of contempt. "I didn't need to. Not with my talent."

His meaning suddenly became clear to me. "The paintings are fake. You painted them yourself."

"You couldn't tell by looking at them, could you?" He sounded proud of himself. "I could have made a killing off them."

I shivered at his choice of words. "But Daniel Hathaway knew something was up."

"That's not even his name." The contempt had returned to his voice. "He's related to Gregor Marriott. Somehow, he found out that I had Marriott paintings for sale."

"And he knew that wasn't right," I said, remembering what I'd read online. "Because there haven't been any Marriott paintings on the market for years. I found that out earlier today. You told me that you got the artwork through an estate sale, but that wasn't true. There hadn't been any such sale, and Daniel knew there shouldn't be any of his great-grandfather's paintings in your gallery."

"Too many people not minding their own business," Victor grumbled.

"Like Irma?"

"She was always trying to collect dirt on people," he groused. "It made her feel superior. Well, who had the last laugh?"

I tried not to let the cold cruelty in his voice shake me. "How did she even know about the forgeries?"

"She peeked in the back window of my gallery in the middle of the night and saw me working on the autumn landscape. Then I guess she put two and two together when she saw the painting in my gallery, attributed to Gregor Marriott. I thought someone had been at the window of my workshop, but I never saw who it was. Then she hinted that she knew what I was up to, and I realized it was her."

Irma must have been on her way to work at her bakery that night. Her route would have taken her past the gallery. If only she hadn't taunted Victor with what she'd seen, she might still be alive.

Victor jabbed the butt of the gun into my back. "Are you

happy now that you've got all your answers? Was it worth sticking your nose where it didn't belong?"

I didn't answer. My growing fear had stolen my voice.

We'd reached the forest. I was running out of time.

Victor gave me a push when I hesitated, and I moved in among the trees. The snow wasn't so deep beneath the thick canopy, but the tall evergreen to my left still had its branches weighed down by snow. I pushed one branch aside and let it go as I passed by. It didn't snap back with as much force as I'd hoped, but the movement was enough to dislodge a pile of snow from a higher branch. The snow slid off in one icy clump and crashed down onto Victor's head.

He let out a cry of surprise and anger.

The pressure of the gun against my back eased up.

I took my chance.

I whirled around and shoved Victor while he was still wiping snow from his face. He stumbled off to the side and I charged out of the forest.

When a gunshot rang out, I veered to the left.

I ran around the curve of a nearby hill and realized I was short on options.

I could run across an open stretch of deep snow, hoping to get to the parking lot without getting shot, or I could go up.

Without any hesitation, I clambered up the steps that had been cut into the snowy hillside so people could reach the top of Snowflake Canyon's famous ice slide. I stumbled and fell to my knees, but quickly scrambled back to my feet and kept going. I could hear Victor huffing and puffing not far behind me. The terrifying sound sent me climbing faster.

I reached the top of the hill and dove behind the wooden storage structure. It was really just a bin with a post at each corner and a roof overhead. The rolled-up carpet sleds were stored inside, awaiting the next day's sliders.

I crouched behind the storage bin just in time. Victor crested the top of the hill and paused, looking around, the gun still held in one hand. Light from the moon reflected off the snow, making it easier to see than I would have liked. If he took two steps to his left, Victor would spot me.

To my relief, he moved forward instead, walking along the far side of the storage bin.

"I know you're up here," Victor said, his voice sending a chill along my spine. "I'm ending this tonight, so why don't we get it over with?"

As he continued his slow steps forward, I crawled on hands and knees in the opposite direction. He made a sudden lunge to the back of the storage bin. I scurried around to the front of it at the same moment.

I got my feet under me, but Victor was faster. He darted to the front of the bin again so we were face-to-face. I stood up slowly as he pointed the gun at me. I rested a hand on the snow-covered edge of the bin.

"You're strong-willed, I'll give you that," he said. "But this stops here."

Not if I had anything to do with it.

I scooped snow up off the edge of the bin and thrust it in Victor's face.

Before he had a chance to recover, I grabbed one of the carpet sleds, ran past Victor, and jumped onto the slide, landing awkwardly on the half-unrolled sled. Victor shouted behind me. There was a loud bang, and a bullet whizzed past me. I careened around a corner, gaining speed as I tried to center myself on the sled.

I had no idea if Victor was following me or if he was waiting for me to round another bend to get a clear shot at me. All I could do was keep myself on the sled as it raced down the twisting slide. Somewhere above me, the gun fired again. I gasped, but nothing struck me. I zipped around another bend and then the slide straightened out. I shot out the end onto flat ground. The sled kept sailing forward. I hit a bump and flew into the air.

I landed hard in a snowbank and my breath whooshed

out of me. I was too stunned to move. A second passed, then another. My right cheek was pressed against the cold, hardpacked snow. The icy temperature against my skin helped revive me. I needed to move.

Planting my hands under me, I pushed myself up to my feet. The snow gave away beneath my left foot with a crunch. My leg dropped straight down until it was knee-deep in the bank. I tried to pull it out of the hole, but my foot was stuck.

I tried again, but I couldn't get my foot to budge.

Frantically, I dug at the icy snow with my hands.

A whooshing sound came from my left. I jerked my head up in time to see Victor shoot out from the bottom of the slide. As his sled lost momentum, he rolled off of it and up to his feet.

He saw me struggling in the snowbank and a cold, cruel smile spread across his face. He raised his gun.

I stopped digging and closed my eyes.

Chapter Thirty-Five

"POLICE! DROP THE GUN!"

My eyes flew open at the sound of Sawyer's voice.

I almost cried with relief when I saw him and three other police officers converge on Victor, their weapons drawn.

Anger flashed across Victor's face, but he knew he was beaten. He dropped the gun and followed the officers' commands to put his hands behind his head and kneel down. Within seconds, Sawyer had him in handcuffs.

While one of the other officers read Victor his rights, Sawyer jogged over to me.

"Becca! Are you okay?"

"I'm fine," I assured him. "Aside from having my foot stuck."

Sawyer dug into the snowbank with his hands and had me freed in no time. I slid down the bank and stood up on wobbly legs. He must have noticed my unsteadiness, because he put his hands on my upper arms.

"You're sure you're okay?" he checked again.

I nodded as I watched the other officers lead Victor

away. I didn't want to think about how close he'd come to killing me, so I tried to focus on other details.

"How did you know we were here?" I asked, turning my attention back to Sawyer.

"We were trying to find Victor so we could arrest him. His car was spotted up here in Snowflake Canyon, so we headed up this way. Just as we arrived, I got a call from Dizzy. She said you'd disappeared and she was worried about you. Then we heard gunshots, so we came running."

"Thank goodness you did."

All the energy drained out of me in a sudden whoosh. I leaned into Sawyer and he put his arms around me.

"Did I miss the parade?" I asked.

"You did."

"That's all right," I said with a sigh. "I'm just glad I'm still here."

"Me too."

There was an undercurrent of fierceness behind his words that sent a rush of happy warmth through my chest despite the cold night.

Sawyer stepped back and held me at arm's length. "Let's go find Dizzy."

I smiled at that. "Sounds good to me."

IT FELT AS THOUGH THE ENTIRE TOWN HAD PASSED through my grandparents' cottage that afternoon. Lolly and Pops knew almost everyone in Larch Haven and they were well loved, so their Christmas Eve open house always drew a big crowd. Even though many people had already come and gone before the sun set, now that darkness was falling over the town, the cottage was still full of familiar faces, laughter, and happy chatter.

Dizzy was ladling eggnog into a glass over by the dining room table, which was laden with food and drinks. Stephanie was chatting with her and selecting finger sandwiches from a platter. Over by the fireplace, my parents were catching up with Dizzy's mom and dad, and Gareth and Blake stood near the Christmas tree, laughing and talking with a couple of our grandparents' neighbors.

When the neighbors wandered off toward the spread of food, I joined my brother and brother-in-law.

"How's your wrist?" Blake asked me.

"All better," I replied with a smile. I hadn't felt a single twinge of pain for the past week.

"How are you doing otherwise?" The question came from Gareth.

He'd been checking up on me almost daily since my unpleasant encounter with Victor and his gun. Sometimes my brother's overprotectiveness could be annoying, but this time I appreciated his concern.

"Good," I assured him. "It helps to know that Victor is locked up and Daniel—or Philip—is going to be okay."

"Is he out of the hospital?" Dizzy asked as she appeared by my side.

"Not yet, but he's going to be transferred to a rehabilitation facility soon," I said. "Sawyer talked to him the other day."

"Did he get more answers from him?" Blake asked.

After Victor's arrest, I'd told my friends and family everything I knew about the forged paintings and why Victor had killed Irma, but there had still been gaps in the story at the time.

"He did," I confirmed. "Apparently, a friend tipped off Philip to the fact that Victor was selling Gregor Marriott paintings in his gallery. Philip knew they must be fakes, so he came to Larch Haven in the hope of proving that. He bought one of the paintings so he could take it to an expert and have it declared a forgery. He also had a contact in the FBI who came and met him at the Christmas tree farm's café. Irma noticed Philip keeping an eye on Victor around town. She approached Philip about it at the baking competition, probably thinking it would make him squirm, but when he acted like he didn't care, Irma got annoyed and walked off. He never saw her again, and he doesn't think she tipped Victor off. Somehow, though, Victor eventually became suspicious of Philip."

"So that's why Victor stabbed him," Dizzy finished for me.

"Thank goodness he didn't kill him," I said. "The knife nicked one of Philip's lungs, but missed his heart."

"I'm curious about Roman," Dizzy said to Blake and Gareth. "Why did he tear that page out of Irma's notebook? What did she have on him?"

Blake answered. "She caught him stealing cash from the till back when Roman worked at her bakery. Roman came clean about that after Victor's arrest. At the time of the theft, Roman's mom needed surgery and he was trying to help her pay for it."

"But Irma never told the police?" Dizzy guessed.

"She preferred to hold the information over him," Gareth said.

"As was her habit," I added before my brother spoke again.

"Roman was worried that if anyone found out, he'd lose his job with us."

"But he's still working for you, right?" Dizzy said.

Gareth nodded. "Aside from a small wrinkle or two at the start, he's been a good employee since we hired him a year ago. Unless he pulls a stunt like that at the restaurant, we're happy to keep him on."

"Sawyer told me that Victor admitted to cutting a page out of the notebook," I said. "He stole it from Irma's cottage after killing her. He was worried that she'd made a note about seeing him forging the Marriott painting in the workroom at his gallery. When he got his hands on the book, he found out that was exactly what she'd done. He read through the notebook to make sure she hadn't written anything else about him, and then he discarded it."

"Why didn't he destroy it instead?" Blake asked. "That would have been smarter."

"He was hoping to throw suspicion on the other people mentioned in the book. He ended up leaving it near Roman's cottage, hoping he'd pick it up and get his fingerprints on it. That way, if the police ever found it, Roman would become their number one suspect."

"Which he did," Dizzy said. "So Roman really did find the notebook in a snowbank."

"Apparently."

"But then Victor attacked Philip when Roman had a solid alibi," Gareth said. "That wasn't too smart."

"Nope," I agreed. "He wasn't as careful as he thought he was being."

Dizzy spoke up again. "What about Juniper's jewelry?"

"Once Victor was charged with Irma's murder, Juniper explained that to Stephanie, and Stephanie shared it with me. Irma withheld some jewelry that Juniper had inherited from her maternal grandmother." I explained that part for Gareth's and Blake's benefit. "On the night of Irma's death, Juniper used the spare key—which was hidden by the back porch—to get into her mother's cottage so she could take the jewelry. She had no idea that Irma was being murdered at the town hall at almost that exact time. Afterward, Juniper didn't want to admit what she'd done, because she was afraid it would make her look guilty of killing her mother."

"What a tangled mess," Dizzy said. "And poor Irma. She wasn't very likable, but she didn't deserve to be killed."

We all agreed with that.

Angela and her husband, Marco, joined our group and the conversation turned to more pleasant topics. Outside the front window, the Christmas lights sent a happy glow into the growing darkness and illuminated the fluffy snowflakes that had been falling steadily for the past couple of hours. Gareth had shoveled the front path before the open house began, and Blake had done the job again as the fresh snow started piling up, so I decided it was my turn to head outside.

I left the others and opened the door to peek out and assess the situation. Two or three inches of fresh snow had accumulated since Blake had been out, but it looked so fluffy and light that I figured I could shovel it aside within a matter of minutes.

I decided not to bother bundling up and instead slipped outside and grabbed the shovel that Blake had left leaning against the house. I had the porch steps cleared in under a minute and then moved onto the pathway. I zipped up one way and down the other, shoveling the snow aside as I went. With the path clear, I hurried back to the shelter of the covered porch. I'd just set the shovel against the house again when I heard approaching footsteps. I turned around to see Sawyer coming along the path to the cottage.

A smile took over my face. I hadn't seen enough of him in recent days.

"Isn't it kind of cold to be out here without a jacket?" he asked as he jogged up the steps.

"A little," I admitted, pulling my cold hands up into my sleeves.

He stood in front of me on the porch and I looked up at him, still smiling.

"I'm glad you made it," I said.

He tugged off his beanie. "I'm not too late?"

"Not at all." I went up on tiptoes so I could tame his dark hair. "There's still plenty of food." I brushed the last strand of hair into place. "Everyone will be glad to see you." I made a move to go to the door, but he stopped me with a hand on my arm.

"There's just one thing . . ." He pointed upward.

My gaze traveled to the sprig of mistletoe hanging above us.

"Oh," I said as my heart thumped about in my chest.

"Pops must have done that. He always likes to catch Lolly under the mistletoe. But we don't have to . . ."

Sawyer's gaze locked on mine. "We wouldn't want to break tradition."

"No?" I said in little more than a whisper, my heart still thudding.

Sawyer leaned in and touched his lips to mine for the briefest of moments.

Tingles ran through me, right out to the tips of my fingers.

When he pulled back, I couldn't look away from his eyes, couldn't seem to catch my breath.

The front door opened.

I sprang away from Sawyer, startled out of our little bubble.

"Rebecca, you'll freeze out there without your coat," Lolly said. Her face lit up. "Sawyer! You made it!" She ushered us into the cottage. "Come on in and we'll get you something to eat."

Once inside, Sawyer shrugged out of his coat, and Lolly took it away to put with the others in the spare bedroom. Dizzy hurried over to give Sawyer a welcoming hug and then she took us both by the arm and tugged us into the thick of things in the living room.

We were quickly surrounded by friends and family.

Warmth glowed inside of me as laughter and familiar voices flowed around the room.

I was safe and I had all my favorite people with me.

That was the best Christmas gift of all.

ACKNOWLEDGMENTS

I'm truly grateful to everyone involved in taking this book from idea to publication. Special thanks to my agent, Jessica Faust, and my editor, Leis Pederson, for believing in this series and helping me bring it to life. Thanks also to Jody Holford for reading an early draft and for always believing in me. Jody, that ending is for you! A big thank-you to Linda Reilly for answering my Vermont-related questions, and to Carina Chao for answering my questions about chocolate and the process of making bonbons and truffles. Any mistakes in that regard are mine alone. Last but not least, thank you to my review crew; my friends in the writing community; and all the librarians, Bookstagrammers, BookTubers, BookTokers, and bloggers who help spread the word about cozy mysteries.

RECIPES

Candy Cane Truffles

- 4 oz milk chocolate
- 4 oz whipping cream
- 1 9-inch candy cane
- 2 tablespoons crushed candy cane
- 8 oz white chocolate

Finely chop the milk chocolate and place it in a heatproof bowl. In the top of a double boiler, heat the cream over medium-low heat until it's just starting to bubble. Remove the cream from the heat, add the 9-inch candy cane, and let the cream steep for approximately 5 minutes. Then return the cream to the stove and heat again until it's just starting to bubble. Remove and discard any undissolved candy cane. Pour the cream into the bowl of milk chocolate. Mix the cream and chocolate together until all the chocolate has melted and the ganache is smooth. Add the crushed candy cane and stir to combine. Leave the ganache to cool to room temperature. Then put the ganache in the fridge until it is chilled and completely set.

Remove the ganache from the fridge and use your hands to quickly roll it into 1-inch balls. Set the balls on a baking tray lined with parchment paper. Place the tray in the fridge and chill the ganache balls. Leave them in the fridge until you're ready to dip them.

Roughly chop the white chocolate and set approximately one-third of it aside (this is the seed chocolate). Put the remainder of the chopped chocolate in the top of a double boiler set over simmering water. Melt the chocolate and heat it until it reaches 113–22°F (45–50°C). Remove the bowl from the double boiler. Add the seed chocolate and stir until the chocolate cools to 84–86°F (29–30°C). At this point, the chocolate should be in temper.

Line another baking tray with parchment paper. Using a truffle fork or regular fork, dip each ganache ball into the tempered chocolate, making sure it is completely coated, and then set it on the prepared tray. Leave the truffles to set at room temperature or, if necessary, chill the truffles just long enough to set the chocolate.

MAKES APPROXIMATELY 24 TRUFFLES.

Almond Creams

- 1 oz unsalted butter (at room temperature)
- 1 teaspoon golden corn syrup
- 1 tablespoon water
- ½ teaspoon liquid invertase*
- ¼ teaspoon almond extract
- 7 oz confectioners' sugar, sifted
- 8 oz milk chocolate

In the bowl of a stand mixer, beat the butter, corn syrup, water, liquid invertase, and almond extract until combined. Stop the mixer and add the confectioners' sugar. Mix on low speed until the mixture comes together in a ball. Taste the mixture. If you want a stronger almond flavor, add more almond extract a drop at a time, mixing after each addition, until you achieve the desired flavor. (I usually add two more drops.)

The mixture should be soft but not too sticky to handle. If necessary, add a small amount more of confectioners' sugar to reduce the stickiness.

Line a baking sheet with parchment paper. Using your hands, roll the fondant into 1-inch balls and place them on the covered baking sheet. Place the fondant balls in the refrigerator for at least an hour. Keep them in the fridge until you are ready to dip them in the chocolate.

Roughly chop the milk chocolate and set approximately one-third of it aside (this is the seed chocolate). Put the remainder of the chopped chocolate in the top of a double boiler, over simmering water. Melt the chocolate and heat it until it reaches 113–22°F (45–50°C). Remove the bowl from the double boiler. Add the seed chocolate and stir until all the chocolate has melted and it has cooled to 86–87°F (30–31°C). At this point, the chocolate should be in temper.

Line another baking tray with parchment paper. Dip the chilled fondant balls in the tempered chocolate, making sure they are completely coated. Place the chocolates on the prepared tray to set at room temperature or, if necessary, chill them just long enough to set the chocolate.

Store in an air-tight container at room temperature for 2–3 days to allow the filling to liquify. Then enjoy!

*If you don't have liquid invertase, you can leave it out. The filling will just have a different texture as it won't liquify.

MAKES APPPROXIMATELY 24 CHOCOLATES.